THE DUKE DARE

LOVE'S A GAME
BOOK TWO

VALERIE BOWMAN

JUNE THIRD ENTERPRISES, LLC

The Duke Dare, copyright © 2024 by June Third Enterprises, LLC.

Print edition ISBN: 978-1-960015-28-0

Digital edition ISBN: 978-1-960015-27-3

Book Cover Design © Lyndsey Llewellen at Llewellen Designs.

She took the dare.

Lady Gemma Brooks was still in her awkward phase when a spiteful young woman dared her to ask the unattainable Duke of Grovemont for a dance. Gemma accepted, not for herself, but to protect the other wallflowers from malicious gossip. But what began as a harmless dare spiraled into scandal, and Gemma soon finds herself forced into an unexpected marriage with a man she barely knows.

He paid the price.

Lucian Banks, the Duke of Grovemont, was still grieving his mother's death when a simple wedding invitation turned his life upside down. Never did he imagine that his friend's younger sister would draw him into a compromising situation, one that led to a hasty marriage. As a gentleman, Lucian will do his duty, but he's convinced that Gemma trapped him, and has no plans to play the role of doting husband.

Can love bloom from obligation?

Lucian leaves London without a word, abandoning his new bride. But when he returns a year later, he's shocked to find that the awkward girl he left behind has transformed into a stunning beauty and the toast of the *ton*. When the truth about their marriage finally comes to light, Lucian embarks on a mission to win his wife's heart. Will Gemma be able to resist the man who once spurned her, especially when he turns from cold and distant to irresistibly charming?

AUTHOR'S NOTE

Dear Reader,

I hope you enjoy spending time with Gemma and Lucien. This book is particularly special to me because it has a similar plot to one of my favorite romance novels of all time, the incomparable Judith McNaught's, *Something Wonderful*. This book is meant an homage to Ms. McNaught, an author whose books helped me through many difficult times in my life.

With this note, I'd like to address the fact that a divorce would have been extremely unlikely during the Regency. One would not have been granted without Lucien's approval, if not his instigation. However, there were some successful divorces during the era, and I'd like to think that Gemma, the daughter and sister of a duke, a duchess in her own right, and an eternal optimist, would have believed she might very well be one of the lucky ones who succeeded in procuring one.

I've written this before, but it bears repeating that, as a storyteller, I'm more concerned with the 'what ifs' than the 'why nots'. I greatly enjoy taking a bit of license in order to bring you the most amusing romp-like 'what if' my imagination can conjure.

Thank you so much for reading my stories. You are the reason I spend my time writing.

Valerie

CHAPTER ONE

London, May 1817, The Duke of Southbury's Wedding Ball

L ady Gemma Brooks had endured all she intended to from Lady Mary Costner. The young woman was a veritable snake. And while her behavior was somehow tolerated at *ton* balls, *this* was Gemma's older brother's *wedding*, and Gemma refused to allow Lady Mary to employ her usual antics to keep the wallflowers from dancing. The nasty chit had the lot of them frightened half out of their slippers.

But Gemma wasn't frightened.

And she intended to let Lady Mary know as much. *Immediately.*

Gemma already had an entire Season's worth of experience dealing with Lady Mary. Unfortunately, neither of them had received offers last year, but Gemma wasn't about to let Lady Mary ruin another Season.

Gemma's brother, Griffin, and his best friend, Meredith, had married yesterday morning at St. Paul's. It had been a huge affair and tonight's celebratory ball at Griffin's town house wasn't much smaller. The large house was packed to the rafters with well-wishers. But the dance floor in the center of the ballroom was nearly empty at the moment. Lady Mary had made it clear that any young lady who danced would have vicious rumors spread about her. She wanted all the eligible gentlemen for herself. It was ridiculous, and it was time to put a stop to it.

Gemma possessed two faults. Well, at least two. But there were two that she readily acknowledged, the two that frequently got her into trouble. The first was that she had a tendency to insert herself in business that was not her own, especially when she felt the person or persons whose business it was required assistance. And the second was that she was impatient. *Supremely* impatient. Her mama always told her she was so impatient she'd been born nearly two months earlier than expected. Her birthday was in the late spring. And there was no lovelier season than spring. Gemma liked to tease that she simply hadn't wanted to miss it.

Tonight was no different. Once she'd decided to confront Lady Mary, Gemma refused to let another moment pass without doing so. She marched directly up to the young lady and tapped her on the shoulder. The shorter blond woman turned with an ice-cold fake smile frozen on her face.

Mary was everything Gemma was not. Mary was petite. Gemma was too tall. Mary was blond. Gemma was dark-haired. Mary had heavenly blue eyes. Gemma's eyes were dark-brown. Mary's bosom was perfect. Gemma's was flat as a saucer. There were a dozen other differences, but only one counted as far as Gemma was concerned. Lady Mary might be the image of perfect womanhood, according to the collective tastes of the *ton*, but Gemma had a much better temperament. She actually cared about people and pets and making friends. Lady Mary didn't have a friend to her name. And she didn't appear to care about anything either. Other than making the best match, of course.

Gemma didn't give a fig that her own looks weren't up to snuff. There were much more important things than beauty, after all. She was about to turn twenty and she'd still yet to blossom. She was to be a "late bloomer," Mama assured her. Mama had been one too. Of course, Mama had bloomed into one of the *ton*'s most noted beauties in her day. Gemma could only hope she'd inherited half of Mama's loveliness. In the meantime, despite her large dowry and esteemed family name, she might not be attracting any of the *ton*'s most eligible bachelors herself, but she certainly refused to sit on her hands and allow Lady Mary to keep Gemma's friends from finding good matches.

"Why, Gemma, whatever could *you* want?" Lady Mary blinked at Gemma condescendingly, the fake smile still plastered to her face.

"May I speak with you privately for a moment, Mary?" Gemma attempted to keep her face entirely blank. She'd never been much good at pretending, but Lady Mary never acted the slightest bit awful in the presence of her mother. Though something told her that Lady Mary's mother would approve. They both seemed to be cut from the same nasty cloth.

"I suppose," Lady Mary sighed before picking up her peach-colored skirts, excusing herself to her sour-faced mother, and making her way toward the far wall with Gemma at her side.

When they were alone, Gemma crossed her arms over her chest and glared at Lady Mary. Why the awful girl had even been invited to Griffin and Meredith's wedding was anyone's guess, but Gemma suspected it had been Mama's insistence that *everyone* be invited to her only son's wedding. After all, it was an event Mama had anticipated for *far* too long if you asked her. And despite the fact that Lady Mary was more reptile than human, she was the daughter of an earl which, unfortunately, qualified her as "everyone" in their world.

"I want you to leave the other young ladies alone tonight," Gemma said succinctly, scowling at the girl.

Lady Mary's light brows shot up. Then her face transformed into the picture of innocence. "Whatever could you mean? Am *I* bothering the *other* young ladies?" She touched her pearls and blinked her thin blond eyelashes at Gemma.

Gemma narrowed her eyes and tapped her white slipper against the marble floor. "You know you are. Now, tell me what you want in exchange for leaving them alone tonight."

Mary's mouth formed a small O. She lifted her nose in the air and sniffed, nearly as if she was affronted by the notion. "I have no earthly idea what you're talking about."

Oh, no. Mary wasn't about to feign ignorance. Gemma had been watching her all evening. Mary would sidle past some poor unsuspecting girl who had dared to dance with an eligible bachelor and quietly say something nasty to her. Something only the two of them could hear. Then her victim would lift her skirts and rush from the ballroom, a panicked look on her face. If the poor girl dared to re-enter the ballroom at all, she would remain firmly ensconced along the far side of the room with all the other wallflowers. It was a pattern Gemma had seen repeated time and again, not just tonight but the entirety of last Season. And Gemma was tired of it. Mary had no right to tell all the other unmarried young ladies what to do. The marriage mart was not her personal playground.

But tormentors like Mary were predictable. They did things out of fear. Fear that they wouldn't get what they wanted. And everyone in the *ton* knew what Mary wanted. She wanted an offer from the Duke of Grovemont, the most eligible of all the bachelors, now that Griffin was spoken for, of course.

Last year, during their debut, Grovemont had been called away to the country to tend to his ailing mother. Mary had remained unmarried all Season, awaiting his return. Grovemont's poor mama had died last summer. And now that their second Season had begun and Grovemont was out of mourning, Mary had made it clear to one and all that she, and she alone, intended to wring an offer from him.

Of course, it didn't matter that Grovemont had shown absolutely no interest in Mary. Until he *did* show interest, Mary intended to continue to keep a firm grip on the social prospects of the rest of the young ladies, scaring them away from every other eligible gentleman, simply out of spite as far as Gemma could tell. If Mary wasn't getting any offers, neither would any of the other girls.

"You know precisely what I'm talking about," Gemma retorted, tapping her gloved fingertips along her arms as she kept them tightly folded across her chest. "What do you want in order to leave everyone alone? Name your price." In addition to being predictable, tormentors like Mary *always* had a price. It was simply a matter of learning what it was.

"Price? Ha. I hardly want *money*. Besides," Mary's assessing gaze swept Gemma up and down, obviously finding her lacking, "*you* couldn't get me what I want."

"You don't know that," Gemma replied, cocking her head to the side, arms still tightly folded. She might be the younger sister of a duke, but Gemma knew she was too tall, too gangly, too inelegant, and far too plain for Mary to be threatened by. But that was precisely why Gemma wasn't afraid of her. Well, that and the fact that fear just wasn't in the blood of the Southbury family. Griffin had fought valiantly in the Peninsular War when he had no good reason to. Gemma wasn't about to allow an overly pampered debutante who acted like a queen to frighten her away. "What do you want?" she reiterated.

Gemma watched as Mary contemplated the matter. Her mean little brain was clearly hard at work. She would come up with something humiliating and ridiculous. Gemma already knew that. But Gemma didn't care. Because Gemma had something Mary could only dream about: the absolute absence of giving a toss what others thought of her. Gemma would do any silly, outlandish thing to ensure Mary allowed the other girls to enjoy themselves tonight.

Gemma knew when Mary had settled on the perfect torment. A bright gleam illuminated her pale-blue eyes, and a devious, catlike smile curled her thin lips. "Fine," Mary said, barely able to contain her snide little glow. "I dare you to convince Grovemont to dance with me."

CHAPTER TWO

Gemma rolled her eyes. She should have known Mary wouldn't have understood how such things worked. She would just have to explain it to her pea-sized brain. "I cannot control *other people*," Gemma elucidated slowly as if speaking to a child. "Grovemont hasn't danced with *anyone*. He hasn't even been seen in public until tonight. He's been in mourning for his mother."

"I know that, of course," Mary retorted, smugness oozing from every pore. "But that's hardly *my* problem. It's *yours* now."

Gemma shook her head. Of course, Mary didn't care that the poor Duke of Grovemont was no doubt still sad about his dead mother. She was truly awful. She'd clearly only chosen the dare because she knew it was impossible to win. "Look, I assumed you would ask me to do something embarrassing or outlandish. What if I ask him to dance with *me*? Won't it be enough that he's certain to refuse?"

Gemma expelled her breath in frustration. Did Gemma truly have to explain to this girl how to use her offer against her? You'd think a young woman as well-versed in terror-izing others as Mary would have already puzzled out such details. But it seemed that in addition to being a nasty bit of baggage, Mary was also a dullard. The nastiest people always were, weren't they?

Mary pursed her lips and contemplated this new bit of information for a moment. "But I want to dance with him." She stamped her foot. "What would *I* get out of making *you* ask him to dance?"

"The pleasure of seeing me embarrassed when he rejects me?" Gemma offered, blinking at her rapidly and giving her a tight smile. Lord save her from dolts.

Mary tapped at her chin for a few moments before another catlike smile popped to her pinched face. "Hmm. Perhaps I *was* too hasty," she finally said. "You're right. Grovemont hasn't asked *any* of the debutantes to dance last Season or this one. There's no chance he'll dance with you. Seeing you humiliated shall be quite entertaining. Very well. I dare you to ask him to dance." She emitted another nasty little laugh.

Gemma expelled her breath. Honestly, that had been far too simple. So simple she didn't trust the offer one whit. She'd do it, of course. But first, she needed Lady Mary's word, whatever *that* was worth.

"Let me ensure I have the right of it," Gemma said, tugging at her naked earlobe. Much to her mother's dismay, she refused to wear earbobs. They made her ears ache, and she was forever worried she'd lose one of them. "If I ask Grovemont to dance, *regardless* of whether he agrees, you give your *word* that you'll leave all the other girls alone for the rest of the evening?"

"Yes," Mary replied far too quickly.

"You'll allow them to dance with *whomever* they please

and say nothing to any of them?" Gemma further clarified, her gaze still narrowed on Mary.

"Yes," Mary said more slowly this time, her pale-blue eyes gleaming. "You have my *word*."

"Very well." Gemma nodded and promptly turned to search the large crowd for the Duke of Grovemont. Frankly, the offer seemed far too good to be true. All Gemma had to do was *ask* the man to dance? Easy enough. A bit unconventional, of course, but certainly not unheard of. Grovemont would no doubt quickly decline, Gemma would thank him for his time, and that would be the end of it. Mama wouldn't like it if she got wind of it, but she would understand once Gemma explained the situation. Probably.

Honestly, the request seemed entirely *too* easy. Only Mary was too senseless to know that asking Grovemont to dance, and even being turned down by him, wouldn't bother Gemma one whit. What did she care if some arrogant duke with more money than sense refused to dance with her? Mary had made a classic mistake. She'd assumed the thing that would mortify *her* would also mortify her opponent. But nothing could be further from the truth.

Gemma completed her search of the ballroom. "I don't see him."

Mary stamped her foot again and scowled. She, too, was searching the crowd. "Where did he go? I had my eye on him until you came traipsing over with your silly offer."

"Don't worry," Gemma said, rolling her eyes again. "I'll find him. But do keep an eye out. I have no intention of having to prove to you that I've asked him to dance. And I'm only going to do it once. So pay attention."

"Oh, I'll be watching," Mary confirmed. Her catty smile had transformed into more of a crocodile's, all gaping lips and far too many visible teeth.

Gemma distinctly disliked the young woman's tone. But no matter. It would be well worth enduring Mary's gloating if she would leave Gemma's friends alone to enjoy the rest of wedding ball. Without another word, Gemma lifted her skirts and took off in the direction of the wedding party. Someone there had to know where the Duke of Grovemont had got off to.

CHAPTER THREE

"**H**ave you seen the Duke of Grovemont, by chance?" Gemma asked Lord Trentham in her most nonchalant voice. The Marquess of Trentham was the bride's older brother and the fourth person she'd asked this same question in nearly as many minutes.

"Seems as if I've seen him round here somewhere," Lord Trentham answered, glancing about.

Drat. Trentham's answer was the same as the others. Apparently Grovemont had left the ballroom. Gemma had searched everywhere. What if he'd left the ball? She hadn't been watching him the way Mary obviously had, but Gemma had *seen him*. He'd looked melancholy. Poor man. He'd waited the requisite six months after his mother's death before returning to Society, of course, for propriety's sake, but Gemma could only imagine how sad *she* would be if *her* mother died. She didn't even like to think of it.

No doubt Grovemont had merely made a brief appearance at Griffin's wedding ball because they were friends. Perhaps Grovemont had already left. Honestly, Gemma wouldn't blame him.

She *hated* to interrupt Griffin and Meredith on their special day, but Griffin was sitting at the head table waiting for Meredith to return from the lady's retiring room. Now was as good a time as any to ask him a question.

She lifted her pink skirts and made her way over to Griffin.

"Gemma, dear, there you are!" Griffin nearly shouted. Her brother, who was rarely intoxicated, was clearly feeling very little pain tonight. He had been drinking champagne and dancing with his lovely bride all evening. It was a joy to see Griff so happy. It had taken him forever to admit his love for his best friend, Meredith. He'd finally declared himself last year, and Mama had spent the entire autumn and winter planning the wedding. There was much to celebrate.

"You look happy, Griffin," Gemma said, giving him a tight hug.

"I am happy, poppet." His smile was enormous.

"You'd best enjoy yourself," Gemma continued. "I've little doubt Mama will be over soon insisting that you and Meredith go to bed." They all knew Mama had been counting the days until a grandson could be born.

Griffin's eyes widened. "What do you know of it, poppet?" he asked, watching her from the corner of his eye.

"Enough to know you'll be in trouble if there isn't an heir to the dukedom born in precisely nine months," Gemma replied. Oh, she already knew all about what happened between a man and a woman in bed. She'd overheard Mama's whist-playing, wine-drinking lady friends talk about such things when they thought she was abed. But the real education had come from Meredith. Meredith had grown up without a mother and had apparently been woefully ignorant of how such things worked. She'd sat Gemma down last Season to ensure she was fully educated in what went on between a couple in the bedchamber.

Honestly, from what Gemma had heard, the entire act seemed slightly ridiculous. But she wasn't the one getting married tonight. She had ages before she would have to worry about such things. Not only was she in no rush to marry, but she also hardly expected to be asked until she finally blossomed, which, according to Mama, might well be another entire *year* from now, if not longer.

Which was why Gemma was so set on helping the other young ladies. As the sister of a duke and a lady in possession of a large dowry, she would have no issue procuring an offer of marriage *eventually*, even if she ended up being only half as lovely as Mama. But the other poor wallflowers, some of whose families were counting on them to make a good match, shouldn't have to endure Mary's machinations. Hence Gemma's search for Grovemont in order to ask him to dance.

She cleared her throat. She needed to sound entirely indifferent. "By the by, Griff, you haven't happened to see the Duke of Grovemont recently, have you?"

Griffin's brows shot up. "Grovemont? Why are you looking for *him*?"

"Oh, one of the girls was asking after him," Gemma said, waving her hand in the air as if the matter was nothing of import.

After her staunch defense of the wallflowers last Season, both Griffin and Meredith were well aware of Gemma's penchant for looking out for the other girls. Griff would have no problem believing she was only searching for Grovemont because one of the wallflowers had asked. Besides, Griff and Mere tended to treat her like a young girl at times, fussing over her choices and reminding her to be patient. She was a woman of nineteen years old now. They needn't worry about her any longer. Of course, Gemma had no intention of telling her brother that she planned to ask

Grovemont to dance in order to keep Mary from acting like a termagant at his wedding ball. Griffin shouldn't worry about a thing save enjoying himself tonight.

Griffin lifted his champagne glass to his lips and frowned. "Now that I think of it, seems to me Grovemont *may* be in my study. Earlier he asked if he might use it for a bit."

"Oh, well then. I'll have to let my friend know," Gemma replied, trying to seem a bit sorry to hear the news. Of course, under *normal* circumstances, a young lady couldn't go searching for a bachelor alone in a study. That would be scandalous. But what Griffin (and everyone else) didn't know, wouldn't hurt him. And Gemma had every intention of getting her task over with as quickly as possible. After all, who knew if Grovemont intended to return to the ballroom tonight?

But how would she prove she'd asked him to dance? Hmm. Either Mary would have to take her word for it, or she would have to catch Mary's eye and get her to follow Gemma to the study.

Meredith returned to the table just then and after greeting Gemma with a big hug, the bride asked her new husband to dance with her. Which gave Gemma precisely the opening she needed to go in search of Grovemont.

Waving at the happy couple as they took to the dance floor, Gemma made her way to one of the ballroom's side doors. Just before she slipped through it, she glanced around to ensure Mary was watching.

Gemma needn't have worried. The girl's bright eyes were fixed on her. Excellent. Mary could follow and see for herself. That would be best. Gemma tipped her head toward the corridor and nodded meaningfully before disappearing through the door. Even a fool like Mary had to have understood her meaning.

CHAPTER FOUR

L ucian Banks, the Duke of Grovemont, had been reclining in a large, leather chair in Southbury's study for the better part of half an hour. He was enjoying some of Southbury's finest brandy. Alone. Nearly in the dark. Which was his preferred company lately. Tonight was one of the first times he'd ventured back into Society since his mother's death last summer.

The previous nine months still seemed completely unreal to Lucian. He'd loved his mother fiercely. Discovering she'd become unexpectedly ill with a weak heart had been a blow. Her untimely death was something from which he would not soon recover.

Lucian had never cared much for Society events, and this Season he cared even less. His mother had adored all the parties and dinners and dancing and *fêtes*. He smiled wryly. She would have loved it here tonight.

Mama and Griffin Brooks's mother, the recently made dowager Duchess of Southbury, had been thick as thieves. And Lucian was a friend to both Southbury and his new brother-in-law, the Marquess of Trentham. Which was the only reason Lucian was here tonight. To wish his friend and his new bride well. He was happy for Southbury. And the man was obviously in love.

Lucian settled back into the chair and expelled his breath. Soon, he would have to do the same thing Southbury had done—take a wife. For on his mother's deathbed, Lucian had *promised* her that he would, indeed, finally find a wife and settle down. He would produce the Grovemont heir as she'd always wanted. He only wished his mother would be here. Not only to meet the young lady of his choosing, but also to meet his future son. He swallowed hard. Damn. It hurt to even have that thought. *Mama would never meet her grandson.* His chest tightened.

Lucian tossed back the rest of the brandy in the glass. It was his own fault for waiting so long to marry. He was thirty years old already. And no amount of brandy would turn back the clock. He would have to live with that regret the rest of his days.

Frankly, he'd arrived here tonight with the intention of taking a closer look at this year's crop of debutantes. He'd gone to a few parties earlier in the Season with the same inclination. But most of the young ladies were huddled together against the wall. Having avoided it like the pox for most of his adult life, Lucian didn't know much about the marriage mart, but he knew enough from Mama's stories to know that one didn't look for one's wife among the wallflowers.

Tonight, he'd arrived to find the same confounding situation. Almost all the young ladies were packed together against the far wall like a herd of frightened sheep. Even at Southbury's wedding ball. So odd. Lucian had glanced over the lot of them, only to find there was nary a one who caught his interest. They all seemed like a timid lot, not making eye contact with him and outright shying away when he'd strode near them to get a better look. Was he *that* intimidating? Lord save him from simpering maidens. He preferred a young woman who'd look him in the eye at the very least. Was that too much to hope for?

There had been only one young lady—one with blond hair and a pinched face—who had stared at him *so pointedly* he'd been loath to glance in her direction again. Something about her determined look made him hie off in the opposite direction. Quickly.

The bridal prospects were not particularly promising. Which was why he'd taken his leave of the cacophony in the ballroom to enjoy a drink in the quiet of Southbury's study.

Lucian scrubbed a hand through his hair. Should he pour himself another brandy? Probably not. He'd been poor enough company tonight as it was. He didn't need to add being a drunkard. He should simply wish his friend Southbury well once more and go home. He lived just around the corner. It would be a short walk.

Lucian stood and expelled his breath again. His mission to find a wife this Season would not be a particularly pleasant one. But he would go about it in a logical manner. The same way he did everything. He'd put together a mental list of the most promising unmarried ladies, pay a call on each of them, and see which was the least uninteresting and most pleasing to look at. Because most of them seemed uninteresting, honestly. His wife might as well be beautiful. Beautiful *and* interesting seemed far too much to hope for, given the ladies he'd seen to date. He shuddered to think of a lifetime leg-shackled to a woman who couldn't carry on an intelligent conversation with him. How had Southbury managed to find Meredith? Had his friend succeeded in marrying the *last* beautiful, interesting lady in the *ton*? A depressing thought, that.

At any rate, there would be plenty of time over the

remainder of the Season to pick through the debutantes for the least skittish, best-looking one of the lot. Though he did not relish the task. Tonight, however, it was time to take his leave.

And he would…in a moment. He stared out over the desk, lost in thought.

"There you are," came a voice from the slightly open doorway.

The voice shook him from his thoughts. Narrowing his eyes, Lucian stood and made his way to the door. When he pulled it open all the way, a tall, thin, coltish-looking young lady stood there staring at him as if she knew him.

A look akin to relief covered her face. A face that had features that were far too large but somehow still compelling. Her dark eyes were particularly alert and intelligent.

Lucian frowned. She'd said, "There you are." He fought the urge to look behind him. He *was* the only one in the study. She'd been looking for him? That was odd.

She quickly stepped inside and closed the door, causing him to step back. He narrowed his eyes on her, taking in her frame from the top of her head, which was a mass of short, dark messy curls, to the bottom of her extremely expensive light-pink gown that skimmed the floor. She wore an exquisite diamond necklace but, curiously, no earbobs. She was tall and quite thin. The effect being that she seemed a mass of arms and legs. But it was her eyes that made the deepest impression. Expressive, dark, and huge. Almost too big for her face. Intent and full of curiosity and intelligence.

He didn't have long to contemplate the gangly girl because she immediately said, "Your Grace," and bobbed a quick curtsy to him.

Deeply ingrained manners caused Lucian to bow immediately, but the frown remained on his face. Why was she acting as if they knew each other? He'd never seen her before. He was certain of it. She looked quite young, but if he'd seen her in the flock of debutantes earlier, he would have remembered her. *This* young lady didn't have a farthing's worth of retiring shyness in her body. If she'd been there, she would have been standing in front of the herd.

And she looked him *directly* in the eye.

"Good evening, Miss… Miss…" He'd never had an unknown young woman accost him in a study before. Or anywhere else for that matter. She should have been introduced to him formally by either her mother or another older lady who knew them both.

"First," the young lady continued in a rush, completely failing to offer her name, "I should like to say how *very* sorry I am about your mother's death. She was quite a nice lady, and I'm certain you're still ever so sad, even though you're back in Society."

Lucian's frown deepened. She knew his mother? "Thank you."

"I know we shouldn't be alone together," the young woman hastily continued, "but I need to quickly ask if you'll do me the honor of dancing with me."

Lucian stared at her as if she'd just walked out of the pages of a book. A strange sort of book with unpredictable young ladies with large, dark eyes who asked impertinent, unexpected questions. "Pardon?" Had he heard her correctly? She was asking *him* to dance? They weren't even in the ballroom. And again, he hadn't been privy to the intricacies of the marriage mart, but he was fairly certain gentlemen were supposed to do the asking. This was all quite strange.

"If you'll just say no, I'll be on my way," she rattled on.

"Wait. What?" Lucian took a step closer to her. Perhaps, if he heard her more clearly, her words might make more sense. "You're asking me to dance and telling me to refuse you?"

What was happening? Was this young woman mad? Did she require a doctor's care? And where on earth was her mother? She shouldn't be roaming Southbury's house alone asking gentlemen she did not know to dance. Quite imprudent of her.

She waved a clearly impatient gloved hand in the air. "Oh, I'm sorry. I forgot that part. You see? I was dared to ask you to dance. So I'm here, asking you." She met his gaze straight on, and again he was struck by the mesmerizing depth of her eyes as well as her forthrightness. "Will you dance with me?" she finished with a kind of half-smile that would have been endearing had she not completely confused him. Her latest explanation hadn't cleared up much of anything.

Lucian scratched his cheek while he contemplated the matter. He'd had a bit to drink this evening, but he wasn't so foxed he was imagining this young woman and her fathom-less eyes accosting him in this study... Was he?

"Who are you?" he asked again, hoping she would take heed that he *still* had no knowledge of her identity. Of course, he wasn't about to dance with a madwoman in a room devoid of music, and he had absolutely no idea what she meant about a dare. But the more important thing at the moment was learning who she was so he could escort her back to her mother if necessary. Or perhaps he should leave her here and go in search of her mother to fetch her. Yes. That was probably the wisest course.

"Honestly, it doesn't matter who I am," she said, rolling her eyes with impatience that was nearly tangible. "A simple no will suffice, and I'll be gone." She pointed back toward the door with a gloved finger.

Lucian blinked at her. Was it truly that simple? Would she leave if he only said no? Perhaps he was overcomplicating the matter. "No then," he said. No doubt it was rude of him to imply he wanted her gone, but with the insane way she was acting, he couldn't even pretend to wish to remain in her company. Of course, he'd been raised to be far more mannerly than this, but it seemed prudent to see to it that this young woman leave as soon as possible.

True to her promise, she merely nodded, an oddly satisfied look on her face. She turned toward the door, ostensibly to leave. The distinct sound of female laughter echoed in the corridor. Still frowning, Lucian pulled open the door to see the same petite, pinched-face blond girl he'd noticed staring at him in the ballroom earlier. A chill ran through him. She stood in front of the door, smirking and laughing.

Lucian narrowed his eyes on her. The same urge he'd had earlier to hurry away from her overtook him. This entire affair was becoming increasingly strange with each passing moment. What precisely did this blond young lady have to do with the dark-eyed young lady's odd dance request? A skitter of apprehension traced its way up Lucian's spine. Here were two young women, obviously unchaperoned, waylaying him in the study where he'd come to find peace. This was precisely the type of thing Mama had warned him about years ago.

"Some young ladies will stop at nothing to force a marriage proposal," Mama had said. "As a bachelor duke, you must ensure you do nothing to encourage them or facilitate such an encounter."

Tonight, he'd let down his guard. He'd been tired from a long trip from the countryside yesterday, sad as usual about Mama's death, and disheartened by the thought of trying to find a wife within a group of debutantes who looked to be wholly panic-stricken by him. And besides, he wasn't at a *ton* ball tonight. This ball wasn't part of the Season. It was Southbury's wedding ball, for Christ's sake.

But that hardly mattered. Lucian needed to get out of here. *Quickly.*

The dark-eyed young woman was already ahead of him, however. She'd picked up her skirts and stepped toward the door as she said, "You heard him, Mary. Remember your promise."

That strange statement sent alarm coursing through his veins. Promise? What promise?

Still standing in the corridor, pinched-faced Mary opened her mouth to speak just as an older female voice rang out from behind her. "Lady Mary Costner, just what are you doing?"

Mary swiveled on her heel as a woman with a similarly pinched face, who Lucian could only assume was her mother, stepped closer.

"Mama! Noooooo!"

CHAPTER FIVE

"**O**h, dear heavens!" Lady Costner said as she
stopped short after seeing Grovemont standing
inside the study so close to Gemma. Gemma
swallowed and stepped back toward the desk.

"What is the meaning of this!" came Lady Costner's shrill
shriek. She promptly pulled a lacy handkerchief from her
sleeve and waved it about in the air as if she was swatting at
an invisible fly.

Mary's eyes were panicked, and her voice was low when
she spoke. "Calm down, Mama. It's nothing. We were just—"

"It's not nothing!" Lady Costner continued in that same
shrill voice. "*These two* were already in the room together.
Alone!" She gave Gemma and Grovemont a condemning
glare.

Mary turned swiftly toward her mother, her eyes wide
and pleading. "No, Mama. You mistake the case. *I* was alone
in the room with *His Grace*."

Gemma's brows shot up. Well, how do you like that?
Apparently, Mary wasn't half the dullard she'd thought her to

be. Mary had quickly read the situation and was trying to turn it in her favor.

A few long seconds ticked by before the same bright gleam slid into Lady Costner's eyes. "Oh, yes. I do believe you are correct."

"This is preposterous," Grovemont said, his tone thunderous.

He was about to say more when Lady Costner opened her mouth and let out a grand shriek. It was somewhere between I've-seen-a-ghost and my-ladylike-sensibilities-have-been-irreparably-damaged. Impressive, actually.

"Southbury!" Lady Costner screamed at the top of her lungs. "Your Grace! Come quickly!"

Gemma gulped. Southbury? Why was Lady Costner calling for Griffin? Oh, no. This was not good. Not good at all. Gemma, who'd been rooted to the spot as Lady Costner's dramatics unfolded, glanced at the duke. She bit her lip and gave him a look she hoped was filled with as much regret as she felt.

Grovemont's face slowly turned to a mask of stone. A muscle ticked in his jaw. And the enormity of the situation landed like an elephant's foot on Gemma's stomach. Her neck began to sweat, and nausea pooled in her middle. *Dear God. Please don't let me cast up my accounts in Griffin's study in front of these people.* Because if Gemma didn't mistake her guess, this hideous woman and her scheming daughter were about to cause quite a lot of unnecessary trouble for the poor, unwitting Duke of Grovemont. And it was all Gemma's fault.

And that wasn't the only awful thing about to happen. Griffin's wedding celebration would be interrupted by this nonsense. Gemma closed her eyes and prayed.

Griffin was not the first person to heed Lady Costner's

shriek. Instead, Lady Steffland and Lady Cranberry, two of Mama's friends, came hurrying to the study door.

"What's the matter, Harriet?" Lady Cranberry asked Lady Costner. "We were on our way back from the lady's retiring room and heard a commotion."

Lady Costner, apparently satisfied with her audience, pushed her daughter into the study and followed her. Then she placed her curled knuckles on her forehead and declared in a still-shrill howl, "We *must* find Southbury immediately. His Grace was *alone* in this room with *my dear Mary*."

Lady Cranberry, always a devotee of gossip and scandal, peered into the room and locked eyes with Gemma. Gemma kept her countenance blank. But there was no mistaking the judgement on the older woman's face. Lady Cranberry swiveled on her heel and immediately rushed off down the corridor, no doubt in search of Griffin.

Gemma was left with Lady Steffland eyeing the four of them from the doorway with a mixture of obvious disapproval and delight. This would be the talk of the wedding ball in minutes.

Grovemont remained stoic, but anger was clearly etched in his features. His face had flushed dark, and his cobalt-blue eyes narrowed on Lady Costner, but he remained silent. No doubt the man was wise enough to wait until Griffin arrived before making his case. And Gemma had every intention of helping him by telling the truth.

"What is *she* doing here?" Lady Steffland asked, nodding toward Gemma when she spied her standing behind Grovemont.

"I was—" Gemma began.

"She happened along *after* I'd already found my dear Mary *alone* with the duke," Lady Costner lied.

"You did no such thing, and you know it!" Gemma

planted her fists on her hips and stared indignantly at Lady Costner.

When faced with a denial, Lady Costner chose that particular moment to crumple toward the floor in a convincing pretend faint.

Left with little choice, Grovemont sprang forward to catch her.

"Mama!" cried Mary, wringing her hands as she hovered over her mother's prostrate body.

"Oh, dear," Lady Steffland said, peering at Lady Costner. "Harriet, are you quite all right?" Lady Steffland fully entered the room and bobbed her head back and forth in an attempt to watch as Grovemont easily lifted the sizable Lady Costner in his arms. He took three long strides toward the leather sofa near the wall and laid her upon it before stepping back. The muscle in his jaw ticked faster.

One of Lady Costner's pale-blue eyes peeked open to assess the situation before she let out a dramatic sigh. "I am a good Christian woman, and I *will not stand* for such sinfulness. My own, *innocent* daughter has been gravely compromised." She turned her head toward Grovemont. "You do understand, Your Grace, that my Mary is the most innocent, unassuming, *pure* girl."

"Your daughter wasn't even—" Gemma's words were cut off as Griffin, Meredith, and Mama came rushing into the room led by Lady Cranberry.

"What is happening here?" Griffin demanded, glancing about and clearly doing his best to combat the effects of the champagne he'd been drinking all night.

Gemma glanced out the crack in the door to see a veritable crowd standing in the corridor. She swallowed hard as anxiety rose like poison in her throat. Oh, this was even worse than she'd expected, and she'd expected it to be quite bad. Lady Cranberry had obviously wasted no time alerting the entirety of the ballroom's occupants. Dear God. *What* had Gemma done?

She forced herself to take a deep breath and concentrate. This would all be cleared up in a matter of moments. She would help the duke explain the truth to everyone. It was that simple. She cleared her throat and shook out her shoulders, ready to do battle with Lady Costner if she must.

"What's going on?" Griffin asked again, more loudly this time. "*Grovemont?*"

"Gemma?" Mama rushed over and gave Gemma a hug. Grovemont's gaze swung to them as if he had just realized who she was. Gemma bit her lip. *Ooh.* She hadn't told him. Had she? Poorly, done. That.

Grovemont stepped forward. His face remained stonelike. "Don't worry, Southbury." His voice was also completely devoid of any emotion. "While I assure you that *nothing* untoward happened. I take full responsibility for the appearance of impropriety. I was alone in this room with your sister when Lady Costner and her daughter happened along."

"No! You were alone with my dear Mary!" Lady Costner insisted, ever shrill.

Griffin scrubbed a hand over his face. Gemma's heart wrenched. She *hated* that she was the cause of ruining her brother's wedding ball. Griffin turned his head toward her, his face gravely serious. "Gemma," he said, "were you alone with Grovemont?"

Oh, thank heavens. Her eyes fluttered shut momentarily with her relief. She had the chance to tell the truth. And Griffin would believe her. He knew she wasn't a liar. Impatient and impetuous, perhaps. Prone to sticking her nose where it did not belong, granted. But no liar. "Yes." She nodded. "I was alone with Grovemont, but only for a few moments before—"

"No! That's not true!" Mary insisted, stamping her foot. "It was *me!*"

"Ladies." Griffin rubbed his temple with a knuckle before he turned to Lady Cranberry and Lady Steffland. "Since there seems to be some discrepancy, what exactly did you see?"

Lady Steffland's brow furrowed as she obviously attempted to recall what precisely she had witnessed. "When we came upon the scene, Lady Costner and Mary were in the corridor. And Grovemont and Gemma were in here together."

"No, Bertha, you're mistaken," Lady Costner insisted. Her eyes were shooting angry blue fire at Lady Steffland.

"It's what I saw too," Lady Cranberry agreed, clearly relishing her role as witness, perhaps a bit *too* much. "Gemma was *alone* with the duke."

Griffin's narrowed gaze shot to Grovemont. "Seems we have the right of it then."

Grovemont nodded. "I shall do right by your sister, of course, Southbury."

Lady Costner's face fell, and Mary's turned bright red. She looked as if she might wail.

Meanwhile, Gemma glanced back and forth between her brother and Grovemont, waiting to hear what came next. The little drops of sweat that had begun earlier were now rolling down her back and running down her temple.

Do right by?

Why, that sounded like...

That must mean...

No. No. No.

Her breathing became so labored that a wheezing sound issued from her dry throat. Meredith came to her and helped her into a chair.

Gemma looked up into Meredith's pretty gray eyes and

desperately whispered, "Please tell me this doesn't mean…" But she couldn't even finish the sentence. Pure undiluted regret gripped her chest and squeezed…hard. What had she done? *What had she done?*

"Just breathe," Meredith whispered. "Griffin and your mother shall handle this, Gemma. It will be all right."

The serious edge to Meredith's voice caused panic to claw even harder at Gemma's insides.

"I should hope so," Griffin was saying to Grovemont when Gemma focused again on their conversation.

Grovemont's jaw remained tight. He glanced briefly around at the occupants of the study, his face still an unreadable mask. "I'll call on you in the morning, Southbury, and we shall discuss the contract. I do not wish to further intrude upon or hinder your wedding celebration this evening. Good night." He gave an efficient bow to the room in general. "Ladies," he said and then stalked away.

CHAPTER SIX

hat happened? What happened?

W Gemma wasn't entirely certain because Mama hustled her upstairs to her bedchamber without saying a word. Gemma had only caught a glimpse of the concern on Meredith's face, the anger on Griffin's face, the disappointment on Mary's face, and the helpless frustration on Lady Costner's face, before Mama whisked Gemma out the back door of the study toward the servants' staircase. And thank God for the servants' staircase because Gemma was not forced to face the curious gazes of all the partygoers who were huddled in the corridor outside the study.

She and Mama seemed to have made a silent pact to remain quiet until they reached Gemma's bedchamber. But the moment the door closed, Gemma turned to her mother, her breathing still coming in short, painful gasps. "Please. Please. Please," she begged. "Tell me that did not mean what I fear it meant."

Mama stepped toward her and wrapped her in a fierce hug. She didn't let go for several long moments. It served to calm Gemma's nerves a bit.

Mama was so lovely with her dark hair shot with gray, her long, graceful limbs, and her high cheekbones. So pretty and so calm and comforting. She was everything Gemma hoped she'd be one day. But that day was not today. Today Gemma was a gangly, impatient mess who may have just ruined the life of a man she barely knew.

"First, breathe," Mama said when she finally pulled back, clutching Gemma's shoulders and meeting her gaze.

Gemma nodded and tried to concentrate. Breathe in. Breathe out. Her lungs hurt, but she wasn't quite as panicked as before.

"Now, let's take a seat." Mama grasped her hand and pulled her along beside her to the edge of Gemma's bed covered in its yellow-flowered coverlet. Daisies. Gemma's favorites. The happiest of flowers.

Gemma took a seat, but her leg bobbed up and down frantically beneath her skirts. "Tell me, Mama. Tell me the truth," she begged.

"Of course, I shall tell you the truth, Gem. Haven't I always? But first, I believe you owe *me* an explanation. What exactly happened in the study tonight?"

Yes. Of course. She *did* owe Mama an explanation. Gemma took another deep breath and gave her mother a very brief explanation of her interactions with Mary and what had happened with Grovemont.

"It was all extremely innocent," Gemma finished. "We can explain it to Griffin, can't we, Mama? Can't we?" Her voice sounded utterly desperate. She searched her mother's face for some small indication of agreement.

Mama's shoulders lifted, and she expelled a long breath. "Griffin is not the problem, Gem, darling."

Oh, God. Gemma's lungs stopped working again. She leaned forward, wrapping her arms around her middle.

Clutching at her sides, she stared unseeing at the rug-covered floor.

"Lady Cranberry, Lady Steffland, and half the ballroom heard the interaction between your brother and Grovemont. Gemma, dear, you know you cannot be alone with a gentleman. I taught you that." Mama's voice wasn't accusatory. It was more sad, tinged with the hint of disappointment. Which made tears well in Gemma's eyes.

A sound that was half-cry, half-groan escaped her throat. "I know, Mama. I know. And I'm sorry. I wasn't thinking. Well, I *was* thinking, but I was thinking of the wallflowers, not myself and—" She dropped her head into her hands. "Oh, I can tell myself all I like that I'd just been trying to save the other wallflowers, but I could have waited for Grovemont to leave the study. I could have waited. But I didn't. I was too impatient. How many times have you told me not to be impatient?"

Mama patted her back, and Gemma looked up and met her mother's gaze with eyes still filled with tears.

Mama leaned down and gave her another tight hug. "It's all right, dear. It's going to be all right."

"But it's not all right, is it? When Grovemont said he'd do right by me, he meant…" Oh, she still couldn't bear to say the words. She choked on them.

Mama nodded slowly and squeezed Gemma's shoulder. "Let me be clear. I told you it will be all right. And it will be… one day. I'm not at all certain tomorrow will be that day. But Grovemont is a good man. He's Griffin's friend. And you are strong. You are a Southbury. You *will* be all right."

A strangled cry escaped Gemma's throat, and she frantically shook her head. "I didn't want this. I don't want this. I wanted to *blossom*. I thought I'd have at least another year to *blossom*. And now…a man who cannot possibly want me shall be *forced* to marry me." The tears streaked down her cheeks, hot and hopeless. "Oh, Mama. I wanted to marry for love. And Grovemont, he cannot—"

Mama squeezed her hand reassuringly. "We cannot presume to know what Grovemont wants, dear."

But Mama was only saying that to make her feel better. Gemma had seen the look on Grovemont's face when he left. And it *hadn't* been pleasure at the thought of his upcoming nuptials. That was certain.

Only now was not the time to feel sorry for herself. It was Griffin's night. Griffin and Meredith's.

"Go, downstairs, Mama. Please. Go down and make certain I haven't ruined Griffin and Meredith's wedding ball. I couldn't live with myself if I thought I had done that in addition to my other sins."

Mama nodded and stood. "I'll just pop down to see if everything's all right. I want to ensure Griffin and Meredith retire soon. But I'll be back up to check on you, dear." She smoothed a hand over Gemma's unruly hair. The dark curls never stayed pinned into place, no matter how diligently her maid tried to subdue them.

Gemma watched her mother go. As soon as the door closed, Gemma dropped to her knees beside the bed and threaded her fingers together in a tight weave. First, she said a prayer that Griffin's wedding ball had not been ruined because of her misdeeds. Then she prayed as long and hard as she'd ever prayed for anything that a miracle would happen and somehow, someway, the Duke of Grovemont would *not* be forced to marry her.

Gemma stayed on her knees until they ached, and when she finally climbed into bed, she wrapped her arms around herself and tried to calm the rattled breathing that had returned in full force. Because Gemma had an awful sense of impending doom that what she'd done tonight was entirely irrevocable and unfixable.

And the worst part was, *she* deserved it. *But Grovemont certainly didn't.*

CHAPTER SEVEN

L ucian arrived on Southbury's doorstep at half ten the next day. If it hadn't been the morning after the man's wedding celebration, he would have come earlier. He'd had no intention of arriving too early, but he'd also been careful not to arrive too late, lest Southbury send a Bow Street Runner to track him down. He didn't want Southbury to think he'd decided not to come and do the right thing, after all.

Of course, Lucian would do the right thing. He was a man of honor. But doing the right thing and liking it were two different things.

He'd got very little sleep last night. Turns out being forced into marriage would do that to a man. The irony that he'd been in the study contemplating how best to find a wife when one had thrust herself upon him was not lost on him.

Only it bothered him immensely that *he* hadn't been the one to do the choosing. The only good thing about what had happened last night was that the Costner chit and her scheming mother had been called out for their lies. Lucian had already deduced that both Gemma and Mary had obviously conspired to find him alone and force a marriage on him. Apparently, Gemma had got there first. He could only be glad about that. He didn't relish marriage to a schemer. But of the two, Gemma was clearly preferable to Mary. At least Gemma had a decent family. Southbury was a good man. Whereas Lady Costner had been only too quick and willing to lie. Lucian shuddered at the thought.

Of course, Gemma hadn't told the truth merely to save him from marriage to Mary. She'd obviously told the truth to become a duchess herself, which must have been her plan all along. He'd deal with her later. First, he had to deal with her older brother.

After contemplating it last night, Lucian had realized he *had* certainly met Gemma Brooks before. But he'd never looked at her the way he looked at debutantes, young women he considered marrying. Gemma was merely the young sister of his friend, Southbury. A dark-haired, skinny moppet he barely remembered and certainly hadn't been attracted to.

And frankly, to his infinite chagrin, he still wasn't attracted to her. She was all arms and legs, far too thin with too-big eyes, a too-wide mouth, and absolutely no breasts to speak of. But her eyes, those obsidian eyes. They *were* compelling. And he remembered them from the last time they had met.

Last night, Lucian hadn't been expecting to run into Southbury's sister, who was now apparently old enough to be out in Society. And so he hadn't even thought about the eyes. But now they were all he could think about. Those big, captivating eyes. He was going to marry the girl with those unfathomable eyes.

Just as soon as a marriage contract could be agreed upon.

Southbury was reasonable. He would ensure a decent

contract was drawn up, and the whole thing would be put to rest sooner than later. It would all be done with an air of scandal about it, but his wouldn't be the first *ton* marriage forged in scandal, and it would hardly be the last.

While Lucian had tossed and turned last night, there was one thing he couldn't get out of his head. Why had Gemma come looking for him in the study, and why was her friend at the door laughing? Gemma had said some nonsense about a dare and had asked her friend if she remembered her promise. The whole thing had given Lucian the impression of a setup.

It reminded him of when he and his mates had first gone to Eton and the boys in the town had offered to take them hunting for snipe. Lucian had immediately felt the hair on the back of his neck stand up and had ushered himself and his friends away from the group, but other young students hadn't been so fortunate. They'd happily dug into their pockets for coins. Of course, no such animal as a snipe existed. And the town boys had merely taken their coins and laughed at them behind their backs. More little Eton fools to rob at the start of the new year. It was always the lot who didn't have older siblings or cousins to inform them before they'd arrived.

The moment Lucian had seen the pinched-face girl standing in the corridor laughing, the hair on the back of his neck had stood up in much the same way, and Lucian never discounted his gut.

The two young women had been up to something together. And if Lucian didn't mistake his guess, they'd been up to securing an offer of marriage from a duke. It made his stomach turn to think about it, but all the evidence was there. Not the least of which was that the sister of a duke—a young lady who, by all accounts, should know better—had shown up alone to a room she had clearly known he was in. After all, the first thing she'd said when she saw him was, "There you are."

Lucian's gut tightened. Apparently, his good friend Southbury had a younger sister who thought nothing of scheming to get her way. And while Gemma would obviously come with an impeccable family name and no doubt be in possession of a hefty dowry, Lucian had wanted to look for a wife who not only had those things but was also the type of woman he could trust. And one who was beautiful. Mama would roll over in her grave to know that he'd got himself trapped into marriage with a skinny slip of a girl who was only too willing to trap him.

At least Lucian was certain Southbury had nothing to do with his sister's scheming. He'd given Lucian every chance to deny what had happened. It appeared the entire thing had been plotted by the two young ladies themselves.

Lucian needed more time to think it all over, of course. To decide how he would handle his new wife once they were wed, knowing how she'd schemed to force his hand. Once they were married, Gemma would belong to him as sure as any other item in his possession. He could send her off to the country alone if he chose. And frankly, he might do exactly that. God knew it would be a chore to bed her.

At the moment, however, there was only one thing to do. And that was to see to the marriage contract with Southbury. Lucian was a man of honor. After the gossip spread by Lady Cranberry last night, Lucian would not leave his friend's sister to a life of scandal and derision.

He rapped hard on the glossy black door to Southbury's town house. It was opened moments later by the butler. He greeted the man as he'd done dozens of times in the past when he'd come to pay a visit to his friend. Only today, he was here for an entirely different reason. One he'd never anticipated.

"Good morning, Your Grace," the butler said, ushering him into the marble-covered foyer. "His Grace is in his study waiting for you."

"I'll bet he is," Lucian muttered.

"Pardon me, Your Grace?" the butler replied.

"Nothing, Spaulding. No need to escort me. I know the way."

Moments later, Lucian was rapping on the same study door he'd been trapped behind only hours before. He took a deep breath to steel himself for the discussion. Southbury was a reasonable man, but any man who believed his sister to have been compromised should be approached with caution.

"Come in," came Southbury's steady voice.

Hmm. He didn't sound angry. Lucian slowly pushed the door open to see his friend sitting behind the large mahogany desk in front of the mullioned windows.

"Ah, Grovemont, there you are. Care for a drink?"

"It's half ten," Lucian pointed out, arching a brow.

"Yes, but given the subject matter, I daresay we could both use one." Southbury chuckled.

Now *that* was logic with which Lucian could not argue. "Hand me a glass," he told his friend.

Two hours later, the details of the marriage contract had been hashed out quite reasonably, and Griffin sat back in his seat and smiled at his old friend. Grovemont was going to marry Gemma. Griffin shook his head. It wasn't a pairing he'd ever imagined. It wasn't a pairing Grovemont had ever imagined either, he was certain of it.

Griffin knew from talking to Mama this morning that Gemma had been beside herself with guilt over what had happened last night. Apparently, she'd been trying to look out for the wallflowers again and had gone too far. Something about a dance and a dare. Gemma had always been too impetuous.

Grovemont was a good man, however, and he would make a fine husband for Gemma. Only Griffin couldn't help feeling somewhat responsible for the whole turn of events. He hadn't been too foxed to remember that Gemma had come asking him where Grovemont could be found last night. She'd said one of the wallflowers wanted to know and, of course, Griffin hadn't guessed that she'd wanted to seek him out for some misguided attempt at keeping Lady Mary Costner from being a shrew. Nonetheless, Griffin telling Gemma where Grovemont had got off to caused him a certain amount of guilt. He should at least *attempt* to explain.

"I'm sorry this wasn't what you'd planned," Griffin said. "Of course, I believe Gemma will make an excellent wife, but I understand that *you* might not feel the same at the moment. I feel deuced awful about it because I fear I had some part in it."

Grovemont's head snapped up, a wary look in his eye. "How so?" His gaze narrowed on Griffin.

"Gemma came looking for me and asked where you were. I told her you were in the study."

Grovemont's brows shot up. "So she *was* looking for me last night?"

"Yes," Griffin admitted. "She said a friend of hers was looking for you. I had no idea she intended to find you herself. Alone. She's terribly impatient, I'm afraid. Though I do expect she'll become less so when she's older."

"She wasn't alone," Grovemont informed him. "Lady Mary came soon after."

"Ah," Griffin trailed off. What else was left to say? At least he could take comfort in the fact that Grovemont would receive Gemma's indecently large dowry. Not to mention he'd tossed in some property and a new curricle of his that Grovemont had his eye on. But still, it didn't make up for the fact that Grovemont was being forced into this because of Gemma's mistake. Griffin didn't for one moment believe anything untoward had happened between Grovemont and his sister in the study last night. But theirs was a Society that was unforgiving of such things.

Honestly, Griffin couldn't even imagine being forced into an unwanted marriage. There had only ever been one woman he wanted, and that was Meredith. He wouldn't have been able to stand a life with anyone else. He could only hope Grovemont hadn't been secretly pining for a specific lady all these years. If so, he was too much of a gentleman to mention it.

Grovemont slapped his knees and stood. "I suppose that's it then."

"Yes," Griffin agreed. To play down any hint of scandal, they'd agreed to have the banns read over the next three weeks and the wedding would take place in a month's time. It needed to happen quickly to quell the rumors, but a month would be plenty of time. Anything less would be unseemly. At least Mama had recent experience in planning weddings. She'd already assured Griffin this morning that she would be able to plan one quickly.

"I do hope the situation last night did not put a damper on your celebration," Grovemont said politely.

Mighty decent of the man to say so. "Not at all."

Gemma had been worried about that too. In fact, she'd sent Mama down to ensure the party had continued. And it had. Of course, Lady Costner and her pinched-face daughter had taken their leave almost immediately after the scene in the study. But for the most part, the celebration had continued, with Griffin and Meredith staying up far longer than his mother wanted them to. Of course, there had already been rumors flying around the ballroom that Grovemont was soon to wed Gemma, but the ball had continued into the wee hours of the night, long after he and Meredith had gone to bed.

Meredith had been nearly beside herself with worry for Gemma last night, of course. Griffin had finally managed to convince her that while he was also concerned, there was nothing more to be done about it on the night of their wedding ball. He'd argued that they might as well retire for the evening and do precisely what his mother wanted them to do—get to the business of producing the next heir to the Southbury dukedom.

Meredith had laughed and pointed out that she was already with child. A delightful bit of news she'd shared with him earlier in the day.

"What Mama doesn't know won't hurt her," Griffin had replied with a wicked grin before gathering his beloved wife in his arms and taking her directly to bed.

All in all, it had been a terribly entertaining evening. And Griffin had awoken in his darling Meredith's arms, a place he'd never let her leave again for longer than the span of a day. He'd waited far too long to make her his, and he loved her without measure.

Which sparked his guilt again, reminding him of Grovemont and how Griffin's family had just taken away his choice of a wife. Damn. Lucian was a good man to do the right thing.

Griffin strode around the desk and clapped Grovemont on the back. They walked together to the door. "It won't be long now before I shall call you brother."

"Indeed," was Grovemont's stoic reply.

"Before you leave, would you like to speak with Gemma?" Griffin offered.

He almost added that she'd been up all night worried sick but decided against it. No man wanted to hear that his future wife was made ill at the prospect of marrying him. No matter what the circumstances of the betrothal had been.

"No," Grovemont replied. "I shall have plenty of time to speak to Gemma at length soon enough."

CHAPTER EIGHT

One Month Later, St. George's Chapel, London

Walking down the long church aisle gave Gemma far too much time to think. As if she hadn't done enough thinking daily ever since she'd got herself into this predicament.

She could run. She could turn right now, lift her white satin skirts, and sprint back toward the doors of the church, down the steps, into the street, and— Then what? Where would she go? What would she do? And how would she explain herself to the *groom,* who was currently standing at the altar with a resigned look on his face, waiting to marry her?

No. She *couldn't* run. This was all her fault, and if Grovemont was going to go through with it, she owed it to him to do the same. Not a day had gone by since their betrothal that Gemma hadn't been racked with guilt for her mistake. And she remained racked with guilt even now. There had been the hint of scandal, of course. But nothing that a wedding between two dukes' families couldn't squash.

In fact, the closer it got to the wedding day, the more well wishes she'd received. It seemed everyone in town wanted to see the most eligible bachelor marry the least likely debutante. Oh, Gemma knew she wasn't much to look at. Yet. And she could only hope the *yet* proved to be true. Ever since she could remember, Mama had told her the stories of how, until the age of twenty, Mama had been too tall, too thin, and had far too large of features for her face. But once Mama had grown into her swan-like beauty, she'd been declared an incomparable. The belle of the *ton*. She'd been the most sought-after debutante her third Season out, dimming all the younger ladies into the shadows with her gorgeous countenance and graceful limbs. Her chest had developed too, Mama had assured her. Currently, Gemma's was as flat as a platter.

But how was Grovemont supposed to know that Gemma would blossom? She was certain Griffin hadn't mentioned it to him, and Mama wouldn't have done so. Of course, Gemma had no intention of trying to convince him either. What if Gemma wasn't like Mama? What if she didn't turn into a beauty? What if she spent the rest of her days looking like a baby giraffe?

Oh, it was too depressing to contemplate. The only thing that cheered her was the fact that Griffin had assured her that Grovemont had been pleased with her dowry and that Griffin had added a few items to make the wedding contract even more agreeable. What those items were, Gemma wasn't entirely certain she wanted to know. And didn't members of noble families marry each other all the time without the hint of love? She would just have to get used to being in a loveless marriage. She did, however, hope that she and Grovemont would become friendly at least. They could, couldn't they?

But those weren't the only things that worried her. What would her new life be like? How would Grovemont treat her? Griffin and Mama insisted Grovemont was a good man, but they didn't know how he acted behind closed doors. What if he were secretly a monster?

She'd never even spoken to Grovemont. Beyond the few moments they'd shared in the study that night, she'd only seen him a handful of times. Frankly, he always seemed to be…controlled. Stoic. If not grim, then also not particular… happy.

In fact, the one memory of him that she kept replaying in her mind was the moment just before he'd opened the study door wide to find her standing there. He'd been sitting behind the desk, staring across the room, and he'd looked… lonely, alone. It had only lasted for a flash of an instant before she'd spoken to him, but she still couldn't dispel that one moment from her memory. It gave her hope. Perhaps… just maybe…the Duke of Grovemont needed her.

Though if he did, he certainly hadn't given any indication of it. Meredith and Griffin had hosted a betrothal dinner one night. Gemma had sat next to her fiancé and smiled until her cheeks ached, but they barely spoke two words to each other save for "good evening" and "good night." Their interactions had been nothing but awkward and stilted. Didn't he *want* to talk to her? Ask her what had happened that night in the study? Why she'd been running around trying to get him to refuse to dance with her? If she'd been Grovemont, that would have been her first question. Apparently, the duke wasn't even curious. Meanwhile, she was exceedingly curious about him.

One thing was certain. She'd made a lifelong enemy of Lady Mary Costner. If the young woman hadn't particularly liked Gemma before, she was her sworn enemy now. Mary's desire to secure an offer from Grovemont had been common knowledge before the debacle in Griffin's study. Each time Gemma had seen her since, Mary had given her a look that could freeze fire. No amount of explanation on Gemma's part would convince Lady Mary that she *hadn't* tricked her into agreeing to the dare with the sole purpose of wringing a betrothal out of Grovemont that night. Which was ridiculous, of course, but not in Mary's scheming little brain.

And in addition to all of *that*, there was something else to consider... Something quite terrifying.

The wedding night.

A lump formed in Gemma's throat every time she thought of it. She wasn't frighted of the act itself. After all, Meredith, who'd insisted on telling her every detail so she would be properly informed, claimed the act was *quite enjoyable.*

Gemma was much more worried about being seen naked by a man she barely knew. But she'd already decided that she would just have to slip into bed wearing the lacy gown Mama had commissioned for the occasion. She'd cover up with the bedclothes when it came time to disrobe. Surely, she wasn't the first young bride with such qualms. She would figure it out.

"Focus on the good parts," Mama had insisted when it came to her wedding and everything after. Mama had always been one to look on the happy side of any situation. She'd taught Gemma to do the same. And after considering it for a while, Gemma had to concede that there were, indeed, at least two good parts.

First, the Duke of Grovemont was not difficult to look at. In fact, the man was downright swoon-worthy. She'd never really thought much about him before. He was her brother's age and had been declared off-limits by Lady Mary, after all. But that night in the study, when she'd got a close look at him, Gemma had to admit he was uncommonly good-looking. With his dark-blond hair and hooded cobalt eyes, his chiseled jaw and perfectly straight nose. He had a way of sweeping her with his gaze, too, that was downright disconcerting. It made her shudder in a very good way. Perhaps the wedding night would be *quite enjoyable*, after all.

Second, marrying the Duke of Grovemont meant that Gemma would become a duchess. And while the thought was somewhat daunting, she had Mama and Meredith to help her. They'd both been duchesses long enough to know what they were about. And if one had to marry a man one didn't know, becoming a duchess wasn't the *worst* thing that could happen. Duchesses wielded great power in Society and could do things others could not. She just might enjoy being a duchess once she got the right of it.

Gemma took another deep breath and forced herself to lift her chin and look down the final length of the aisle. Her bridegroom stood at the altar, his hands folded in front of him, his perfectly fitted black morning coat, white shirt, waistcoat, and cravat looking dapper and expensive. His hair was slicked back, and those hooded blue eyes bore into her as she came closer. He had an inscrutable look on his face. There was no smile. Nothing. Was he angry? Indifferent? Apprehension bubbled in her middle.

For a moment, she paused and held her breath. The urge to turn and flee was nearly palpable. Griffin felt her hesitance and stopped with her. *You must do this*, she told herself. *This is your fault*. Grovemont would be humiliated if she ran away. Swallowing the large lump that had formed in her throat, she forced herself to take her next step, then the next, then the next, until she and her brother made it to the altar.

When they stopped in front of the archbishop, Griffin took her arm and placed it on Grovemont's black sleeve. She glanced up at him, attempting a smile. The look of cold, hard indifference on his face made her smile instantly whither. She swallowed.

Oh, God. It was too late to run.

CHAPTER NINE

That Night, The Duke of Grovemont's Town House

Lucian stared at his wife over the rim of his wine glass. She was on the dance floor, laughing and jesting with her brother and sister-in-law. She looked completely carefree. Happy even.

Good. She should enjoy it while it lasted.

Lucian had planned this ball tonight to keep up appearances. As far as the *ton* knew, Lady Gemma had been his choice of bride—minus the slight hint of scandal involved in their match — and he intended to keep it that way. The only person who would know he was angry with her, unhappy about being forced into the match, was his *wife*.

After the wedding this morning, Gemma had been bundled off in a coach with her mother. Later this afternoon, both women had arrived at his town house. He hadn't bothered to greet them. The servants had brought Gemma's trunks to the bedchamber that adjoined his. Where else would the new duchess sleep, after all? Lucian had called for the housekeeper and promptly informed Mrs. Howard that

Gemma's things were not to be unpacked. Mrs. Howard's brow shot up, but she'd nodded and done as she was told.

Lucian had a plan. After several days of obligatory revelry to celebrate their nuptials, he intended to send his new duchess and all of her belongings to one of his most remote estates. Cumberland, perhaps. He smiled to himself.

Gemma might have successfully garnered herself the title of duchess, but *he* would see to it that she enjoyed none of the other advantages that came with the position.

Oh, he would visit her upon occasion, out of obligation, but those visits would be few and infrequent. No more than he regularly visited his distant estates. Once a year. Twice, perhaps. *Someday*, he would have to get her with child, he supposed. But not tonight. Or anytime soon. Something told him a baby would only please her, and he had no intention of pleasing the woman who'd forced him into marriage.

His new wife may have had the upper hand in ensuring their union, but it would be the last time she had the upper hand. Lucian intended to show her, clearly and unmistakably, that from now on, *he* was in command of their marriage. She would do as she was told.

He'd been careful these last weeks, calculated. He'd ensured that he hadn't seen her much. He certainly hadn't spoken more than a few words to her. That had been intentional. He'd wanted her to wonder how it would be. While she'd no doubt been having visions of marriage to a handsome duke and becoming the toast of Society, he'd been entertaining visions of living his life as if he hadn't even married. And that's precisely how he intended life to be with his new wife. Completely unchanged.

Southbury and his duchess came off the dance floor, and Lucian watched from the table where he sat as Lord Pembroke approached Gemma, bowed, and then obviously invited her to dance. The next thing Lucian knew, Gemma whirled away in Pembroke's arms. Lucian narrowed his eyes on the young earl.

"Shouldn't you retire soon, Your Grace?" came Southbury's voice from beside him, shaking him from his thoughts.

Lucian turned and gave his old friend a tight smile. "I suppose so." He lifted the glass and swirled the wine inside as he watched his wife dancing in the arms of another man. She still looked happy. It was time to wipe that smile off her face. Whispers had begun. He was being watched. It was his wedding night, and he had an obligation to take his new wife upstairs. Upstairs, but not to bed.

Setting his half-full wine glass upon the table, Lucian stood and smoothed a hand over his white satin waistcoat. "Good evening," he said, inclining his head to the Duke and Duchess of Southbury.

The two nodded back, but Lucian was already stalking toward the dance floor. Pembroke was a good-looking, young upstart who'd recently inherited his father's earldom. The latest rumors had him as the next most eligible bachelor looking for a wife. The man was wide of the mark dancing with Lucian's wife. What did he want with a gangly married lady?

Lucian came to a stop a few paces behind Pembroke on the dance floor and waited until the earl had nearly backed into him before he lifted a hand and poked the younger man sharply on the shoulder with one finger.

Pembroke immediately stopped and whirled around to see Lucian glaring at him with a narrow-eyed stare.

Lucian gave the earl a fake, tight smile.

"Good evening, Your Grace," Pembroke said in an overly enthusiastic voice. "I do hope you haven't come to fetch your wife. I am *so* enjoying our dance."

"Then I'm here to dash your hopes because that's

precisely why I'm here. To fetch *my wife*," Lucian replied through a tight jaw. He glanced at Gemma to see her already large eyes go even wider. She was looking at him as if she was frightened of him. Fuck. That's all Lucian needed. To have the rumor start that he'd scared his new bride half to death by escorting her upstairs on their wedding night. He needed to do something to calm her fears.

"Care to dance?" he asked, directing his question to Gemma and completely ignoring her erstwhile dance partner.

"Y…yes," Gemma stuttered.

Lucian fought the urge to roll his eyes. She didn't just look scared of him; she sounded frightened too. Very well. He would have to spend a few unpleasant moments pretending to be the delighted bridegroom. He'd had plenty of practice pretending in life. This would be no different.

"I'll just leave you—" Pembroke said, but Lucian didn't wait to hear more. Instead, he stepped forward to take Gemma into his arms.

At first, she was wooden. One gloved hand on his shoulder, the other captured in his, and both felt as if they'd been cast in iron. But soon, after they'd spun around the floor a few times, her hands relaxed and she dared a glance up at him.

"Having fun?" he forced himself to ask with an equally forced smile on his lips.

"Ye…yes," she gulped. It was clear from the tremor in her voice that she was having no such thing.

"After this dance, we should retire," he said, ensuring his voice was neither eager nor angry. Indifference was the key. Always indifference. Show no emotion. Ever. His father had taught him well.

"Very well," she replied, but her voice cracked on the last word, and she swallowed audibly. Dear God. What did the girl think he was going to do to her? Pounce on her on the staircase? Surely, her mother had properly prepared her for the wedding night. Not that he intended to give her a traditional wedding night, but he realized *she* didn't know that. All the more vexing that he hadn't been able to choose his bride himself. If he had, he would have chosen someone beautiful, someone he *wanted* to make love to tonight. Someone he would have spent the last weeks flirting with and getting to know so that the culmination of this evening would be welcome to her, instead of anxiety-provoking.

Though it served her right to be filled with anxiety. She deserved no less. Still, she was young, and he didn't relish torturing anyone, least of all a young, innocent female. The moment the music stopped, he took her hand and guided her toward the staircase that led up and out of the ballroom.

Once they were standing in front of the double-doors, Lucian turned to say good night to his guests. He could feel Gemma perched at his side. He could only hope she didn't look as frightened as she'd sounded a few moments ago.

The ballroom clapped for them as he bowed, and she curtsied. Then they took their leave together. Normally, his mother would be here to handle the guests. Instead, Gemma's mother, the dowager, had stepped in to handle things this evening. If she were alive, Mama would be a dowager tonight too, now that he'd married. The thought saddened him. Was it better that Mama hadn't lived to see him marry a woman he hadn't chosen himself? Oh, what did it matter? It was done now. He was married to this lanky, scheming girl. For better *and* for worse.

Silently, he escorted her into the corridor and through the house to the foyer, where they ascended the main staircase to the second floor where the bedchambers were. As they walked, her gloved hand hovered at his arm but barely rested there. Her weight was not upon it, as if she were hesitant to touch him.

When they made it to the door to his bedchamber, Lucian stopped. "This is my room," he explained before pointing to the door several paces down the corridor. "That's yours."

"Yes, that's where I dressed earlier, isn't it?" she asked, blushing slightly.

"Yes," he assured her. He led her down to her door before he stopped again. Instinctively, she pulled her arm away from his.

He bowed to her. "Good evening, Your Grace."

Her brow furrowed, but she nodded. "Good evening, er, *Your Grace*." He had not given her permission to call him by his Christian name. Likewise, she hadn't given him permission to call her Gemma. It would probably be better that way. At least for now. Just another way to establish that their marriage was to be in name only.

After his bow, Lucian turned on his heel and walked away, smiling to himself at the memory of the tiny frown marks between his new wife's brow.

GEMMA JUMPED AT EVERY SOUND. She'd been in her bedchamber, dressed in her fancy lace night rail, for at least an hour. Her maid, Anna, had helped her dress. Mama and Meredith had given her an encouraging talk earlier, and now she was...waiting. Waiting and waiting, but the duke didn't come. She knew he was in the adjoining room. The moment she'd gone into her room and shut the door, she'd immediately turned to peek out. She'd watched him go into his bedchamber not ten paces away. And she'd heard several noises coming from the door between their rooms for the first quarter hour after she'd changed. But now there was only…silence.

Her nerves were winging about in her belly. The anticipation was making her ill. She wasn't frightened any longer. Now it was the anticipation making her jump. When she'd spied him from the dance floor earlier, butterflies had taken flight in her belly. He might be quiet. He might be difficult to read, but there was no doubt that the man was handsome. The truth was she'd been dreaming about kissing him for weeks now. She'd even practiced on her pillow at home. And now, well, she was *ready* for her wedding night. Looking forward to it, actually. She'd pictured him sitting on the side of the bed, leaning down to capture her mouth with his. She wanted to get started.

In fact, she'd stolen glances at him all day, biting her lip and shivering with anticipation when she thought about them being alone together tonight. Now it was time. But he was dawdling. This wasn't normal for a groom on his wedding night, was it? How long did it take a groom to prepare? Surely not longer than the bride. She should have asked Mama and Meredith how long it would take. But, honestly, it hadn't occurred to her to ask.

Perhaps he was being solicitous, making certain she had adequate time. But as the clock on her mantelpiece ticked closer and closer to the hour, she began to fear he was not coming.

Frowning, she tiptoed over to the adjoining door and placed her ear on it. *Silence.* Scowling, she dropped to her knees, leaned down, and peeked under the door. *Darkness.* She lifted her head and blinked. Had he left? Gone back downstairs? Surely not.

She climbed back to her feet and paced for a while, biting at her thumbnail and considering her options. Had she been misinformed? Should *she* be the one to knock on the door? It seemed unlikely, but perhaps he was waiting for her to indicate that she was ready.

Oh, yes, that must be it. Relief slid through her. She summoned every bit of nerve she had and hurried back to the door. She closed her eyes, straightened her shoulders, and raised her fist to knock. She was just about to strike the first blow when she heard it, distinct and unmistakable. *Snoring* was coming from the other side of the door.

Gemma's mouth dropped open. She shook her head. Surely, she was mistaken. She stepped forward and pressed her ear to the door, holding her breath. No. There was no mistaking it. The clear sounds of snoring echoed from the other side of the door.

It was her wedding night, and *her groom was asleep*.

CHAPTER TEN

The Next Morning, The Duke of Grovemont's Bedchamber

"Would you like your evening clothes tonight, Your Grace?" Lucian's valet, Franklin, asked as he finished helping Lucian dress for the morning.

"Yes, please. We'll be going to the Timberlys' affair tonight."

"Very good, Your Grace." Franklin nodded, bowed, and left the room.

Lucian took one last look at himself in the Cheval glass. Not too shabby. He looked perfectly rested. Most unlike a groom on the morning after his wedding. How would his new bride look? Would she still be frowning when he encountered her this morning? He looked forward to finding out, actually.

Whistling, he made his way down to the breakfast room and pushed open the double doors.

His wife was sitting there. She straightened her back against the chair when he entered the room. The rest of the dining room was empty, save for the servants. The guests had all gone home last night to their own townhomes, including Gemma's family. It was just the two of them this morning in married splendor. He bit his lip to keep from smiling.

"Good morning," he said in an overly bright voice.

"Good morning," she replied in a murmur.

A footman began dishing his plate from the sideboard while Lucian glanced over at Gemma. Her plate was covered with food as if she'd barely eaten anything. At the moment, she seemed to be pushing some unfortunate eggs around with her cutlery.

"I trust you slept well," Lucian added congenially.

"I did," came his new wife's curt reply. "You?"

"Quite well." He took a seat at the far end of the long table opposite her. And just as he did every morning, he snapped open the paper that had been sitting next to his coffee.

Lucian had read a few paragraphs when his wife cleared her throat in an excessively loud manner. He folded down the edge of the paper and glanced over to meet her gaze. "Are you quite well?" he inquired.

"Are you?" she replied, a bit of a saucy sardonic tone in her voice, surprising him.

He nearly smiled at that. *Nearly*.

"Yes. Quite." He lifted the paper again and resumed reading.

GEMMA STARED at the back of the paper covering her husband's handsome and highly slappable face. What in the world was going on? Who had she married? At her brother's house, her family spoke during breakfast. They joked and laughed and talked about the contents of the paper, last night's amusements, and anything else that caught their fancy. But here was this man *reading* as if she weren't even in the room.

And he hadn't even *mentioned* anything about why he hadn't arrived in her bedchamber last night. Not that she expected him to discuss it in the middle of the breakfast room with the servants hovering about, but he hadn't come to her room earlier this morning either to say…anything.

And now, when she'd attempted to begin conversation, he'd answered in a few clipped words and gone back to reading *with the paper covering his face*. She'd never encountered anything like it. *Purely rude.*

"Are you enjoying the paper?" she forced herself to ask as a solicitous footman poured her more tea.

"What's that?" her husband called without so much as dipping the paper to look at her again.

"Nothing," she shot back as the footman gave her a sympathetic look.

She sat there, stirring more sugar into her teacup for what felt like endless moments, and becoming more and more annoyed, before she finally dropped her teaspoon to the saucer with a clatter.

"What are your plans today?" she asked in an overly loud voice. Perhaps her new husband was hard of hearing. She doubted it. But it was possible.

"I'll spend the morning in the study as usual, and then I like to go to the club in the afternoon," he replied without so much as a tremor in the paper.

Well, far be it for having a new wife to distract the man from his usual pursuits. Fine. If he was going to play the role of the consummate nobleman going about his day, so would she. Gemma lifted her chin. She took a sip of tea and placed the cup back on the saucer before she said, "I suppose I'll meet with the housekeeper today."

"No need. Mrs. Howard is quite well-equipped to take care of things here."

No need? Gemma scowled. They both knew that it was proper for the lady of the house to take over such things as seeing to dinner menus and orders from the merchants. Of course, there was a need. What could he possibly mean?

"I was hoping Mrs. Howard would give me a tour of the house," Gemma added. There. He couldn't possibly have an objection to *that*. "Unless you'd like—"

"She'll be more than happy to show you about," her husband said.

Gemma had been about to ask the man if *he* would like to show her his home, but apparently *that* was beneath him. A sudden pang of homesickness hit her. How was she supposed to fit in here with this enigmatic man who didn't do any of the things she'd been raised to expect in the household of a duke? How was she to be happy here?

She couldn't go ask Mama or Meredith. Or, perhaps more correctly, she *wouldn't* go ask them. First, that would be disloyal. And she had no intention of being a disloyal wife. No matter how strange this household was, her surname was Banks now, and she would be loyal to her new family. But it wasn't just that.

She also didn't want either Mama or Meredith to think she couldn't handle her own new home. They'd both worried about Gemma enough in the past few weeks. In addition to giving her plenty of advice, they'd often given voice to their concerns that the marriage to Grovemont might be too much for Gemma. Gemma had no intention of proving them right and certainly not on her *second* day. She'd grown up as the baby of the household, constantly being told she was too young or inexperienced to do anything. She'd got herself into this mess with her stubbornness and impatience, and she had every intention of handling it with the grace and bearing of a true duchess. There would be no running back home and begging for advice or assistance.

How would a regal duchess act under such circumstances? Gemma thought for a few moments. A regal duchess certainly wouldn't allow her new husband to know she was flustered. Or affected in the least, actually. Which meant no more clattering teaspoons and barely veiled anger. *That* was beneath her.

"After my tour, perhaps I'll pay a call on my mother and brother," she said in the most nonchalant voice she could muster.

She stood, folded her napkin, and tossed it on the seat. There. That should show him that his plans had absolutely no impact on her. She wouldn't allow him to see that his disregard of her hurt. "Good day," she said as she moved past him toward the corridor.

"Be back and ready by nine," he instructed, folding his paper as the footman moved to place his plate in front of him. "We're going to the Timberlys' ball tonight."

CHAPTER ELEVEN

Three Nights Later

Gemma paced in front of the door that led between her bedchamber and her husband's. It had been three days. Three days of them barely speaking to each other. Three nights of them attending *ton* balls as if they were a happily married couple.

Grovemont hadn't told her anything about himself, his life, or even how he expected them to conduct themselves as a married couple. It was truly strange. All he'd done was eat breakfast with her in the mornings, his face stuck behind the newspaper, with no words spoken past, "Good morning."

Then he'd escorted her three nights in a row to a *ton* ball. They'd ridden in his luxuriously appointed coach together, speaking only of things such as the weather and the traffic in monosyllables. Then, once at the ball, he'd take off in one direction and she'd been forced to go in search of her family and friends in another. At some point, her husband found her, danced one waltz with her, left her again, and then gathered her at the end of the evening for the same boring ride home.

Was this how her marriage was to be? Day after day of hardly speaking and barely spending time together? It was maddeningly dull.

And to add insult to injury, her new husband *still* hadn't visited her bed. Each night, she'd put on the frothy lacy concoction from her wedding night and waited until she heard the snoring. Then she'd sunk into the mattress and pulled the covers over her head, completely frustrated and confused. What was *wrong* with him?

Oh, God. Was he impotent? She'd heard about such things. From Meredith, actually. Apparently, her first husband had been, *ahem*, unable to perform. But something told Gemma that impotence was not Grovemont's issue. In fact, she got the distinct impression it had something to do with *her*.

Gemma wanted to ask Meredith about it. But her pride kept her from it. If she explained to either Meredith or her mother what was going on here, no doubt they'd be appalled. Those two ladies lived quite different lives. Lives with talking, and tea sharing, and newspaper discussions, and laughter. And while she didn't want to contemplate how her mother and father had ever spent time in their bedchamber, Gemma was certain Meredith and Griffin shared plenty of time in that room. And from what Meredith had intimated, they greatly enjoyed themselves there.

This, whatever it was, with Grovemont was something else entirely. Some sort of purgatory of pleasantries that made one feel as if one were going mad. Her husband had never said anything unpleasant toward her or indicated he was unhappy with her, but surely there was something wrong if he hadn't seen fit to visit her bed at night. Even if she hadn't yet blossomed, he should at least see fit to *consummate their marriage*.

Gemma had tolerated it impassively the last three nights, but now here she was on night four and she was quite tired of the uncertainty and waiting. Either her husband would bed her, or he'd explain to her why not!

Before her nerve left her, she took a deep breath, turned, and stomped to the door. She knocked on it loudly, so sharply her knuckles hurt.

Silence.

She put her ear to the door. The snoring had stopped. She must have woken him.

A few moments passed. She lifted her hand to knock again when she heard "Come in" muttered sleepily.

Gulping and willing her pounding heart to settle, she pushed open the door between their rooms and stepped into the quiet darkness.

The light from her bedchamber illuminated a small space around her.

"Yes," came her husband's deep voice from the bed. "What is it?"

What is it? She fought the urge to stamp her bare foot. Did he truly not know? He had to. "I… I…" Oh, God. For all that she'd been impatient enough to knock and enter, she'd thought very little about what she would say once she arrived.

"Are you all right, Gemma?"

It was the first time she'd heard him say her Christian name. She'd begun to wonder if he even knew what it was. But at least he'd given her an opening.

"No. I'm not all right," she blurted. Oh, so much for acting the regal duchess. Regal duchesses must not have the temper Gemma was born with.

"If you're ill, I'm certain Mrs. Howard can get you something to—"

"I'm not *ill*," she said in a far louder voice than she'd meant to. "I'm…"

The man didn't even have the decency to light a candle so she could see his face.

"I'm confused," she finished.

"Confused?"

Here it was. She'd come this far. She might as well say it all. She took a few steps closer to the bed and peered toward him through the darkness. "It's been four nights since we married, and we haven't…" She stopped, half-hoping the floor would open and swallow her. But South-burys weren't cowards. She must press on. "You haven't…" She bit her lip. How exactly should she put this? "We haven't shared a bed."

"Correct," came his steady voice in the darkness while her heart pounded like a drum.

Wait. What had he said? Correct? Correct. She already knew she was correct. What the devil did that mean?

"And?" she prodded, her hands on her hips now. She'd been nervous when she'd first walked into the room, but she was quickly becoming annoyed.

"And that's the way I intend for it to remain…for now."

The complete nonchalance in his voice made her blood boil. He intended? That's the way *he intended* for it to *remain*? Dear God, the man sounded as if he was talking about a busi-ness arrangement rather than an intimate evening between husband and wife.

"I don't understand," she continued. "I may not know much about it, but I am under the distinct impression that a man should take his wife to his bed after their marriage."

He had the audacity to sigh. Audibly sigh. "There are several things about our marriage that are not traditional."

Her hands had curled into fists at her sides. Not traditional? What did that mean? "Such as?" She angrily blinked at him. Oh, do tell, *Your Grace*.

"Such as the manner in which we married," he offered.

She took a deep breath. Oh, yes. There was that. That needed to be discussed. She was nothing but pleased that he'd brought it up. "Yes, that's something I would like to discuss with you. I never meant to—"

"Never meant to what?" His voice rose and dripped with anger-edged skepticism, sounding so harsh that it made her take a step back. "Never meant to trap me into marriage? Save your breath, Gemma. I know you and your friend were scheming that night in your brother's study. I heard what you said to her."

Gemma's eyes flew open wide. He *was* angry. Angry and holding the way they'd married against her. Fine. That stood to reason, but why hadn't he given her the courtesy of asking her about it first? She would just have to set him straight. "First, Lady Mary Costner is *not* my friend and second, it wasn't—"

"The only thing that will make this worse is if you continue to lie to me." His voice was calm but hard.

Her brows snapped together. "Lie to you? I never—"

"I *abhor* liars."

"So do I." She crossed her arms tightly over her chest and glared at him. She might not be able to see him, but she hoped he could see the anger on her face in the light from her room.

A flint struck and the lamp on the table next to his bed flared to life. In an instant, he pushed the covers off and stood. He was wearing only a loose pair of linen trousers obviously meant for sleeping. His chest was entirely bare, and Gemma couldn't help but notice the muscles that stood out in stark relief along his abdomen and the light dusting of blond hair that formed a V and disappeared in an intriguing line down his trousers. She stared. She couldn't help herself. She'd never seen a man's bare chest before. And this one... well, it looked particularly fine. Her mouth went dry, and she completely forgot what she'd been saying.

His dark-blue eyes flashed like sapphires in the dimness and his voice was a low growl. "Allow me to make this clear. Our marriage will in no way be conventional. I have kept you here in town to keep up appearances. I will not have the *ton* gossiping about me or my wife. But make no mistake, you may have taken away my choice of whom to marry, but *I* will be making all the decisions from now on. Including where you live, where we go, and when, where, and *if* I bed you. *Do you understand?*"

White-hot anger exploded behind Gemma's eyes. Then it spread quickly through her body until she felt as if she might burst into flames right in front of him. *Do you understand?* The pompous, demeaning words played themselves over and over in her head. Oh, she understood all right. She understood that her husband was under the mistaken impression that she would be the sort of wife who would allow him to treat her like an inconsequential piece of property. She understood that he was a haughty, condescending, pompous horse's ass!

This duchess, regal or no, was not about to accept such treatment.

"Do you understand, Gemma?" he repeated. His jaw was clenched, and his voice remained low.

"Perfectly," she shot out before turning sharply on her heel. She stomped back through the doorway and ripped the door shut behind her. The slam of it reverberated through both rooms. No doubt the servants had even heard it. Good.

Clearly, regal was not the sort of duchess she would be. Angry. Angry was more like it. At least at the moment. She paced in front of the large fireplace in her bedchamber. *That man*! She'd given him every benefit of the doubt up 'til now, but the truth was glaring. Her new husband didn't want to be married to her. He blamed her for ruining his life, and he intended to make her pay without so much as bothering to listen to her explanation of what had happened that night in Griffin's study, or the apology she'd fully intended to provide.

Lucian Banks was the worst kind of man. And she was married to him. *Forever*.

CHAPTER TWELVE

When Lucian arrived in the breakfast room the next morning, his wife wasn't there. Was she still abed? Or was she purposely staying away? He guessed the latter. Clearly, she'd been angry last night after their encounter. She'd slammed the door hard enough to wake the dead. He'd ignored that. He had no intention of entertaining her moods. She would just have to learn that what he said was final.

But he couldn't concentrate on reading the paper. A memory kept nagging at his mind. Her eyes in the candle-light last night. Those dark, expressive eyes had been easy to read. First, they'd been filled with worry, anxiety. Then annoyance. And then, for just a few fleeting moments, sadness. And finally anger.

But it was the sadness that stuck in his mind. She'd come to ask him why he hadn't bedded her. A normal query for a new bride, perhaps. But they were anything but a normal couple.

Those few moments of sadness he'd seen haunted him.

He shook his head to dispel the memory. He'd do well to remember that she was a good actress. Perhaps an excellent one. Hadn't she acted the part of the innocent debutante the night she'd found him in her brother's study?

She'd pretended as if encountering him had been nothing more than a lark, but her words had reverberated in his head every damn day since then. *"You heard him, Mary. Remember your promise."* She and her friend had planned the entire thing. He could only guess what Mary's "promise" had been. No doubt to bring her mother and the other matrons running in order to cause the exact scene that had ensued.

Yes. His wife was an actress. He wouldn't be fooled. He needed to stay on his guard in her presence. He couldn't trust anything she said or did. She simply hadn't liked being dismissed last night. Frankly, he'd been surprised she'd had the temerity to come knocking on his door. But just because she didn't like his answers didn't mean he would change his mind. Gemma needed to learn that she would not be getting what she wanted out of this marriage. And the sooner she realized it, the better.

There was only one thing she'd said last night that gave him pause. The part about them not spending the night together for four nights. At first, he'd avoided her bed to make his point clear. But the more he thought on it, the more he realized he probably should bed her before sending her away to the countryside. After all, their marriage wouldn't be legal until that deed was done. Unpleasant or no.

Of course, that might result in a child. The thought of using a French letter or pulling out occurred to him. But he found those choices distasteful. She was his wife, and if ever he declined to use protection, it should be with her. Perhaps he'd been wrong about it at first. Perhaps he *should* try to get her with child before sending her off. God knew he wouldn't relish doing it again anytime soon.

Very well. He would get it over with. He would bed his wife. But he would also set the boundaries. Very clear ones. It would be a perfunctory act. Nothing more. With a woman as scheming as Gemma, he had to remain in control.

CHAPTER THIRTEEN

That Night, The Kents' Ballroom

Gemma was prepared to make the most of it. The Kents' ball, that was. Her terrible husband had already taken off toward Lord Kent's study the moment they'd arrived. But that would not keep her from having a wonderful time. Her friends and family were here. She intended to enjoy herself in their company. The devil take Grovemont.

She breezed through the crowd, lifting the skirts of her sky-blue gown. She was wearing her favorite diamond necklace tonight. One that made her feel like a regal duchess. One that Mama had given her. She was still without earbobs. And now that she was married, Mama would no longer have a reason to try to coax her into wearing the hateful things. Her husband might be awful, but there were some perks of being a duchess.

Gemma craned her neck, searching for Griffin and Meredith. But she kept getting distracted. Every time she thought about the haughty way Grovemont had insisted she'd tricked him into marriage, she wanted to scream with frustration. She'd no more wanted to marry him than he'd wanted to marry her. She'd assumed she would have time to explain it to him, to ask his forgiveness for the way they'd started in life. But now she realized he wasn't interested in listening to her explanation. He'd already made up his mind. She was guilty.

"Gemma, there you are," came Meredith's pretty voice behind her. "Where is Grovemont?"

Gemma turned to greet her sister-in-law and brother with a big, false smile. "Oh, he must be around here somewhere. I just saw him."

Gemma spent the next hour chatting and laughing with Griffin and Meredith. Of course, she didn't mention a thing about her unhappy marriage. It would only make Griffin feel guilty if he knew how bad it was. And it was her fault, not his. He deserved no guilt.

"Is Grovemont planning to take you to his country estate in Devon?" Griffin asked.

Gemma still had the fake smile pinned to her face, but her brother's question made her frown. One of the many hideous things her husband had said to her last night came winging back through her brain. "I *will be making all the decisions from now on. Including where you live.*"

She hadn't given that part of his diatribe much thought, but now she couldn't forget it. "*I have kept you here in town to keep up appearances,*" he'd also said. Did he intend to send her away? If so, where? And when?

It would be an outlandish thing for him to do. Surely, he wouldn't — Oh, dear. Another memory came to her then. A memory from the day after her wedding, when she'd asked Mrs. Howard if the maids would be moving her things from the trunks to the wardrobe and the dressing room. Mrs. Howard had lowered her gaze and replied, "Not at this time, my lady."

Gemma had assumed she meant *that day*. She'd guessed the maids were busy helping with the wedding ball, which stood to reason. But as the days progressed and her items were still in the trunks, she'd questioned Mrs. Howard again and had received yet another vague answer.

Now, Gemma had a sinking feeling she knew why the housekeeper had been so vague. Grovemont intended to send Gemma away. Where? Who knew? For how long? It was anyone's guess. But she was certain about it, and she intended to confront the man at the earliest opportunity.

"Excuse me," she said to Griffin and Meredith. "I think I see Cecily."

Gemma couldn't leave fast enough. She didn't want Griffin and Meredith to see the panic that was undoubtedly in her eyes. And she *had* seen her good friend Cecily Grundy standing near the entrance. She made her way over to her friend, intent upon rescuing poor Cecily from her awful mother.

"He's going to send me away," Gemma whispered as soon as she and Cecily were alone near the wall a few minutes later.

"Who?" Cecily asked, blinking her bright cornflower-blue eyes at Gemma.

"Grovemont, of course," Gemma replied.

Cecily's mouth formed a perfect O. "Where is he sending you?"

"I don't know. But I intend to find out. I—"

"Oh, don't look now, Gemma. But Lord Pembroke is coming this way. You know that Lady Mary has set her sights on him now that Grovemont is lost to her. She's warned us all away from him, of course."

Gemma fought the urge to roll her eyes. Apparently, Lady Mary was back to her old foibles. "I was hoping Mary would stop with that nonsense."

"Oh, no. Not Mary," Cecily replied, shaking her head. "Seems Pembroke is her new prey. Which means, I, for one, intend to stay far away from him. I'll see you later." And with that, Cecily disappeared into the crowd just before Pembroke arrived at Gemma's side.

"Your Grace," Pembroke said, bowing over her hand. "It's good to see you this evening."

"Good evening, Lord Pembroke," Gemma replied, smiling at the earl.

"You look beautiful tonight as always. Will you do me the honor of dancing with me?"

Gemma gave him a beatific smile. Cecily might want to stay far away from Lord Pembroke, but Gemma was a duchess now. She had absolutely nothing to fear from Mary Costner. Of course, she would dance with Lord Pembroke. Besides, better to dance with a gentleman who seemed to want to dance with her than with her ill-tempered husband, who did it out of obligation.

"I'd be delighted," she easily replied, placing her arm on Lord Pembroke's proffered one. Pembroke led her to the dance floor.

Lucian glared at the dancers. Was that *Pembroke* with his wife *again*? That made three nights in a row. It was unseemly for a married woman to dance so often with a man who was not her husband. Did Pembroke *want* his nose broken? Lucian stalked toward the dance floor.

"Get lost, lad," he said to Pembroke in a tone that brooked no further argument. "I want to dance with *my wife*."

Pembroke, who was at least a head shorter than Lucian, gulped, quickly bowed to Gemma, and scurried off into the crowd.

Gemma allowed Lucian to take her into his arms, but she remained stiff as a fencepost. Her lips narrowed to a thin line, and she refused to look anywhere other than directly at his shoulder clad in black evening attire. "That was ill-mannered of you," she informed him.

"Duly noted," was his unaffected reply.

Ah, so she was angry again, was she? Or perhaps she'd never stopped being angry from before. No matter. She would learn soon enough that her moods would not affect his behavior in the least.

"Smile, won't you?" he demanded. "It's unseemly to allow everyone to think we're unhappy."

"We *are* unhappy," she shot back. "And I have no problem being unseemly."

Lucian kept the false smile pinned to his face. Good God. Had her mother not taught her any better manners than that? Fine. He would discuss it with her later when they were alone. For now, he would simply finish their dance for the sake of appearances.

When the music came to an end, he formally bowed to her. "I'll be back to fetch you in an hour to escort you home."

Her smile was tight and fake. "I shall remain on tenterhooks."

TRUE TO HIS WORD, Lucian was back to fetch her in one hour. This time, he was forced to gather her from the center of a group of wallflowers, where she appeared to be delivering some sort of speech.

"And that is precisely why each of you should do as you wish, without regard to Lady Mary—"

She stopped the moment she caught sight of him out of the corner of her eye.

"My lady," he drawled, bowing to her.

A slight sigh sounded through the gathered wallflowers before they all scattered, but not before he noted many of them staring at him with dreamy eyes.

Meanwhile, his *wife* nearly rolled her eyes at the sight of him but dutifully excused herself to the remaining ladies and said good night.

Within a quarter hour, they were in the coach headed home. As usual, Lucian spent the ride staring out the window into the darkened streets of London. Tonight, he had one annoying thought on his mind.

Why had it bothered him to see Pembroke fawning over his wife? Lucian had never been the jealous sort, and he did not intend to become one now, especially when his wife was a plotting schemer who had only married him for his title. But something about seeing her enjoying herself in Pembroke's arms earlier had made Lucian want to snap the younger man's neck. And for the hint of a moment, he'd wanted that dazzling smile of Gemma's directed at him.

It made no sense. She'd only be faking her affection, but somehow when she laughed and danced with others, she seemed…believable. As if she was truly enjoying herself. And that laughter, that happiness. It was…attractive, captivating. It made her face light up. Made the whole room light up.

"Are you planning to send me away?" came Gemma's simmering voice from the other side of the coach.

"Pardon?" He frowned. Where the hell had *that* question come from? He certainly hadn't mentioned anything about it to her, or anyone else, for that matter.

"Tell the truth. Are you planning to send me away or not? I deserve to know when and where."

He forced his voice to remain measured, calm. It was the only way to deal with Gemma. "If and when I decide to—"

"No." She stopped him. "That is an unacceptable answer to me. If you plan to send me away, I want to know the specifics. Now."

Lucian folded his arms over his chest and glared at his demanding wife. First, he didn't have the bloody specifics. He hadn't worked them out yet. Second, he was under no obligation to share his thought process with her. Why did she insist upon constantly questioning him? It was almost as if she *enjoyed* arguing. He'd hoped for a biddable wife. Clearly, he had got the opposite. She was recalcitrant even. And he'd put up with far less egregious behavior from far more beautiful ladies.

"You are in no position to demand anything from me," he replied simply.

"Oh, far be it from me to question *His Grace, the Duke of Grovemont.*" Sarcasm dripped from her voice.

His eyes narrowed on her. "You are currently being treated with a level of respect due your station, but I have no intention of allowing you to demand anything from me, including my decisions."

Her eyes flew wide, and a hand fluttered to her chest. "I should be *grateful*? Is that what you're telling me? Perhaps thankful that you have not tossed me in a dungeon with only moldy scraps of bread for meals and no abuse of my person?"

"You're dramatic," he ground out.

"You're made of stone."

Lucian didn't have long to contemplate *that* loaded statement before she added, "I'm getting out of the coach. I'll *walk* home."

"The devil you will."

But Gemma lunged for the door.

In her haste, she flew across his lap, and her gown stuck on his boot, stopping her flight. She sprang backward and landed atop his lap, where she immediately began wriggling and fighting like a cat trapped in a burlap sack.

"Damn it, stop squirming," he said, unintentionally becoming aroused by the feel of her on his lap.

"Let go of me then," she replied, still struggling.

"I'm not holding you. Your gown is caught—"

And just like that, the fabric tugged free. There was a horrible ripping noise, and Gemma ended up on the seat beside him with the back of her gown ripped and a sleeve hanging haphazardly off her shoulder.

She stared down at the mess, aghast. "Why...why...look what you've done? My gown is ruined."

"Nothing the maids can't fix, I'm certain." He tugged at his cuff, desperately willing his cockstand to subside. What in the hell had caused it? It was unwanted. And unwelcome.

She continued pulling at her ruined sleeve. "That's your answer to everything, isn't it? Order a servant to fix it. Some things can't be fixed, *Your Grace.*"

She narrowed her eyes on him. She clearly wasn't talking about the gown any longer.

"Like what?" he ventured.

She hoisted her ripped sleeve and moved back to the opposite seat, where she stared out the window, ignoring him.

He *should* have left well enough alone. He *should* have kept his damn mouth shut and enjoyed the quiet on the ride back to the town house after she'd thankfully abandoned her idiotic plan to exit the conveyance. But instead, he found himself saying, "I find it ironic that *you're* angry with *me.*"

Her nostrils flared. He could see that she wanted to say something. She wanted to, but she was warring with herself.

"When *I* am the one who should be angry," he continued. It wasn't like him to goad anyone into a fight, but there was something about the way she was trying not to say anything that made him want to push until she said whatever she was clearly thinking. And something about the way he'd become attracted to her so easily made him want to punish her.

"Oh, yes, because you have the moral high ground, don't you?" She was kicking her foot beneath her skirts, the light-green satin fabric rising and falling with each kick.

His brows shot up. "I do, actually."

"You are a pompous, arrogant blowhard who is under the mistaken impression that the world revolves around him. You think you have the right to punish me, but you haven't even heard the whole story, and I'm certain you don't even care because that might make you wrong. And how could a know-it-all ass like you ever be wrong? If you want to order your wife around like a piece of chattel, you're welcome to try, but I'm here to tell you that I have no intention of taking orders from you now or ever. And if you don't like it, you should send me away sooner rather than later because it's not about to change."

During her speech, Lucian had *tried* to interrupt her several times. But each time he opened his mouth to speak, he couldn't get in a word. She wouldn't stop. She'd clearly been pushed to the edge and had let the tide rip.

She was somewhat magnificent, he grudgingly admitted to himself, when she was on such a tangent. Her eyes were bright and fierce and compelling. Color had risen in her cheeks, giving her a warm glow. She was pointing her finger in the air, and she looked like an angry goddess who had descended from the heavens to wreak damage on the mortals who'd displeased her. In that moment, he did the only thing he could think of to get her to stop ranting. He reached across the space, pulled her sharply into his arms, and kissed her.

The moment his lips touched hers, Gemma shut up. She shut up and made a small gasping sound in the back of her throat. He'd intended to stop the moment she shut up, but the feel of her soft lips on his did something to him. Something to his groin, specifically. His lips moved on hers forcefully, pushing open her mouth and invading the wet warmth inside. Another tiny gasp and she opened for him. *That's it.* His mouth slanted over hers, his tongue possessive. And without thinking, he pulled her onto his lap, this time to grab her hips and hold her steady against him. To press her softness against his hardness. He heard himself groan.

The kiss turned wild. His mouth slanted across hers, and her fingers went up to thread through his hair. His hand moved down to push up her skirts and rest on her warm thigh through her shift. She seemed ravenous for him. How could that be? And he? He was equally ravenous for her. What the hell was happening to him? He didn't even like her, but in that moment, he wanted to bury himself deep inside of her and thrust until she was moaning his name and they were both spent.

Thankfully, the coach pulled to a stop, shaking Lucian from the lust-induced haze that surrounded him. The last thing he wanted was for the footman to open the door and see him fondling his wife. He quickly pulled his mouth from Gemma's, removed his hand from beneath her skirts, and set her on the seat beside him. She made an *oof* noise and was staring straight ahead with a completely dazed look on her face, her lips swollen and her eyes as big as wagon wheels.

"Your Grace," came the footman's voice moments later as he opened the door and folded down the stairs. Clenching his jaw, closing his eyes, and willing his erection into nonexistence, Lucian counted to ten, cleared his throat, and then descended the steps before he turned back to help his wife out of the coach. Gemma came along, still looking as if she didn't know where she was. And she didn't say a word. He'd rendered her speechless. Interesting.

The moment her feet touched the ground, Lucian quickly whipped off his coat and covered Gemma's shoulders to hide the ripped gown. Then he took her hand and led her across the graveled path to the steps up to the town house, where he helped her climb the stairs. She was silent the entire way.

Somehow, they made it up the stairs, into the house, and all the way up to the corridor beside their bedchambers where Lucian was able to hand Gemma off to her maid, who was waiting for her mistress.

Moments later, when the door to his own bedchamber closed behind him, Lucian leaned back against it, closed his eyes, and groaned. Damn it. What had *that* been about? That kiss had been explosive. Unlike any he could remember in recent memory. Hell, in former memory either.

He was pulling his cravat from his neck when his valet came hurrying in. Franklin helped him undress, and Lucian pulled on the soft linen trousers he preferred to wear to bed before dismissing the servant.

But Lucian didn't go to bed. And after pacing for the better part of half an hour, he knew why. He was sexually aroused, damn it. And, amazingly, he wanted...his wife.

That was a mad thought. But that kiss had done something to him. Specifically? It had given him a raging cock-stand. One that he was still trying to tamp down. And that was confusing too because his wife was not his sort of woman. She was thin and tall and without curves. Her eyes were too large and her hair was too short and she, well, just wasn't his sort. But there was something about her eyes, something intriguing, something compelling. And the way she'd been so forceful and determined. The way she'd delivered that diatribe… And then that kiss. It had been beyond passionate. And he wanted…more.

He'd already decided he would bed her before sending her off, hadn't he? This would be in keeping with his plan. It didn't mean anything. Being sexually aroused by her would only make it easier.

His decision made, Lucian stalked over to the adjoining door and knocked.

CHAPTER FOURTEEN

The knock startled Gemma. She hadn't been expecting it. Though, admittedly, after that kiss in the coach, she didn't know what she had been expecting. In fact, she didn't know much about anything after that kiss.

It was as if she'd been struck dumb by it. She'd somehow managed to make it out of the coach, up the stairs, into the town house, and into her bedchamber without remembering how she got there. Thank heavens, Anna had been there to help. She had a brief memory of her maid removing her gown, her shift, and then her stockings. A few words had been exchanged about the ripped sleeve, and then a new silky night rail had been slipped over her head, and somehow she was in bed and Anna was gone.

Gemma had been sitting there for several moments staring at the wall in awe. What in the world had happened in that coach? A kiss? She knew it was a kiss. It had all the indications of a kiss and yet…it had been something so much more. Something that had swept over her and made her entire body hot and achy and restless. One moment she'd been wanting to jump from the coach to escape that vile man. The next moment, she'd been melting in his arms, her fingers threaded through his soft hair as his mouth owned hers. It made no sense.

The knock made her heart jump into her throat.

"Come in." Her voice was barely a whisper. She cleared her throat and was about to repeat herself when the door opened, and Lucian came striding inside.

She lifted her gaze and once again was confronted with the man's bare chest. God save innocents from such a sight. Earlier she'd told him he was carved from stone. Marble was more like it, and at the hands of a master. Michelangelo himself could not have done more admirable work.

Lucian began pacing in front of the bed. He scrubbed a hand through his hair, mussing it in a way that made her want to touch it again. "I was wondering what you thought of that kiss?"

She blinked. She might as well be honest. "I… I have no words."

He nodded. "I feel the same."

"Is it normally like that?" Her brows knitted together. "I have nothing to compare it to."

He continued his pacing. "No. It's *not* normally like that."

Gemma gulped. "It had to be a mistake. Right?"

"It didn't feel like a mistake." He stopped pacing and strode over to her side. "In fact, I was wondering if we might…try it again."

Her throat went dry. He wanted to kiss her again? "I suppose there is no harm in trying again." She swallowed hard. "Just to confirm."

"Yes, to confirm. Quite logical."

He lowered himself to sit on the edge of the mattress facing her. His nearness made her suck in her breath. He reached out and wrapped a warm hand behind her neck.

Their eyes met. An undeniable spark leaped between them. Gemma felt a shudder work its way through her body. His blue eyes were mesmerizing her.

He leaned forward, closer, closer.

His lips touched hers like a whisper, barely felt. Barely there. A hum moved through her body. When the tip of his tongue licked across the seam of her lips, coaxing them to open, the hum became louder. And when his tongue plunged into the heat of her mouth, possessing her, it turned into a full roar. She couldn't hear anything anymore... She could only feel. The pressure of his mouth against hers, the heat of his hand behind her neck, the rasp of his skin against the softness of her chin.

Her hands went up to his hair again, just as they'd done in the coach. It was a mindless response. She'd longed to feel the soft thickness between her fingers, but this time she soon let her fingers move down along his rough cheeks, gliding down the thick muscles in his neck. She let them splay across his rock-hard bare shoulders and stay there. Her fingertips curved around his shoulders, and she pulled him toward her. He moved, down, down until he was atop her, the bedclothes between them inconvenient until she felt him fling them away. And then his weight settled atop her, and she clung to him, reveling in the welcome weight pressing into her, never wanting him to leave.

When his mouth moved to her ear and dipped inside the delicate shell, Gemma's body bucked. She moaned. Then his mouth moved to nip at the lobe, then down the side of her neck, where he lightly sucked the skin there as if he were tasting it. She arched her neck to give him more access.

Her eyes rolled back in her head. How in the world did that feel as good as it did? She'd never imagined anything like it. He was nipping at her skin, licking her, lightly sucking. She let her hands venture from his shoulders to his chest, reveling in the feel of the muscles that jumped beneath his hot skin at her touch. She splayed her hands wide to feel as much as she could, and a tremor stole through her body. The man's muscles had muscles. She pushed her hands back up to his shoulders and then down his thick arms. The barely restrained power there made her shiver with delight.

His mouth moved down to the bodice of her night rail. "How much do you like this garment?" he asked in a husky voice that sent another shiver through her.

"Not much," she breathed against his ear.

The sound of the night rail ripping in two followed, and she was bared to him.

"Gemma," he breathed as he took in her body.

"I know I'm not very..." She bit her lip. "The women in my family blossom later." She felt like a fool trying to explain herself, but it seemed like the right time.

"You're perfect," he whispered.

He pushed himself away and stood to discard his trousers. Gemma gasped when she saw his nude body. He was the perfect one. But she wasn't about to quibble. His manhood stood out large and thick between his strong thighs and his legs were as masterfully sculpted as the rest of him.

Standing next to the bed, he gently pulled the pieces of her night rail away and tossed them on the floor. Then he moved back onto the bed atop her, bracing his strong arms on either side of her head.

She felt him hot and thick against her thigh.

Gemma held her breath. Meredith had explained the act to her. She knew what would happen next. But would it hurt? Meredith hadn't mentioned that, but Gemma didn't see how it couldn't hurt given the sheer size of the thing.

One of his hands moved down between her thighs. His fingers parted her and when he touched a spot so delicate, so perfect, she cried out, "Oh." She grasped his shoulders tight and closed her eyes.

"You like that?" he rasped against her throat.

All she could do was gulp and nod, and then his finger was pressing against the spot in tiny little circles, and Gemma forgot the entire world and everything in it.

The pressure between her legs built. It grew and grew until she was mindless, wanting something, more, more.

When one of his fingers dipped inside her, she gasped against his rough cheek.

"Do you want me, Gemma?" he asked.

"Yes," she breathed, nodding. Her eyes closed. She did. She so did. She hadn't expected it to feel like *this*. Any of it.

"I want you," he whispered into her ear. "Come for me," he said, intently watching her face just before stars burst behind her eyes and a feeling unlike any she'd ever known exploded between her legs. Her body jerked and a shudder ran the full length of her. Her breathing hitched with tiny gasps and she clung to him until the tremors eased slowly away.

He kissed her again as her body settled. And then his thick heat was there, probing between her legs. The first slide of him inside her made her gasp again. She'd thought she couldn't feel anymore, but when he slid in farther, farther, inch by inch, she adjusted her hips to meet him and wrapped her arms fiercely around his neck. She clenched her teeth together.

He kissed her cheek. "I'm not hurting you, am I?"

"No." She shook her head. It didn't hurt. It was more like…fullness. Complete fullness.

When he shifted his hips to go all the way in, there was a tiny pinch, but Gemma quickly forgot about it. Because she had opened her eyes and watching his face had become her new obsession. His eyes were closed, and he wore a nearly pained expression. His features stood out in the shadows in stark relief. His lashes, so dark and full, feathered along his cheeks and his jaw was clenched. But the best part, the very best part, was how he was shaking ever so slightly. As if he couldn't control himself.

"Oh, God," he moaned. "Gemma. You feel so good."

She felt so good?

Truly?

The power of those words was heady. She had this beautiful man at her mercy. He was completely lost. *She'd* made him feel this way.

When he began to move, Gemma realized what Meredith had been talking about. Quite enjoyable indeed. His hips pulled back and thrust, eliciting an "Oh" from her. The next thrust garnered an "Oh my." And so it went. He pumped into her, again and again, sliding in and out, clearly reveling in the feel, his eyes still tightly clenched shut as she gasped with pleasure beneath him.

He was strong and sure and seemingly indefatigable as he thrust into her. The groans coming from the back of his throat captivated her. She lifted her hips to meet him thrust for thrust, crying out each time he drove inside her.

When she felt a tremor shoot through him and his arms, still braced on either side of her head, trembled, she truly felt powerful. She was heady with it. He pressed his forehead to hers hard and his mouth captured hers as he pumped into her again and again before groaning, "Gemma," against her lips and collapsing atop her with one final deep pump.

Gemma lay there in a sweaty heap. The gorgeous man on top of her was breathing heavily. Dear heavens, *that* had been surprising. Surprising and exhilarating and satisfying and... intimate. So very intimate. Grovemont...Lucian...was a completely different person in bed. How was it possible that this was the same man who walked around in life with a clenched jaw and an unaffected look on his face? How could a man who could be so passionate and unreserved in bed be so controlled and dominating outside of it?

He rolled to the side and gathered her in his arms, snuggling her head under his chin. Gemma pressed her nose to his neck and breathed him in. Surely, what they'd just shared had changed things between them. He couldn't send her away after that. This *had* to mean he'd changed his mind.

Gemma fell asleep with a smile on her face. Perhaps marriage wouldn't be so bad, after all.

CHAPTER FIFTEEN

The Next Morning, The Duke of Grovemont's Study

Lucian scrubbed a hand through his hair. Fuck. Fuck. Fuck. He'd been attempting to read a report from his solicitor all morning, but he'd barely got through the first paragraph, and he'd read the damn thing ten different times. The report was filled with information he'd been looking forward to reading, information about his holdings in India. He needed to plan a trip there. Had intended to after he'd chosen a wife and married. Things may not have gone according to plan, but he *was* married. He couldn't leave Gemma alone here, could he? Damn it. Gemma. He couldn't concentrate. His mind betrayed him, constantly replaying memories of his time in bed with her last night.

He'd expected it to be pleasant. Sort of like scratching an itch. After all, he hadn't been with a woman since before he'd returned from the countryside months earlier. But what had started out as an experiment had quickly turned into one of the most satisfying sexual experiences he'd had in his life.

Gemma was surprising in bed. That was the best word for it. She'd been passionate and giving and uninhibited in a way that he had not expected. The truth was he'd been unable to control himself. The second his mouth touched hers, he'd been lost. He'd intended to give her a second orgasm, but after he'd slid into her tight sheath, his mind had gone numb. Something about the way she'd responded to him, holding nothing back, had inflamed him. Years of rigidly implemented self-control had disintegrated in moments, and he'd become a lust-crazed beast.

It had to have been the months of celibacy. That was the only explanation for it. At least that's what he intended to tell himself. Because any other reason for his performance in bed with his wife last night was too unsettling to contemplate.

She'd definitely been a virgin last night. Not that he'd thought she wasn't, but he'd felt her maidenhead give way, and he'd seen the evidence on the sheet.

He'd awoken in the middle of the night lying on his back to find her cuddled against his chest, one arm flung over his waist. His first thought had been to roll her over, slide down, and give her an orgasm with his mouth. No doubt it would scandalize her. Then delight her. The thought had brought a sexy smile to his lips.

But he'd quickly shaken his head. That was a bad idea. A very bad one. His time in bed with Gemma had been an unexpected pleasure, but he couldn't allow himself to enjoy it too much. It would only complicate things. They still had a score of unresolved issues between them. She was still the schemer who'd trapped him into marriage. And he was still the husband who intended to show her who ruled the household.

One thing she'd said last night in the coach kept popping into his mind. *"You haven't even heard the whole story, and I'm certain you don't even care."* It had been part of her rant telling him exactly what she thought of him. Showing her true colors. But what had she meant by those words? No doubt it was just more acting on her part. She was determined to play the role of the victim in their marriage.

Either way, spending more time in bed with Gemma would be nothing but a mistake. It might make her believe they would have more to their marriage than he intended.

Early this morning, he'd quietly slipped out of her bed, pulled on his trousers, and left the room while his wife was still sleeping. He'd slept the remainder of the night in his own bed. This morning, he'd called for his valet and bathed, dressed, and breakfasted before coming down to the study.

And now he'd made a decision. He'd already intended to send her off to the countryside. This morning, he realized he needed to do so more quickly than he'd planned. He did not trust himself not to take her to bed again...not even tonight. And that wouldn't do. He had no intention of making what had happened between them last night a habit. It had been too enjoyable. Theirs would not be a passionate marriage. It couldn't be.

Which meant that Gemma needed to go. Immediately.

He rang the bell for his butler and asked the man to summon Mrs. Howard.

Within an hour, the plans were made for Gemma to leave for his estate in Cumberland this afternoon.

Within an hour and a half, Gemma came looking for him.

She didn't knock, just opened the study door and boldly strode inside, appearing like an angel of vengeance. She was wearing a sunny yellow day dress, and her short curls were scattershot as usual. The look on her face was decidedly unhappy. She planted her hands on her hips and glared at him. "When were you going to tell me that you're banishing me to the countryside?"

"Didn't Mrs. Howard—?"

"*Mrs. Howard* is not the one who should have to tell me. Are you such a coward?"

His brows shot up. "Pardon?"

"You heard me. It's cowardly to send your wife away without telling her."

His nostrils flared as he swiftly sucked in air and braced his hands on the desk to push himself up, wrestling with a temper he hadn't even known he had. "Look, Gemma, I told you. We have an unconventional marriage."

She crossed her arms tightly over her chest and cocked her hip. "Oh, I don't know. It's not so unconventional to send your wife packing. Lots of noblemen do it. Don't give yourself too much credit for being unique."

He narrowed his eyes on her. "Is that the only reason you came in here? To call me names?"

"No, I came in here to tell you that you can't control me. You're so worried about appearances. How will it look when you banish your new wife to the countryside?"

"I feel it's best if—"

"Feel? *Feel?* Ha. You've never had a real emotion in your life. You may think you can send me to Cumberland to break my spirit, but that won't happen."

Break her spirit? That was a bit dramatic, wasn't it? But he'd already learned that she was dramatic. He doubted there was anything he could say that would convince her that he had no intention of "breaking her spirit."

"I've nothing more to say to you on this topic." He took a seat and made a show of hovering his quill above the papers in front of him, as if he were already engrossed in his work again.

"Good, then you may just listen to what I have to say. I've spent my whole life in the company of my friends and family, and if I am sent away from them, I shall be miserable. Which,

I am guessing, is your entire objective. You may be a miserable man, devoid of happiness or hope, but I won't allow you to make *me* miserable. You can send me away, but you will not break me." She turned and flounced toward the door. "Good-bye, *Your Grace*."

Of course, the door slammed behind her.

Lucian stared at the space where she'd just been standing, her words echoing in his head. Break her? Miserable? He wanted to make the point that they would not be together. He would spend time with her when he saw fit. He hadn't planned to make her *miserable*. Not to mention she'd accused him of being "devoid of happiness or hope." Where the devil had she got that idea? Just because he hadn't taken kindly to being manipulated into marriage, she'd made a judgement about his entire demeanor?

Growling, he pushed back in his chair and drummed his fingers against the top of the wooden arms. He contemplated the situation for several long moments.

He *was* happy.

He *had* hope.

Didn't he?

There *was* another way to handle this. Perhaps a way where they would both get what they wanted. He couldn't stay with her here, not after how she'd responded in bed last night. Not after the things she'd just said to him. But he also didn't want to make her miserable by sending her away.

Not to mention that she made a good point. How *would* it look to send her away so soon after their wedding? No doubt it would be gossip fodder within days. He hadn't thought about that.

Lucian shook his head. Hopefully, he had got her with child last night because it would be *quite* a long time before there would be any opportunity to do so again.

He'd been putting off his trip for far too long. It was time. He was going to India. His new duchess could stay in London.

CHAPTER SIXTEEN

Fifteen Months Later, The Duchess of Grovemont's Dressing Room

Gemma stared at her reflection in the looking glass. It had taken a full year, but it had happened. She'd finally turned into the beauty that Mama had promised she would. Of course, her husband hadn't been here to see her transformation. That ass had never even told her he was leaving. He'd simply left a note.

At first, Gemma had felt relief. After all, she'd won the battle. He wouldn't send her to Cumberland. She should have been nothing but pleased when she'd read the short missive he'd left on her nightstand the night after they had consummated their marriage.

> *Gemma,*
>
> *I have reconsidered our arrangement and have decided to go to India to attend to some business that requires my attention. I expect you'll have*

everything you need for your stay here in London. Mrs. Howard can assist with any questions or concerns.

    Yours,

    Lucian

It was strange, his valediction. He'd used the word *yours*. That was amusing. He wasn't hers. Not at all. Perhaps she legally belonged to *him*. But he wasn't hers. Was he mocking her by using that word? Or did it flow from his fingers as a lie so easily? Or perhaps he'd merely written it in the event someone else read the note. A servant or her relatives. Her husband did *so* like to keep up appearances. She'd learned that about him in the short amount of time they'd spent together.

Regardless, she'd taken the blasted note and put it in the far recesses of her wardrobe. Hidden it inside a glove she rarely wore. And then she'd done her best to forget it. Forget him. Because Lucian Banks wasn't worth the space in her memory.

After making love to her so tenderly, an act that had shattered her emotionally, then threatening to send her far away like an unwanted horse being put out to pasture, the man had left the country without so much as discussing it with her. Leaving nothing more than a three-sentence note that ended with a false "yours."

It shouldn't have surprised her given his previous behavior, but it had angered her. She couldn't help it. He'd left her to rot.

But slowly, as the days turned to weeks, and the weeks turned to months, her anger had turned into indifference. Just like a good member of the Grovemont clan. Over the last fifteen months, Gemma had learned to *perfect* indifference.

In addition to his other sins, he'd never written. Not once in all these months. Not even one note to say he had made it to India safely. She only knew he had because from time-to-time Mrs. Howard mentioned letters *she* received from him, ordering her how to go about some of her duties in taking care of the household.

Of course, Grovemont didn't know that she and Mrs. Howard had become thick as thieves over the last fifteen months. She'd heard all about Mrs. Howard's family in Somerset. And Mrs. Howard had heard all about Mama and Griffin and Meredith. Gemma had even told the older woman about Richard, Gemma's eldest brother who'd died in a horse race before Griffin had come back from the war. Grovemont might be instructing the housekeeper by letter, but Gemma was now the lady of the house. She and Mrs. Howard and Mr. Warwick, the butler, consulted each other on all things. The three of them even had dinner together every Monday night. She quite enjoyed their company.

Which was how Gemma knew Grovemont hadn't so much as asked after her health or well-being in the letters he sent the servants. She'd ask them from time to time and would be met with a blush and a subject change from dear Mrs. Howard, or a bit of stammering and an offer to refill her wine glass from Mr. Warwick. Apparently, asking after his wife's health would be far too considerate of Grovemont. He'd merely written to the servants to ask them to complete their duties. Gemma could be dead for all he cared.

He hadn't even inquired whether the one night they'd spent together had resulted in a child. Though Mrs. Howard would certainly have told him as much if that had been the case. And, at first, Gemma had wished it *had* been the case.

For that first month before she got her menses, Gemma

had prayed she would be with child. Because she refused to let her husband touch her ever again. Not without a fight. Because Gemma had a plan. A plan that made her smile to herself each time she considered it.

Grovemont was off gallivanting around the world, no doubt thinking his absence would make her pliable and willing. He may have had the upper hand before he left, but upon his return, he would not find her turned into a meek woman willing to do his bidding. On the contrary, he would find a wife who had every intention of *divorcing him*.

A divorce would result in a scandal, of course. But Gemma no longer cared. Of course, she hadn't told Mama or Griffin or Meredith yet. They would try to talk her out of it. But her mind was already made up. Which meant the less her family knew about her plans, the better. She'd have to tell them eventually, of course, so they could prepare themselves for the inevitable gossip, but she would wait for the right time.

She didn't even care if she had to plead guilty to criminal conversation. A charge that would be tantamount to admitting she'd been with another man. She hadn't, of course, but it would be worth everyone thinking she had to be free of *him*.

And other than the scandal, what would Grovemont care? The man had clearly never wanted their marriage. Had thought so little of it that he'd abandoned her. He should be happy that she would so easily agree to a divorce.

And now, she would finally have her chance to inform him of her decision. True to his behavior of only communicating with the servants, the ass had sent a note last week. One that indicated he would be arriving home soon. One that asked the servants to prepare his rooms. Gemma hadn't even known about the note. She'd only discovered his plans after she asked Mrs. Howard why the housemaids were dusting in his rooms more frequently than they had before.

But no matter. She was done waiting around and wondering what Grovemont would do next. She intended to take the reins of their marriage and steer them firmly toward divorce.

Gemma stared into the looking glass. She was still tall, of course, but no longer lanky or awkward, and her breasts had filled out quite nicely indeed. The belle of the *ton*, they called her these days. She was more popular than ever, and she'd used her power to keep Lady Mary from terrorizing the wallflowers. She'd become fast friends with Mary's most coveted suitor, Lord Pembroke. Just this Season, Mary had finally given up on Pembroke and become betrothed to a long-suffering baron, who was no doubt fated to be even more long-suffering as Mary's husband. But at least the unmarried ladies of the *ton* were free to dance with the men of their choosing again.

Gemma dabbed a bit of her new favorite perfume behind her ears. If her *husband* would not give her the common courtesy of informing her of his return, she would not give him the courtesy of telling him where she was when he arrived. She would go to her brother's town house for the afternoon, and from there, she intended to go to the Monroes' ball tonight.

CHAPTER SEVENTEEN

The first thing Lucian noticed when he entered his town house was the unfamiliar scent. It smelled like some sort of intoxicating perfume. A mixture of flowers and fruit and something indefinably...feminine.

The next thing he noticed was the flowers themselves. Ridiculous amounts of them. Crystal vases filled with them. Not in an ostentatious way, but in a tasteful yet lovely way. Had Gemma done that?

There were little things too—a new rug, an unfamiliar vase. All tastefully done with an eye to detail. Hmm. Were those Gemma's work as well?

Leaving the trunks to the footmen, Lucian bounded up the stairs two at a time in search of Mrs. Howard. He found the lady in the doorway to his bedchamber, clearly overseeing the final details to ensure the rooms were ready for his return.

"There you are, Mrs. Howard." He gave the woman a wide smile as she turned to face him.

"*Your Grace.*" She curtsied and an equally large smile lit up her familiar face. "Welcome home. We're nearly finished here and—"

"No need to hurry on my account. I intend to spend most of the afternoon in my study seeing to the correspondence I missed. I merely wanted to find you and tell you that I had arrived."

"Might I say how well you're looking, Your Grace?" Mrs. Howard said next, eyeing him up and down.

He bowed slightly. "Thank you, Madame. I do believe the sun agreed with me."

"Indeed," Mrs. Howard replied.

He inclined his head toward the staircase. "Walk with me down to the study?"

The two turned and made their way downstairs as Lucian fired off two dozen questions about the house, London, his correspondence, the mews, the coaches, the other servants, the shopkeepers' deliveries, and a number of other things he wondered about.

By the time they made it to his study, Mrs. Howard had answered all of his questions to his satisfaction.

"Thank you, Mrs. Howard," he said, giving the lady a final bow. "I'll take things from here."

Mrs. Howard's brow shot up in a disapproving manner. One Lucian was quite familiar with. It would take longer than fifteen months for him to forget his trusted servant's most telling facial expression. The woman had known him since he was born.

"Don't you want to know about your *wife*, Your Grace? You haven't asked so much as one question about her." There was an unmistakable note of disapproval in her words.

"Oh, yes. How is she?" Lucian said absently, already rifling through the stack of correspondence he'd found atop the desk.

At Mrs. Howard's silence, he glanced up. The housekeeper was staring at him with obvious judgement in her hazel eyes.

"You may want to ask her *yourself*, Your Grace."

Lucian frowned. Mrs. Howard had never reprimanded him. She'd never had to. This was the most disapproving thing she'd ever said to him. Point taken.

"Very well," he replied, expelling his breath. He *should* say something in way of greeting to Gemma. "Where is the duchess?"

"She's gone out for the afternoon."

"Mm." Lucian had already turned away and was headed around the side of the desk to take a seat. He had much to get to. "I shall speak with her later then."

He'd expected Mrs. Howard to leave, but when her shadow remained in the doorway several moments later, he glanced over. "Yes, Mrs. Howard? Is there something else?"

Mrs. Howard folded her hands together and inclined her head. "Ahem. There is…something you should know."

Lucian stopped sorting through the post. "Yes?"

"The duchess has become…quite a favorite of the servants."

Lucian frowned. "In what way?"

"She, uh, plays cards with the footmen on Tuesdays and has tea with the maids on Sundays."

Lucian blinked at her. A duchess? Playing cards with the footmen? He'd never heard of such a thing. "Thank you for bringing it to my attention, Mrs. Howard. I'll take care of it."

"No, Your Grace," she said, clearing her throat. "You misunderstand me. I mention this not to indicate it is a problem. But to let you know how very *beloved* Her Grace is in this household. Mr. Warwick and I don't know what we'd do without her." With that, the housekeeper turned and exited the study, leaving Lucian to stare after her in wonder. If he didn't mistake his guess, he'd just been taken to task for the treatment of his wife and then warned that the servants were on the duchess's side. Good God. He'd clearly been gone too long. Had his entire household descended into chaos?

Regardless, he'd see Gemma at dinner. He would ask after her health. Ask after her health and then inform her of the decisions he'd made about their future while he'd been gone. There was no reason they couldn't be civil to each other and live separate lives as they'd already learned to do in the last fifteen months. It would all be quite tidy. And the *ton* wouldn't suspect they were anything but happy. A marriage exactly like his parents had.

Hopefully, his wife had matured in the last year. Perhaps she was no longer as dramatic or as eager to argue. He could only hope she'd changed. But even if she hadn't, Lucian intended to succinctly inform her how their marriage would be from now on. She would simply have to accept it.

Meantime, he would see to this mountainous stack of correspondence and then he would go to his club. The long travel had been hell. He needed a drink, and he looked forward to catching up on the latest news about London, about Parliament, and about his friends' lives. There would be plenty of time to deal with Gemma later.

CHAPTER EIGHTEEN

Later That Afternoon, Brooks's Club

Lucian sat in a large leather chair, wedged between half a dozen of his friends, with a marked frown on his face. He'd spent the better part of the last hour being regaled by story after story about his wife.

It had all begun innocently enough. He'd arrived at the club to find several of his old friends lounging about. One of them had offered to buy him a drink. The others had gathered round to welcome him back, and now he was sitting in the middle of a storytelling session, and Gemma was the protagonist of *every single one*.

"It's a good thing you're back, Grovemont," Lord Hightower said with his deep chuckle.

"Why's that?" Lucian grumbled, already dreading the answer. It was certain to have something to do with Gemma's popularity. That had been the theme of all the stories so far. His wife. His beautiful, popular, beloved-by-everyone wife. Apparently, they called her the belle of the *ton* now. In addition to having befriended all of his servants,

Gemma had also apparently charmed all of Society. What was left? The King's court?

"I daresay your wife's had more marriage proposals than this year's crop of debutantes combined." The older man laughed heartily at his own words.

"What?" Lucian scrubbed a frustrated hand across his brow. How was that possible? "She's married to *me*. She cannot entertain marriage proposals," he shot back.

"Perhaps, but more than one chap has been hoping your ship got lost at sea, if you know what I mean," Lord Bellingham added with an annoying wink and an even more grating laugh.

"We've all been wagering on when you'd come back. Surely, you'd heard?" Lord Markham added.

"Heard what?" Lucian hadn't heard anything, of course. And these fools should know it.

"How gorgeous your wife has become. You should know she's had a least a half dozen offers from gentlemen to take a lover," Lord Markham continued, significantly lowering his voice on that last bit.

"The duchess's dance card is never empty, that's for certain," Lord Hargate added.

Lucian's fingers curled into a fist, and he eyed them all with supreme distaste. So far he had been able to glean that apparently, Gemma, his tall, coltish wife, who'd been too thin and too awkward, had turned into a great beauty.

He couldn't picture it. Wasn't even certain how such a thing could have happened. She *had* been quite young when he'd left. Was it possible that in the year since he'd been gone, she'd changed that much? According to every man at this club, it wasn't just possible. It was a fact.

Add to that, the news that Gemma was apparently the darling of the *ton*. She had a full social calendar, according to these chaps. She hosted parties and attended them, knew everyone and was known by everyone. And apparently she was adored by all of Society.

Damn it. He'd clearly made a mistake not shipping her off to Cumberland.

"I must admit," came Lord Tinsley's reedy voice, "I didn't understand when you first married her. Other than her being of good family, that is. But now I realize that *you* were the cleverest of the lot all along, Grovemont. You managed to marry the most beautiful lady the *ton*'s seen in an age *before* she was beautiful." Tinsley nearly laughed himself hoarse while Lucian glared at him from behind his half-filled brandy glass.

"And I've had more than one lad ask me if you'd look askance at your wife taking a lover," Lord Berbrook said. "Though I did remind him that you've yet to sire an heir, so he will probably have to wait."

Wait indeed. Lucian tossed back the rest of his drink. Was he having a fever dream? Had he contracted ague, that dread illness common in India due to the humid air? How was it possible that his wife—his scheming, disobedient wife—had become the toast of the *ton* in fifteen short months?

Lucian didn't know. But he was damn sure about to find out…immediately. He signaled to the footman that he was leaving.

"Who did you say was having a ball tonight?" he asked his friends as he stood up.

"The Monroes," they shouted in unison.

Lucian lifted his chin by way of good-bye. The Monroes were having a ball tonight. That's where Gemma would be. So *that's* where Lucian was going.

CHAPTER NINETEEN

ucian ignored the stares and whispers directed his
way the moment he stepped into the Monroes' ballroom. When the butler announced his name, a
collective gasp went up around the room. All pairs of eyes
were on him now as he slowly descended the marble staircase to the lower level of the room where most partygoers
were gathered. So much for being discreet.

He made a show of smiling and nodding to anyone who
welcomed him back. He went from group to group, shaking
hands and exchanging small talk, but all the while his gaze
impatiently darted about the large room. Where was
Gemma?

He'd been at the blasted ball for the better part of an hour
before Lord Tidwell, who was obviously deep in his cups,
had the temerity to blurt out, "I should think you'd want a
word with your duchess, Grovemont. I believe she's out on
the balcony with Pembroke at the moment."

Lucian's head snapped up. He just so happened to be
standing at the far side of the ballroom next to the floor-to-
ceiling windows that overlooked the Monroes' verandah. He

slowly turned his head to look out the window. Two figures were there, standing outside against the balustrade. A man and a woman. The dark-haired woman was wearing a bright-turquoise gown. Her head thrown back, she was laughing uproariously. The man was down on one knee, holding her hand.

Lucian's jaw clamped tight. Was he to believe that *his wife* was out there alone with a man who appeared to be... proposing marriage? After the stories he'd heard at the club, he didn't doubt it.

"Yes, there she is. With Pembroke," Tidwell verified, pointing to the couple and slapping Lucian on the back. "They're thick as thieves."

Lucian didn't wait to hear more. Without so much as excusing himself to the group, he turned on one heel and stalked toward the French doors.

A collective hush fell over the ballroom.

GEMMA WAS LAUGHING SO HARD she thought her sides might burst. Pembroke had become one of her closest friends over the last year, and he'd escorted her out onto the Monroes' balcony tonight when she'd mentioned that the ballroom was too hot. Now he was on one knee, drunkenly pretending to propose to her with a large pink peony that he'd somehow procured from a nearby bush.

Pembroke had asked for Gemma's help in ensuring that his proposal, when it came time to make one to the lady of his choosing, would be adequate. Gemma, of course, had happily obliged, and Pembroke was even now practicing.

"My dearest, Lady Gemma," he said, bending over her hand with an exaggerated swagger. "Will you *please* do me the honor of becoming my wife?"

The next thing Gemma knew, Pembroke was flying across the balustrade. He landed on the grass below in a tangled heap. And her *husband*, of all surprising people, was standing in front of her looking like an angry god. His face was dark, clouded with fury, and his nostrils were flaring. Otherwise, he looked annoyingly fit and tanned. A state that made his blue eyes even more arresting.

"She's already married," Grovemont spat down to Pembroke without so much as looking at him.

Pembroke jumped up and scrambled away into the darkness, muttering, "Quite right."

Gemma turned to face her husband. She crossed her arms over her chest and glared at him, careful to keep the long-practiced indifference on her face.

So, he was back? And he'd seen fit to arrive here tonight? It was probably no more than a coincidence. She doubted he'd known she was here. He wouldn't cross a roadway to greet her. But it was no matter. The Monroes' verandah was as good a place as any to have this long-awaited discussion.

Her husband was about to find out that she was no longer the uncertain little bride he'd abandoned fifteen months ago. And she would enjoy letting him know it. "Pembroke was only jesting," she insisted, giving Grovemont a false, tight smile.

"He's *not* amusing," Grovemont shot back.

Gemma narrowed her eyes on him. She let her gaze wander from his head to his feet, sizing him up. He wore straight black boots, tight buckskin breeches, a white shirt and cravat, and a cobalt waistcoat that matched his eyes. He was not dressed for a ball. That was interesting. Why had he come?

Unfortunately, in addition to being muscled, fit, and tanned, he was still as devastatingly handsome as he'd always been. Months in another land hadn't changed his sharp jaw, perfect nose, and hooded blue eyes that could tempt a saint. Now he looked as if he'd *added* muscle, and with his darker skin, he looked more like a dangerous pirate than an English aristocrat. Fine. He was exceedingly handsome. Too bad his disposition ruined the effect.

"I found Pembroke quite amusing," she replied, arms still tightly crossed.

"You shouldn't be out here alone with a man," Grovemont ground out.

"Come all the way back from India, did you, to tell me as much?" she asked brightly, blinking at him. "You could have saved yourself the trouble and merely written to me." She touched a fingertip to her chin. "Oh, wait. *That* was too much for you, wasn't it?" She tapped her fingertip along her jaw as if she'd just thought of it.

He narrowed his eyes on her. "We're going home."

He turned on his heel, apparently expecting her to follow. *Ha*.

Gemma moved her hands to her hips and stood with arms akimbo. "You may go home if you wish, but I'm staying here."

He stopped immediately, and when his head snapped back to face her, surprise flared in his eyes.

Good. She wasn't through surprising him. Not in the least.

"I said we're going home," he repeated. "*Now*."

"And I said I'm staying here." She tilted her head and pasted the *most* indifferent smile to her face. The same indifferent smile she'd practiced in the looking glass, so she knew it was good. "You don't tell me what to do any more, Your Grace." With that, she picked up her skirts and flounced past him toward the French doors.

CHAPTER TWENTY

L ucian forced himself to count to ten. Slowly. But anger surged through his veins. It was not lost on him that he was never angry unless his *wife* was involved. In fact, he couldn't remember being angry a day in India.

But the moment he'd seen Pembroke proposing to Gemma, it was as if a red veil had descended over his eyes. He'd stalked outside and tossed that fool into the gardens. How dare Pembroke take such a liberty? And someone had said Pembroke and Gemma were thick as thieves. Did that mean she'd taken him as a lover?

If Lucian found out that was true, Pembroke's life wouldn't be worth a farthing.

One thing was clear. The chaps at the club were right. Gemma *had* become a beauty in the last fifteen months. An extraordinary one. The moment he'd seen her in the light from the candles scattered across the verandah, he'd sucked in his breath.

Where she had once been tall and awkward, she was now graceful and poised. Where she had been flat-chested, she was now generously curved. Her hair, which had once been a short mass of wayward curls, was now long and luxuriant. It was swept up behind her head, but he could tell how much longer it had grown. The curls had been tamed into a sophisticated chignon. She'd grown into her features, and her eyes were now luminous in a face of such ethereal beauty it hardly seemed real. High, sharp cheekbones, delicate dark brows, sooty lashes that framed eyes so dark they looked exotic. She had the face of an angel. The body of a siren.

And the temperament of a demon.

She was wearing a satin turquoise gown with an empire waist. The color was splendid with her dark hair. Lucian understood why all the gentlemen at the club had been so ready to tell him about her. He'd left a duckling and returned to a swan.

She might be beautiful and popular, but Lucian had no intention of allowing his wife to run about town accepting proposals and taking lovers. Quite the opposite, actually. She was *his*. He would not allow her to cuckold him or make a mockery of his family's name. The sooner she realized that, the better.

He'd wanted to get Gemma alone to discuss that and everything else he'd heard about her at the club. He intended to provide her with a set of rules. And if she failed to follow the rules, he would send her to Cumberland. He would make that clear. She should *not* try him.

Only before he'd even had a chance to speak to her, she'd immediately defied him. Which meant she *hadn't* changed from the headstrong chit he'd left all those months ago. Unfortunate, but still an obstacle he was ready to surmount.

She'd given him a blank look at first, then a tight smile. She was angry as well. She'd mentioned that he hadn't written her in all these months. What precisely did she think he had to say to her? But even as he had the thought, he could admit that it stood to some reason that she was angry.

She'd stalked away from him, refusing to go home in order to get a bit of her own back after having been ignored for so long. Fine. Even Mrs. Howard had implied that had been poorly done of him. He would acknowledge that he may not have handled his communication with his wife in the best manner, but that was all he'd acknowledge. Gemma's refusal to leave with him had been maddening. But she couldn't ignore him for long. They'd be back home together soon enough. And when they left here tonight, he would make everything clear. Over the last year, she may have had *carte blanche* to act however she liked, but he was back in town, and her inappropriate behavior was about to be *severely* curtailed.

Lucian straightened his shoulders and smoothed a hand down the front of his shirt. The entire ballroom had no doubt just witnessed his duchess leave him outside. Perhaps some of them—the females—thought she was in the right. But he had no intention of allowing the ballroom to think there was a problem in their marriage. She might not agree to go home with him yet. But by God, she would dance with him.

He turned on a heel and stalked back toward the ballroom.

CHAPTER TWENTY-ONE

G emma was near the refreshment table with a host
of people around her skirts when she spied
Grovemont glaring at her. He stood several paces
away talking to Lords Harwell and Kitson.

She tried to ignore her husband's glare, but she could *feel*
it on her. What did he think he was about? Stalking back into
her life and demanding she go home with him? She wouldn't
go home with him if he begged. Got down on both knees,
even.

Besides, what did he have to say to her? He hadn't had a
word to impart in fifteen months, and *now* he wanted to talk?
Doubtful. He probably only wanted to take her home to ruin
her evening. She was only glad he hadn't made a scene. If
he'd tried to force her to go with him, it would *not* have
ended prettily. That was certain.

Gemma took a sip from her champagne glass and laughed
at the jest Lord Harwell had just shared. She wanted her
husband to think she was having the *best* time without him.
Grovemont would have to think again if he thought she
would snap at his slightest command. She'd been naïve, full

of guilt and apprehension when they'd first married. Now, she realized she'd been a fool. A far-too-compliant fool, and she had absolutely no intention of allowing her husband to have the upper hand. *Ever again.*

OVER AN HOUR LATER, she'd just finished dancing with Lord Bidwell when Grovemont appeared at her side. "My lady," he said, bowing perfectly over her hand. "Will you do me the honor?" He glanced toward the dance floor.

Scores of eyes watched her. The entire ballroom seemed to be holding its breath. Very well. She would not make a scene. *That* would only make it seem as if she gave a toss, and she decidedly did *not*. Besides, indifferent people did not make scenes.

Reluctantly, she put her hand on his arm. His other arm snaked around her back to pull her close as a waltz began to play. She fought the urge to groan. *Why did it have to be a waltz?*

"Seems you've become quite popular since I've been gone," he drawled.

"Seems *you're* still an ass," she shot back, blinking at him innocently.

His nostrils flared. "If you cannot smile at me, at least keep your face blank."

"Oh, yes, *must* keep up appearances." She rolled her eyes. "Tell me, Grovemont, why are you here?"

"I returned from India this afternoon."

"No, I mean why are you *here*? At this particular ball tonight?"

"I came here looking for you."

Her brows shot up. "Did you come simply to ruin my evening or do you have something to say to me?"

"I wanted to see you."

"Ha. I hardly believe that. You haven't written me since you left. Don't pretend as if you care if I'm alive or dead."

"You are *my wife*," he ground out.

"Not for long, I'm not."

His eyes narrowed sharply. "What is *that* supposed to mean?"

She gave him the most fake-beautiful smile she could muster and lowered her voice to a hostile whisper. "It means I want a divorce, Your Grace. And I intend to get one at any cost."

CHAPTER TWENTY-TWO

M any hours later, Gemma leaned back against the velvet squabs of the coach and sighed. She was on her way home from the Monroes' ball. Alone. The remainder of the evening had been quite enjoyable, actually. Grovemont had left soon after their waltz had ended, and she couldn't have been more pleased.

Oh, several of her friends and acquaintances had asked her if she'd missed him or how she felt about his return. She'd answered all of them with vague words that sounded somewhat pleasant. She might want to slap her husband's arrogant, handsome face, but she had no intention of letting the *ton* know that.

Grovemont didn't realize it, but she had been raised to keep family issues within the family. There was no chance she would tell other people their secrets, but she drew the line at pretending with *him*. If he wanted a wife who believed in false pretenses, he had married the wrong lady.

And, of course, he *had* married the wrong lady. It had been clear from the start. A divorce was the only option, really. She smiled to herself as she remembered how his face had flinched for just one moment when she'd mentioned the word. His infallible confidence had slipped just a notch. And *that* had been a delight to witness.

She'd surprised him. Good. All this time, he'd been in India thinking he was punishing her by staying away and refusing to write. Instead, all it had done was firm her resolve to end their marriage. The ensuing scandal would be awful for both their families, but he would live through it. He had no choice. Besides, a duke in need of a duchess and heir could always come back from a scandal. *She* would be the one to take the brunt of it. No man would want to marry her after she'd been ostensibly tossed over by Grovemont. Which meant she would never have a baby. The pain of that thought throbbed through her. It was the thing that saddened her the most. But baby or no, she was still determined to divorce him. That's how desperately she wanted out of this marriage.

Her family wouldn't like it, but they would accept it eventually. They loved her. If she explained to them how awful her husband had been to her, they would agree it was for the best. Eventually. She hoped.

When the coach pulled to a stop in front of her town house, a footman opened the door to the conveyance and pulled down the steps. Gemma alighted and made her way across the graveled path and to the steps leading up to the door.

Once inside, she gave her bonnet and pelisse to the butler, who smiled at her warmly.

"Good evening, Your Grace. Did you have a nice time tonight?"

She returned his warm smile. "I did, Warwick, thank you. How is your tooth?" Just yesterday, she'd seen the man grabbing at his jaw, and she'd given him a poultice to place on his sore tooth. He'd thanked her mightily.

"Doing much better now, Your Grace. Thank you again. Terribly kind of you."

"I'm glad to hear that, Warwick. Remember to use the same recipe for five days in a row."

"I will, Your Grace. I will." He nodded.

She made her way across the marble foyer and ascended the staircase. When she got upstairs, she warily eyed the door to Grovemont's room. Was he in there? Skulking about? Or had he gone back to his club? She could only hope he was gone. But no matter. What he did with his time had no bearing on her. She was going to sleep.

She pushed open the door to her room, expecting to see Anna waiting for her as usual. The maid liked to sit in the chair in the corner with her sewing. Instead, the room was pitch dark. Gemma frowned. Where was Anna?

Gemma fumbled around in the darkness, trying to pick out the path to her nightstand so she could light the flint. She'd barely taken three steps when a scratching sound caught her attention. Seconds later, a candle flared to life next to the bed.

She sucked in her breath.

It wasn't Anna.

Grovemont was there, sitting in a Chippendale chair next to her nightstand with a snifter dangling from his fingers.

"Jesus, you scared me," she exclaimed, pressing a hand to her chest.

"It's after two," came his dark voice.

"You know how long these things go." Obviously, he'd dismissed Anna and decided to lurk around in the dark. Too bad. Gemma fully intended to ignore him. She went directly to her dressing room and shut the door. She would just have to undress as much as she could by herself and then call for Anna. Hopefully, he'd be gone by the time the maid arrived.

"What do you think you are doing?" came his voice from the other side of the dressing room door.

She rolled her eyes. "I'm preparing for bed." She managed to unbutton the top few buttons behind her back. The bodice of her gown gaped away to show quite a bit of her *décolletage*.

"That's not what I meant, and you know it," he shot back.

She couldn't help but smile. "Not really. Tell me what you meant then."

"You said you want a *divorce*." His voice was low, accusatory.

She wrenched open the door. She was fully prepared to say it to his face. "I do want a divorce."

His gaze dropped momentarily to her bodice just before he gave her a long-suffering stare. "*Why* do you want a divorce?"

She couldn't stop her humorless laugh. "Are you quite serious?"

"Humor me."

"Fine. I want a divorce because you are an ass, and I have no intention of living the rest of my life under your thumb with your ridiculous rules and your broody temper."

"I didn't send you to Cumberland."

Her brows shot up. "Do you expect my thanks? You did something much worse than send me to Cumberland. First, you made lov—" She shook her head. That part didn't matter. "You refused to listen to me when I told you I did not trap you into marriage. You're a presumptuous, holier-than-thou, pompous bastard, and I don't want to be married to you."

He blinked at her strangely as if surprised by what she'd said and trying to determine if she was telling the truth. She rolled her eyes. Of course, he would think she was still being deceitful. He was *such* an ass.

"You *did* trick me into marriage," he finally replied evenly.

She pressed her palms together and spoke as if she were addressing a small child. "No, you see. That is where you are wrong. I understand why you may have *thought* I tricked you into marriage, but you never even gave me a chance to explain. If you had, you would know I was trying to *help my friends* that night by convincing Lady Mary to leave them alone. Contrary to your arrogance, the entire world does not revolve around *you*."

He shook his head. "That story makes no sense. How would you finding me in the study affect Mary and the wall-flowers?"

Gemma folded her arms over her chest. "Oh, now you want to know what happened that night?"

"As I said…humor me," he ground out.

"Fine. Mary dared me to ask you to dance. I went searching for you. It was impetuous of me and ill-advised—believe me when I say I know that now—but it was not ill-intended, and I certainly wasn't trying to *force you to marry me*. In fact, after Mama told me that we would have to marry, I cast up my accounts if you want to know the truth."

He frowned at her, scowling. Clearly, he didn't believe that either.

"I did," she continued, completely indignant now. "Right there in the bowl in my bedchamber. What reason would I have to lie about *that*?"

His only answer was more skeptical staring.

"But, of course, you're not going to believe me because you're so supercilious you honestly believe that I was scheming to get you to marry me. Did you ever stop to consider that I didn't want to marry you either? And while I won't say there aren't ladies out there capable of such trickery, *I* don't happen to be one of them. Lady Mary is, by the by. No doubt you'd be happier with her right now, ordering her about and acting put upon. But I have no use for it. And I have no intention of staying with you." By the time she finished, Gemma's chest was heaving and her cheeks were hot. Her forehead had even begun to sweat. But she'd said it. Everything she'd been waiting to say to him and then some. And it felt good. Quite good.

Grovemont took a maddeningly slow sip from his glass. "A divorce is out of the question."

Gemma reached around her neck to remove her diamond necklace. She'd been prepared for his refusals. And she was prepared with her own strategy. Ignoring them. "I've thought about it a lot, and we can do this one of two ways. You can say the marriage was never consummated, or—"

"That's not true," he ground out.

She gave him a long-suffering look before taking a deep breath. "You know that and I know that, but no one else does."

"A divorce is out of the question," he repeated.

"As I was saying…you can either say the marriage was never consummated, or I am willing to admit to criminal conversation."

He surged to his feet and slammed his glass to the tabletop beside him. "*You cuckolded me?*"

She plunked her hands to her hips. "No. I have not, you pompous ass. Contrary to what you think of me, I am not the sort who would cuckold my husband; however, I *am* the sort who would allow everyone to *think* I did if it gets me what I want."

His eyes narrowed on her. "And that is?"

"To never see you again."

Blue fire leaped in his eyes as he stared at her and a muscle ticked in his jaw. *Not so indifferent now, Your Grace?*

She moved toward the bed and pulled the bell to summon

Anna. "I'll give you a day or two to think about it. Now, I'm certain you know how to see yourself out."

With that, she flounced back into the dressing room and shut the door.

A sly smile popped to her lips. Oh, how she'd enjoyed seeing his face when she told him he had two choices. How did *he* like being ordered about?

CHAPTER TWENTY-THREE

Lucian wanted to stab the bloody ledger with his quill. He'd been trying to concentrate on his letter writing this morning, but all he could think about was Gemma's curt speech in her bedchamber last night.

She wanted a *divorce*?

That was ludicrous. Outlandish. Was she truly so naïve she thought she could threaten him with something so utterly insane?

She *had* managed to surprise him. He'd give her that. Of all the things he'd thought she would say to him when he returned, asking for a divorce had *not* been one of them.

Seemed that in addition to her beauty, the last year had also given his wife fangs. She was clearly not intimidated by him. Of course, she hadn't been particularly meek when they'd married, but now she was the *opposite* of meek. She was combative.

He sighed and scrubbed a hand through his hair. Perhaps he'd handled her incorrectly. Perhaps ordering her about and insisting on his way was not the best maneuver. She'd called him an arrogant, holier-than-thou ass. Perhaps he needed to be a bit more circumspect.

She'd seemed truly angry last night when she'd accused him of not giving her the benefit of the doubt. He'd actually spent a moment wondering whether she was telling the truth. Was it possible she *hadn't* schemed to get him to marry her? Could it actually be true she *hadn't* wanted to marry him any more than he'd wanted to marry her? Had she truly *vomited* when she found out they would be forced to marry?

That last part had been almost too much to believe. After all, he had been an eligible duke, and even a man as arrogant as he apparently was had heard others call him handsome. It was not an opinion he'd formed entirely on his own. He'd been a desirable choice for a husband. The papers had named him most eligible. Then again…if everything Gemma had told him last night *was* true, he'd made a terrible miscalculation.

The words she'd said that night in Southbury's study, the words that had haunted him ever since, floated back to his mind. *"You heard him, Mary. Remember your promise."*

Soon after, Lady Costner had come running and shrieking and accusing him of ruining her daughter. *That* was why he hadn't listened to Gemma's attempt at an explanation. *That* was why he'd assumed she'd schemed to get him to marry her. It had been obvious that she and Mary had both been trying to corner him in the room alone… Hadn't it?

But even if he'd made a mistake, he had no intention of granting her a divorce. Such a thing would bring shame upon the Grovemont name, the title, and his entire family, past and future. It was unthinkable. No, he would *never* agree to a divorce, but he *did* need to find out if she was telling the truth about the rest of it. Because if Gemma *hadn't* wanted to marry him, that would change everything.

CHAPTER TWENTY-FOUR

There was one person Gemma could talk to. One person who would keep her secret, not judge her, and never attempt to talk her out of it. Which was why Cecily Grundy was the only person Gemma had told about her desire for a divorce.

It was impossible not to love Cecily. She was a sweet girl with the very best intentions and love in her heart for everyone. She was also easy to talk to. And over the last year, since Grovemont had been gone, Gemma had spoken to her friend at great length about her marriage. With Cecily, Gemma knew her secrets would go no further. Cecily was the only person who truly understood how unhappy Gemma had been since the moment she'd married Grovemont. Oh, Mrs. Howard and Mr. Warwick suspected, but Gemma had never dared share her unhappiness with the two trusted servants. They were Grovemont's servants, after all. They owed him their loyalty.

But Cecily was Gemma's friend. The two young women had forged a bond during their first Season. Gemma had become the champion of the wallflowers against awful Lady

Mary. United against a common enemy, Gemma and Cecily had grown especially close. Cecily came from a genteel family who'd lost its fortune, which meant she was a *decided* wallflower.

But then darling Griffin had stepped in and danced with Cecily at one of the balls, and the girl's dance card had remained quite full ever after. She'd even received a handful of proposals. Unfortunately, her Mama had refused them all due to the fact that Cecily's older sisters weren't married. It was a problem Gemma and Cecily had spent many hours discussing over scones and tea.

Today's problem called for more scones and more tea.

"And then I told him he had two choices," Gemma reported as she lifted her cup to her mouth in Cecily's mother's drawing room. Thankfully, Cecily's two obnoxious older sisters and her overbearing mother were at the milliner's for the afternoon. Cecily had feigned a megrim to skip the outing.

"You didn't!" Cecily exclaimed.

"I did." Gemma lowered her voice. "I told him he could claim the marriage was never consummated."

"Oh, but that's not true!" Cecily interjected, her bright-blue eyes going wide and her round cheeks turning red.

"No, it's not true, and he made that same point," Gemma continued, "but I said he could claim it was true."

"What was the other choice you offered him?" Cecily asked.

"I will admit to crimcon."

"Crimcon!" Poor Cecily went pale as milk.

"Yes," Gemma replied, nodding and smiling.

Cecily drew her hand away from her mouth. "But that would mean you... you..."

"Had lain with another man," Gemma finished for her in a loud whisper.

The bright pink in Cecily's cheeks deepened.

"I'm sorry if I'm upsetting you, dear," Gemma said, suddenly quite aware that she was speaking of things she probably shouldn't in front of an unmarried lady. But neither of them was uneducated. Gemma had shared all she knew with Cecily. "Ignorance is dangerous," Meredith always said.

Cecily plucked another scone from the silver tray in front of them. "No. It's quite all right. I'm only sorry you're being forced to make such a drastic choice."

"It's my own fault," Gemma replied with a sigh. "If I had just had the patience to wait for Grovemont to come out of the study at Griffin's wedding, I wouldn't be in this predicament."

"And he wouldn't either," Cecily pointed out with a sigh of her own.

Gemma pursed her lips. Hmm. Cecily was right. Grovemont wasn't to blame either. Not for the marriage, at least. He was, however, decidedly to blame for being an ass. But if Gemma hadn't made such a mistake in the first place, they wouldn't be married, and she wouldn't even know how big of an ass he was. Oh, dear. Was that guilt tugging at her conscience?

"Do you think you should ask him if there is any other way?" Cecily bit her lip.

Gemma blinked at her friend. "Any other way to what? Justify a divorce?"

"No. To live together. Perhaps declare a truce?"

"A truce?" Gemma blinked again. "It's not a war. At least it shouldn't be. I simply don't want to be his wife."

Cecily pulled the tip off one end of the scone. "Perhaps you could go to the country. I would miss you terribly though." She frowned.

"I do plan to go to the country," Gemma admitted. "But only until the scandal dies down."

Cecily popped the bite of scone into her mouth and chewed and swallowed before adding, "You could divide the house, stay out of each other's pockets."

Gemma scowled. "Divide the house? How would that work?"

Cecily waved her hand in the air. "Oh, my mother and father do it. They're quite adept at the practice. Though I doubt they have ever formally spoken about it. Upstairs, Mama stays to her rooms and ours, and Father stays in his. Downstairs, Mama occupies the breakfast room and the drawing room, and Father remains in his study. It's quite efficient."

Gemma's scowl deepened. She'd never heard of such a thing. "They never speak?"

Cecily shrugged. "Oh, we have supper together, and I'm certain I've heard them exchange words at the dinner table upon occasion. But otherwise, no. I can't say I see them speak."

Gemma shook her head. That was not how she understood marriage to be. It was not the way Griffin and Meredith behaved with each other. They both talked and laughed all day in each other's company. Or they sat in the same room reading and sipping tea, content to be quiet together. It was lovely. And it was precisely how Gemma wanted her own marriage to be. Only she'd ended up stuck with Grovemont, who preferred a newspaper in his face.

"Even if we divided the house, the second half would still be occupied by an ass," Gemma finally explained. "No. I definitely want to divorce."

Cecily looked a bit sad but nodded. "If you think that's best, Gemma. I support your decision wholeheartedly. But if you are divorced, Mama won't allow me to speak with you, you know?"

"I know." Gemma frowned. She knew how serious

divorce was. Only a handful had ever been granted. And the accompanying scandals were legendary. "We'll still be able to write though, won't we?"

Cecily expelled her breath. "Before you decide for certain, you may want to speak with someone who knows about scandal."

Gemma cocked her head to the side. "An expert in scandal?"

"Yes," Cecily replied, nodding sagely. "You should write to Lady Clare Handleton."

CHAPTER TWENTY-FIVE

Later That Afternoon, Brooks's Club

W hen Southbury entered the club, Lucian glanced up. Excellent. Gemma's brother was just the man he was looking for. He'd already spent the first half of the morning making discreet inquiries as to whether anyone had actually known his wife to have cuckolded him.

Turned out, not one man had knowledge of anything of the sort. In fact, they'd all been quick to assure him the duchess had carried herself with nothing but grace and dignity since he'd been gone. She'd been entirely faithful to him, despite the fact that she'd apparently had an abundance of offers to stray.

"She's quite beautiful, you know?" Lord Melmont said after giving Lucian an earful of similar information.

Lucian clenched his jaw. "Yes, I know," he ground out.

Why did everyone insist on telling him how beautiful his wife was? As if he couldn't see it with his own two eyes. He wasn't blind. Far from it. In fact, last night when she'd been railing at him, he'd been struck half dumb by the sight of her. It had been difficult to concentrate on the mad things she'd been saying because he'd been so preoccupied by the view of her gaping bodice. And the alluring flush on her high cheekbones.

Gemma looked so unlike she had last year. It was almost as if she was a different person. Only the eyes made him realize it was her. Those same dark, compelling eyes that had been wide with apprehension after their wedding were trained on him last night with fire flashing inside them.

Yes, she was gorgeous, which was precisely why he needed to know if she had cuckolded him. It was also why he could not take her to bed until he'd been back for at least a month. Any child born to her would have to be proven to be his and his alone. Frustrating but true. Not that the woman appeared to be ready to welcome him into her bed anytime soon, but surely she would see reason after she realized he would not be granting her a divorce.

"I know at least three men who offered her an arrangement," Melmont continued. "Pembroke has been—"

Lucian's hand shot up. "Do not mention Pembroke's name in my presence, if you please."

A delighted smile covered Melmont's face.

Great. That bit of gossip would be making the rounds soon enough…that Lucian was so enraged by Pembroke that he refused to hear his name.

Only it was true. So be it.

Honestly, hearing Pembroke's name made Lucian want to punch his fist through the nearest wall. Instead, he forced himself to smile and nod and thank Melmont and the other men he'd spoken to for the information they'd provided.

Lucian was convinced Gemma hadn't been unfaithful. Now he needed to discover exactly what she had been doing that night in Southbury's study.

And he knew precisely who to ask.

Lucian excused himself, took his drink, and made his way to the next room to find Gemma's older brother.

"Grovemont!" Southbury exclaimed the moment he saw him. "I heard you'd returned." His brother-in-law stood and clapped him on the back, splaying his hand toward the seat next to him. "Please sit."

Lucian lowered himself into a leather chair while Southbury ordered a drink from one of the footmen.

"How was your travel?" Southbury said after they were both settled in.

"Long," Lucian grumbled.

Southbury shook his head. "I don't know how you managed it. I wouldn't be able to stand being away from Meredith for that length of time."

Lucian allowed his silence to speak for itself. He and Gemma clearly didn't have a love match. But at least Southbury had introduced the topic Lucian wanted to discuss. Specifically, he wanted to know if Southbury was aware of Gemma's ludicrous desire for a divorce. Surely, he wouldn't approve. But Lucian had to handle the inquiry carefully on the assumption Southbury didn't know.

Lucian scratched his chin in the most nonchalant way possible. "Have you spoken to your sister?"

Southbury nodded. "I saw Gemma not two nights ago, actually."

Lucian lifted his brows and crossed his right boot atop his left knee. "Did she mention any plans?"

"Plans?" Southbury frowned. "No. What plans?"

Interesting. Apparently, Gemma hadn't mentioned her desire for a divorce to her brother. No doubt he'd say so if he knew. Was she biding her time? Was she intentionally keeping her desire for a divorce from her brother? Or was the entire claim a ruse? One meant to manipulate Lucian.

Regardless, Lucian wasn't about to share the secrets of his marriage with his brother-in-law. "She didn't mention anything to you?" he asked vaguely, tugging at the leg of his breeches.

Southbury scrubbed his chin and leaned a bit closer. "I hate to put my nose somewhere it does not belong, but…I do think she's been quite unhappy about your absence."

Lucian's brows shot up once more. "Funny. I get the impression that she *enjoyed* my absence."

Southbury shrugged. "The few times I've asked her about it, she's mentioned that you never wrote to her."

Lucian expelled a long breath. He might as well admit to that mistake. "It's true."

Southbury's countenance became sharp, his voice serious. "I'll be honest with you, Grovemont. I've worried a time or two whether she's happy in the marriage. Especially given the circumstances of how you two became betrothed."

Ah, there it was, the opening he needed. Lucian lifted his glass to his lips as he considered the most effective reply. "Gemma is the one who wanted the marriage," he finally said.

Southbury's brows drew together into a sharp frown. "That's not true."

Lucian cocked his head. "Of course, it is. She and her friend planned it."

Southbury gave him a look that clearly indicated he thought Lucian had lost his mind. "What? No. Gemma was trying to get Lady Mary Costner to leave the other girls alone that night."

Gemma's words from last night played through Lucian's head. "I was trying to *help my friends* that night by convincing Lady Mary to leave them alone." Then she'd gone on with something about a dare and a dance, but none of it had truly made any sense. "I know that's what she said, but—"

"That's what *happened*." Southbury's voice took on a low,

warning tone. "Meredith and I had both witnessed Lady Mary's antics before. She'd threatened all the debutantes with dire consequences if they didn't stay away from you."

Lucian's frown intensified. "I don't understand. What did I have to do with it?"

Southbury blew out a breath. "Lady Mary had her sights set on wringing an offer from you. I assumed you knew."

Lucian shook his head. "I had no idea. I barely knew who the chit was before that night."

"She certainly knew who you were," Southbury told him. "At our wedding ball, Gemma had managed to negotiate a truce with Lady Mary. Gemma agreed to ask you to dance. Lady Mary expected you to reject her, and once Gemma was duly humiliated, Lady Mary agreed she would leave the other girls alone for the remainder of the evening."

Lucian sat in silence for several moments as he considered what he'd just been told. It was practically nonsensical. But he had to admit that it actually fit with what he'd heard Gemma and Mary say to each other that night. It was all becoming more clear.

Lucian wiped a hand over his face. "You're saying Gemma knew she would be humiliated by asking me to dance, but she still did so?"

Southbury nodded. "Yes. She had no hope that you'd say yes. Lady Mary had dared her. No doubt she intended to report it to the ballroom. Apparently, you had quite a reputation for never dancing with any of the debutantes."

Lucian's jaw locked. The thoughts he'd had alone in the study before Gemma had entered came back to him. "The irony is that I had just decided I would begin asking young ladies to dance."

"Gemma couldn't have known that." Southbury shrugged. "The problem is she's impatient. Instead of waiting for you to return to the ballroom, she went looking for. She shouldn't have done that. She regretted it immensely later that night."

Regretted it enough to…vomit? Lucian considered everything he'd just heard. He'd known Southbury since they were lads in school together. The man wasn't a liar, even if his story would paint his own sister in a better light. More to the point, the story he'd just told was ludicrous enough to be true. If Southbury had invented it, it would be less convoluted. Which left only one conclusion. Gemma *had* been telling the truth when she'd told him she hadn't wanted to marry him any more than he'd wanted to marry her.

So, she was neither a cheat nor a scheming liar.

And here he'd been treating her like a pariah the entire time they'd been married. Fuck. He shook his head. He was precisely the pompous, arrogant, holier-than-thou ass that Gemma had accused him of being. He'd hurt her. Hurt her, refused to listen to her, and pushed her away…to the point that she now wanted a *divorce* of all things.

Damn it all to hell. There was only one thing to do. He had to find a way to make it right.

CHAPTER TWENTY-SIX

Even Later that Afternoon, The Duke of Grovemont's Music Room

Gemma was playing the pianoforte when her husband came home. She had no idea where he'd gone or what he was up to. And frankly, she didn't much care. She only hoped wherever he'd been, he'd spent time contemplating the two choices she'd left him with. She already knew how she would handle the divorce.

First, she would hire a solicitor. One who would assist her not only with the legal aspects, but one who could explain the details to Griffin and Mama. They wouldn't like it, but they would see reason after she explained how unhappy she was in her marriage and how unfairly she'd been treated by her husband. Griffin and Mama loved her. They wanted her to be happy. They would understand once they had a chance to consider it all for a while.

Next, she would convince Grovemont to agree to the divorce. Of course, it would also be the most difficult part. The man was an ass, and he particularly disliked anything that made him or his family look bad. A divorce would be especially appalling to such a man. But she would just have to make him see that a divorce, especially one she was quite willing to assume the blame for, would be far less embarrassing than having his wife go about telling anyone who would listen what an awful husband he was. She didn't relish doing such a thing, but she would if it was the only way to convince him to comply. Hopefully, it would embarrass him more to have his wife traipsing around town speaking ill of him than to grant her a divorce for crimcon. Of course, indicating that the marriage had never been consummated would probably be best. Time would tell which option he preferred.

Finally, after Grovemont agreed to the divorce, she would go to Griffin's estate in the country for a year or two. Just until the scandal died down. Time healed many scandals. By the time she returned, there would be some other scandal, and everyone would forgive and forget *her* little indiscretion. After all, as long as she wasn't in search a new husband, no one would care much what she did. At least that was what she would have to tell herself to get through this plan because, otherwise, she might lose her nerve, and she *refused* to lose her nerve.

Even if it meant she was exiled to the countryside forever, she would not remain married to the Duke of Grovemont. It was undeniably painful to think she would probably never have the chance to marry for love, to have children and a home of her own. It was excruciating to contemplate. But it was also the price she had to pay for her recklessness. She hadn't meant to, but she had been the one to make the mistake, to force Grovemont to propose. It was still her fault, and she had to take responsibility for it…even at the cost of her own happiness.

She was determined, but she had also taken Cecily's advice and written to Lady Clare Handleton. Clare was a spinster and Meredith's closest friend. She'd been ruined during her first Season by a titled man who'd refused to marry her. Ever since, she'd been unwelcome in most of the homes owned by members of Society. Of course, Clare was welcome in Meredith and Griffin's home, and having a duke and duchess as close friends had garnered her a bit of respectability. But Clare had never married and was still treated poorly by most members of the *ton*. If anyone knew what it was like to weather a scandal, it was the woman the papers had nicknamed "Scandalton." She only hoped Clare would write back soon. Time was of the essence. She couldn't get away from Grovemont quickly enough.

When the door to the music room opened and Grovemont stepped inside, Gemma nearly missed a key. She scowled. What in the world did he want in here? He could clearly hear she was playing. It had better not be some new rule or demand he intended to impart. She had no patience for his ridiculous decrees today.

Lifting her nose in the air, she ignored him. She continued to play her sonata until he came to stand directly in front of the instrument. He smiled at her. *Smiled*. And, frankly, it looked…genuine. It wasn't falsely tight or strained in the manner they usually smiled at each other.

Gemma narrowed her eyes. *Why* was he smiling? She'd never seen him smile. Not like that.

No matter. She turned her attention back to her sheets and finished the piece before she allowed her fingers to come to a rest atop the ivory keys.

Grovemont's clapping echoed through the large room.

She narrowed her eyes to *slits*. "Did you want something?" she asked tersely.

"I want to say good morning," he replied in a voice that sounded nearly jovial. "I failed to do so before I left today."

She arched a brow over her still-narrowed eye. He was up

to something. Feeling guilty over failing to say good morning? Not likely.

She expelled a long breath. "Have you made up your mind?" she asked, deciding not to acknowledge his "good morning" comment. "Consummation or crimcon?" She gave him a big, bright, fake smile.

He slid his hands into the pockets of his coat and strolled toward her as if he hadn't a care in the world. He bit his bottom lip and gave her a lazy smile. One she suspected would make a certain type of lady swoon, if she did not know him.

"I have not yet decided," he replied smoothly. "Would you give me a sennight to think about it?"

Her brows shot up. A sennight? That seemed like quite a long time. And she didn't trust for a moment that he didn't have some sort of trick up his sleeve. But allowing him a sennight to contemplate the matter was preferable to him declaring an outright no and starting a war between them, which is what she'd expected he might do. It would also give her time to receive a reply from Lady Clare.

Gemma smiled without showing her teeth, silently letting him know she was suspicious of his motives. "A sennight?" she repeated.

"Yes. Please," he replied.

Please? She pressed a hand to her throat. Had he said *please*? She didn't think he knew what that word meant and certainly had never expected *him* to use such a word? Oh, he was definitely up to something. No doubt he intended to avail himself of the sennight in order to secure a solicitor to savagely fight her on the divorce. But she didn't have much of a choice, did she? "Fine," she finally allowed. "One sennight."

"Thank you." He bowed to her. "You play beautifully, by the by." He nodded toward the pianoforte.

Her jaw dropped, but he didn't see. He'd already swiveled on his heel and was on his way toward the door. She watched him go with her mouth still open. Had he just complimented her? First, he'd smiled, then he'd used the word *please*, and finally he'd given her an actual compliment?

Oh, yes. The man was *definitely* up to something.

CHAPTER TWENTY-SEVEN

That Night, The Duke of Grovemont's Bedchamber

Lucian paced in front of the fireplace across from his bed. No sooner did he reach the far wall than he'd turn on his heel and stalk back. His shoulders were tense, and he couldn't sit down. He'd just sent Gemma a note asking her if she would do him the honor of accompanying him to the Chadworths' ball this evening. He knew she already intended to go because he'd inquired after her plans with her maid.

Normally, Lucian would have *told* Gemma that he was escorting her to the ball. But after learning that she *wasn't* a scheming liar this morning, he'd vowed to himself that whatever his inclination toward Gemma, he should do the exact opposite. Because clearly everything he'd done since becoming a husband had been incorrect. Woefully incorrect. So, where he'd been ordering her about before, he now intended to secure her agreement.

He'd begun this morning after his return from the club. She'd been home playing the pianoforte. He'd paused outside the music room and listened for a while, enjoying the strands of the melody echoing in the corridor. She was a truly talented musician. After enjoying the sound for a bit, he'd stepped inside the room.

Gemma had immediately been suspicious of him, of course. Her face gave away her every thought. She'd stared at him with narrowed eyes as if she expected him to tell her to stop playing, almost daring him to order her to stop. Instead, he'd calmly watched and waited until her song came to an end.

He'd expected her to mention the divorce again, and she had. Which is why he'd asked for a sennight to think about it. He needed time to decide upon the best course of action. He did not want to argue with her. Telling her again that a divorce was out of the question would only rile her. In their short time together, he'd already learned that Gemma did not take kindly to being told what to do.

On the contrary, she liked to feel as if she had the option to do as she liked. Which was why asking for a reprieve on the divorce discussion made the most sense. It would give Lucian time to determine the best way to handle the situation.

He needed to talk her out of *wanting* the divorce in the first place. Simply telling her that he would endeavor to be less of an arrogant, pompous, holier-than-thou ass would not convince her. He was certain of it.

He needed to *show* her his behavior had changed. He needed to charm her. Which, of course, was easier said than done. No one had ever accused him of being particularly charming. Handsome? Yes. Rich? Undoubtedly. Eligible? Indeed. But charming? No. Which meant he must learn how to be charming. He had to.

It couldn't be too difficult. God knew he had friends who

excelled at such things. Like Ashford Drake, the Marquess of Trentham. Ash was a charming bastard.

"Your home is your domain. Everything belongs to you. Everything." Lucian's father's words echoed in his head. He shook it. His father had been the definition of an arrogant, pompous, holier-than-thou ass. One who was preoccupied by the way things looked to everyone else, completely ignoring the feelings of the people he loved. His father had died with a wife and a son who didn't particularly miss him. Of course, to Lucian's knowledge, Mama had never requested a divorce. Which meant…Lucian was *worse* than his father. What a comforting thought. But Lucian was also clever and determined. Determined to act completely opposite from how he had acted toward Gemma to date. And he'd already had a modicum of success.

If he didn't mistake his guess, he'd succeeded in disarming her this morning. Surprise lit her eyes when he'd used the word *please*, for example. But Lucian was no fool. Paying her a compliment and asking for the sennight to think about the divorce would not be enough to change her mind. He had a great deal of work to do.

And he would begin tonight. *If* she agreed to allow him to escort her to the Chadworths'. For all he knew, she'd tell him to go to hell, or she'd tell him she'd changed her mind. Either way, he'd —

The knock at his door nearly made Lucian jump. He smiled to himself. Jesus, was he *that* nervous? He was never nervous. His new wife had him in knots.

"Come in," he intoned.

By the time Warwick stepped into the room holding Gemma's reply on a silver salver, Lucian was at the bookshelf in the corner, thumbing through a tome in an effort to look as if he'd forgotten the errand he'd assigned the butler. As if he'd *hadn't* been anxiously awaiting his wife's answer.

"Your Grace," Warwick intoned as he stepped toward him, bowing his head. "Her Grace's reply."

Lucian moved to meet him halfway across the thick rug. "Thank you, Warwick. That will be all for now," he said in his most unaffected tone. He forced himself to wait for the servant to close the door behind him before he ripped open the sealed vellum.

I'll see you in the foyer at ten.

Short. Not particularly sweet. But not a rejection either. It would do.

Lucian smiled to himself. It was time to woo his wife.

CHAPTER TWENTY-EIGHT

Later That Night, The Chadworths' Ball

The moment Grovemont looked her way, Gemma jerked her head in the opposite direction. Oh, drat. She'd been caught staring. And she *was* staring. Staring at her husband across the expanse of the ballroom.

In addition to *asking* if she would allow him to escort her to the ball tonight, he'd hovered by her side all evening, danced with her *three* times, which was unseemly, and was even now engaged in the pursuit of fetching her a glass of champagne because she'd mentioned she was thirsty.

In short, he was being entirely un-Grovemont-like. Precisely the same way he'd been in the music room this morning. What in the devil's name was he up to? And how would she find out?

He'd asked for a sennight. A request that seemed reasonable on the surface, but he would no doubt use that time to plot a way to thwart her plans. Only she couldn't discern how. She would have to search his study. That's all there was to it. There had to be something there that would give her a clue as to his plans.

Meanwhile, however, he was being entirely disconcerting with his solicitousness. He slid back next to her side, handing her a glass of champagne. "Would you care for anything else, my lady?" he asked. "A finger sandwich, perhaps?"

Was he truly offering her a finger sandwich? And she had no reason to think he wouldn't trot off and get one for her if she said the word. It was not just off-putting. It was…bizarre.

"Why are you being so nice to me?" No one had ever accused her of not being forthright.

"Why wouldn't I be nice to you?" he replied with an angelic smile.

"Wouldn't you rather be…doing whatever it is you normally do at balls?" She waved her hand in the air in a circle.

He poked at the curve of his lip with his tongue. "Normally, I hide in the study, drinking and playing cards."

"Well then?"

"I prefer your company."

"You don't have to pretend when no one is around to hear us," she informed him with a tight smile.

"What if I'm not pretending?"

Gemma didn't have long to contemplate *that* astounding statement before she was jostled from behind. She turned to see Lord Pembroke.

"Ah, Your Grace, lovely to see you," Pembroke said, eyeing Lucian warily.

"Good evening, my lord," Gemma replied.

Grovemont had opened his mouth, but before he had a chance to say anything Lady Mary, of all people, swept into their circle.

"There you are, Pembroke," Mary said. "I've been looking all over for you. You must come meet my friend, Sally. Good evening, Your Grace," she said to Lucian without so much as acknowledging Gemma's existence.

Pembroke looked as if the last thing he wanted was to meet Sally, but he politely excused himself to Lucian and Gemma and turned toward Lady Mary.

"That's right. *Go away*, Pembroke," Lucian growled at the shorter man.

Pembroke glanced back at Grovemont disapprovingly.

After the two strode off, Gemma shook her head at Grovemont. "Why do you dislike him so?"

Grovemont lifted both brows. "What's to like?"

Gemma watched as Mary led Pembroke over to the wall where they began speaking in earnest. No friend named Sally, eh? Gemma shook her head. Leave it to Mary to lie about why she wanted to speak to him. She was up to something as well, but thankfully it was no longer Gemma's concern. Now that Mary was betrothed, she'd stopped threatening the wallflowers. Which meant Gemma could relinquish her role as their unofficial protector.

"Lady Mary was staring daggers at you," Lucian pointed out.

"Oh, I was never her favorite, and when you and I married, I suppose I made a lifelong enemy."

"I would *never* have married *her*." Grovemont took a sip from his champagne glass. "Even if she'd been the one I'd been found alone with in the study."

And with that startling bit of information, he offered his wife his arm for yet another dance.

CHAPTER TWENTY-NINE

The *Next Morning, The Marquess of Trentham's Town House*

Lucian had plans for the day. Plans to learn precisely how to be charming. After last night, he realized it would not be easy convincing Gemma to give him a chance. It would take every bit of his skill and then some. Which is why he'd sent a note round to someone who knew all about charm. Meredith's brother, Ashford Drake, The Marquess of Trentham. It was also why Lucian was even now sitting in Trentham's study.

The marquess had a desk, but it had been turned into more of a sideboard of sorts, with bottles of alcohol and glasses sitting upon it instead of papers, ledgers, and an inkpot. In fact, if the man had an inkpot, Lucian didn't know where it was.

Trentham had long ago declared himself a lifelong bachelor, but he'd also been quite clear that he had no intention of seeing to his estates, attending sessions of Parliament, or doing mundane things like meeting with solicitors. In fact, he'd handed off all his work to his secretary. Ash spent his time carousing, drinking, and being charming.

A more devil-may-care chap did not exist. And Trentham was never without a beautiful woman on his arm. Charm, you could say, came naturally to the man. Which was precisely why Lucian was here. If one wanted to learn to be charming, one went to an expert.

"Tell me again what exactly you're trying to do," Trentham said as he poured them both a large glass of brandy.

Lucian cleared his throat. His errand was embarrassing, but he and Trentham had been good friends since they were lads. Trentham would keep anything he shared a secret. "I wish to win over my wife."

Trentham cupped a hand behind his ear. His brow furrowed. "Pardon? I thought I heard you say you wish to win over your own *wife?*"

Lucian shifted in his seat and bit his lip. "I did."

Trentham cocked his head to the side. "What would you want to do that for? The woman is already *married* to you."

Lucian nodded. Trentham didn't believe in marriage. So much so that one day at Court, he'd announced to the King himself that he had no intention of marrying. Ever. The King had apparently thought it was a jest, but anyone who knew Trentham well knew that he was quite serious. The man gave no cares about his title, his estate, or an heir. In fact, he'd been quite vocal when his father had been alive, telling the previous marquess that he had every intention of letting the estate rot. And Lucian thought he had issues with *his* father. Apparently, Trentham won that contest.

Regardless of his unorthodox lifestyle and choices, Trentham was a decent man and a good friend. He would help. Lucian knew it. Though he'd also be the recipient of a lot of good-natured ribbing in the meanwhile.

"Isn't the entire point of marriage that you no longer need

to be charming?" Trentham continued, handing Lucian his brandy glass. He was giving Lucian a look that clearly indicated he thought he'd lost his mind.

"In some instances, perhaps," Lucian allowed, taking a large sip. It might not yet be noon, but this was damned humiliating. The drink couldn't hurt. "But in my case, I need all the help I can get."

Trentham took a seat behind the desk and pushed away some of the bottles so they could see each other. "It's no great mystery," the marquess said. "Women want what everyone wants."

"Which is?" Lucian prodded.

"Attention, of course."

Lucian nodded. "Sounds easy enough. But in practice, it's much more difficult."

"Not really," Trentham continued. "Women like to be treated as if they are special."

Lucian blinked. "That's it?"

"Essentially, yes," Trentham replied. "And the truth is, they *are* special. So it's not difficult to do. For example, when you're with a woman, you should never mention another woman. At least not another woman you're interested in."

"I'm not interested in another woman," Lucian replied, frowning.

"All the better for you then," Trentham replied with a wink.

"What else?" Lucian demanded, moving closer to sit on the edge of the chair. This was already interesting. He'd come to the right spot. He could learn a lot from the marquess.

Trentham lifted his glass to his lips and took a sip. "Women like to be treated as if you only have eyes for them. They like to be given gifts, complimented, and cherished. Above all, respected." He shrugged. "That's what they want. Simple, really."

"Respected? Cherished?" Lucian breathed. Who knew? But it hardly sounded simple.

"Yes. The problem is they often won't come out and tell you these things. Would make it much simpler if they did, honestly. But I've figured it out through trial and error, mostly." Another wink from the marquess, and he raised his glass as if in a toast. "That and asking pointed questions to the sorts of women who'll give the answers."

Lucian's frown deepened. "*Not* noblewomen, I take it."

Trentham's cheeks puffed with the air he blew into them. "I avoid noblewomen like the plague. They're only interested in one thing... Marriage."

"But the way to charm them is the same?" Lucian clarified.

"I expect so. A woman is a woman," Trentham replied, grinning. "Look, the easiest way to learn what a woman wants is to ask her."

"Ask her?"

"Yes, you know, questions. Ask her how her day was. Ask her what is bothering her. Ask her what she would like for breakfast." Trentham waggled his eyebrows after that last bit of advice.

Lucian cleared his throat and tugged at his waistcoat. Trentham certainly wasn't subtle, but perhaps women liked that sort of thing. "Anything else?"

Trentham shrugged. "Be confident. Most women abhor a man who isn't sure of himself."

Confident? No problem there.

"But not overbearing," Trentham amended.

Oh, well, there was the problem then. Lucian had already guessed he would fare better with Gemma if he was less imperious. He'd been nothing but overbearing since they'd married.

"Ask her opinion on things that matter. And take her advice."

Lucian shook his head. That hadn't been anything his father had ever told him. The old man would be spinning in his grave now if he heard this. He couldn't remember ever hearing his father ask his mother for advice. And if she'd given him any, he wouldn't have taken it.

"And talk to her," Trentham added.

"Talk? About what?"

"The weather, the races, the news of the day. The same things you talk about with any friend."

"Friend?" Was Gemma his friend? Could she be? He'd never thought of such a thing.

"Yes. Friend. Women are friends too, you know."

Lucian expelled his breath and shook his head. "You've listed so many things. I was hoping there would be just one trick to seem charming."

Trentham cocked a brow. "But that's just it. Charm *isn't* a trick."

"Isn't it?" Lucian drawled.

"No. It's not, actually. Charm isn't about pretending to be someone you're not. It's about listening. It's about truly caring about how someone else is feeling. Discovering what's troubling them. Asking them about themselves. Caring about the answer. Charm isn't false. Not true charm, at least. And most people, astute people like Gemma, can immediately spot the difference." He winked again. "Of course, being witty doesn't hurt either."

"I'm *not* witty," Lucian assured him, groaning.

"Then mind how she is feeling. Ask her. Truly *listen* to her answers."

Lucian rubbed his knuckles against his forehead. Emotion. That's what Trentham was saying. Ask about feelings? No wonder Lucian had been rubbish at being charming his whole life. His father had taught him from a young age that showing emotion was strictly forbidden. There'd been no asking about feelings in his household. There had only been one thing: appearance.

"How are *you* feeling, by the by, about what I just said?" Trentham asked.

How was he feeling? How *was* he feeling? God, the question alone induced panic.

"Take your time," Trentham replied. "I know it's difficult for you."

Lucian took a deep breath. He could do this. He needed to begin the sentence with…"I feel…" He took another deep breath for good measure. "Honestly, I feel…frightened. As if I already know I'll fail."

Trentham cocked his head to the side. "And you think you'll fail because…?"

"Because I have no earthly idea how to care about someone's emotions or how to show mine," Lucian blurted.

"That's not true. You just shared an emotion with me. And one that is not easy to share at that."

At Lucian's inquiring look, Trentham said, "You told me you're frightened."

Lucian pressed his lips together. "I did, didn't I?" Trentham had a point. Had he ever told another living soul he was frightened before? And he'd just shared that with another man. Not only that, it felt good to admit it. Freeing, actually.

"Yes. And it gets easier the more you do it." Trentham clapped him on the shoulder. "Just be honest with Gemma. Tell her what you're feeling. Ask her what she's feeling. I promise you'll get much further with her that way than by ordering her about."

Lucian lifted his chin. "Who says I was ordering her about?"

Trentham grinned and lifted his glass. "We've been friends a long time, Grovemont."

Lucian couldn't argue with that. "All right. I'll try it."

"Good. It also helps me to behave toward women in the exact opposite manner my father would have done so."

Oh, now *that* was solid advice.

"Pay attention to your wife," Trentham continued with another grin, tipping his glass toward his friend in salute. "What do you have to lose?"

Oh, only his marriage, his reputation, and his future heir. But who was counting? If paying her attention and sharing his feelings was the way to convince Gemma to give him another chance, Lucian would do it.

He had to.

CHAPTER THIRTY

Four Days Later, The Grundys' Drawing Room

"He asked me to dance three times. He brought me two glasses of champagne. And then, when we arrived home, he inquired as to what I wanted to be served for *breakfast!*"

Gemma imparted all of this while sitting on the burgundy settee in Cecily's drawing room. Gemma was wearing a light-yellow gown. Cecily was wearing a sky-blue one. And both of them were eating far too many scones while drinking far too much tea.

"That all sounds quite lovely," Cecily said from her perch on the matching settee across from Gemma's.

"It all sounds quite *suspicious*," Gemma insisted. "Last night he asked me if I wanted to go riding in the park today."

Cecily took a sip from her teacup. "What do you mean? You love to go riding in the park."

"I know I do, but *he* doesn't know that I do. And I don't think for one moment the man *wants* to ride in the park with me."

Cecily frowned. "Why wouldn't he?"

Gemma shook her head. "That's just it, Cecily. You're thinking of this from *your* perspective. *You* would like to ride in the park with me. But he doesn't like me and thinks I'm a cheating, lying ne'er-do-well."

"But you aren't a cheating, lying ne'er-do-well," Cecily pointed out loyally.

"Of course, I'm not, but he thinks I am. Which is my *entire* point. I told him I wanted a divorce, and now he's being nice to me. He clearly wants something."

"Perhaps he wants to be nice to you," Cecily offered.

"Whenever we dance, he smiles at me. He asks me how my day was," Gemma muttered under her breath.

"And?"

Gemma's arms were tightly crossed over her chest. "And it's obvious that he's planning something."

Cecily frowned. "But didn't you say that's how Griffin treats Meredith?"

"That's precisely how Griffin treats Meredith, but Griffin *loves* Meredith. Grovemont doesn't love me. He couldn't wait to get away from me, and he hasn't been back a full fortnight."

Cecily blinked and tilted her head to the side. "How long does it take to fall in love?"

Gemma shook her head. "I have no idea, but I'm certain one doesn't fall in love with someone one doesn't even *like*."

Cecily bit her lip. "I'm not sure that's true, Gemma. Remember *Much Ado About Nothing*."

"Oh, Cecily, Shakespeare won't help this situation." Gemma sighed and uncrossed her arms long enough to take another bite from her scone.

Cecily nodded. "Very well. What do you think he's up to then?"

Gemma's eyes narrowed to slits. "I don't know. But I

intend to find out. Of course, I've *considered* that it *may* be my change in appearance."

"You are extraordinarily beautiful now," Cecily agreed.

"But I just *know* that's not it," Gemma continued. "First, he hasn't even mentioned my appearance."

"He'd have to be blind not to have noticed," Cecily pointed out.

Gemma shook her head and bit at the end of her thumbnail. "It's something else. I know it. He's worried about his reputation being ruined. He could have his pick of beautiful women to take as a mistress. We both know it."

The door to the drawing room opened just then, and the Grundy's manservant stepped into the room. Mr. Hampton was a jack of all trades at Cecily's house. He served as butler, footman, and groom since the Grundys could no longer afford many servants. Cecily was the only member of the household who treated him with kindness. "Miss Cecily," Mr. Hampton said, "you have another visitor."

"Another visitor?" Cecily sat up straight and nearly dropped her scone. She blinked at Gemma. "No one visits me but you. Not after Mama sent all the suitors away."

"Who is it, Mr. Hampton?" Gemma asked.

The man cleared his throat nervously and glanced away. "Lady Clare Handleton, Miss. If your mother was home, she would not want—"

"Show her in immediately," Gemma demanded, not allowing the man to finish his unwelcome statement.

At Cecily's nod, Mr. Hampton left to do as he was told.

"Oh, can you believe it? She's come to visit," Gemma said, clapping her hands together with glee. "The most I expected was a letter."

"And to think Hampton nearly didn't allow her past the door," Cecily said, shaking her head. "I suppose that's one example of what scandal will do to you, Gemma."

When the door to the drawing room opened next, Lady Clare came striding into the room. She was wearing a gorgeous sapphire-blue gown that hugged her curves and set off her pretty blond hair and dark eyes to perfection. Gemma had only met Lady Clare a handful of times, but each time she'd been impressed with the lady's forthright demeanor and penchant for doing and saying exactly what she wished.

"My dears," Lady Clare said as she strode over to the sideboard and began pouring herself a glass of brandy. "I'm so glad to have found you together. I hope you'll forgive the intrusion, but I felt strongly that I have far more to impart than could be aptly done in a letter. Also, I'm always on the hunt for a reason to escape my mother. I did wait for *your* mother and awful sisters to leave, Cecily. I expect they'll be back soon, so I'd better talk quickly."

Gemma and Cecily could not have been more delighted. They waited with bated breath for Lady Clare to take a seat. She kicked up one leg, revealing an indecent amount of stocking, and boldly sipped her brandy as she spoke. "So, you want to know how it feels to be the subject of a scandal?"

Gemma nodded, staring at the older woman with wide eyes. Clare was Meredith's age, which made her nine and twenty. "Yes, and I hope you'll do as I asked in my letter and not share my intention to divorce with Meredith."

"The first lesson to learn about ladies who've been through scandals," Clare replied, "is that they don't *ever* share *other* people's secrets."

"Stands to reason," Cecily breathed.

"I'd like you to be quite candid, if you please," Gemma urged. "A divorce is certain to cause as big a scandal if not bigger than…" She bit her lip. Oh, she shouldn't have started that sentence.

"Than what happened to me?" Clare finished for her, laughing.

"I beg your pardon," Gemma murmured.

Lady Clare gave them both a bright smile. "The second lesson to learn about ladies who've been through scandals is that there's nothing you can say behind our backs that surprises us. We're quite forthright. It's not as if we think our scandal is a secret. It's quite the opposite. Out there for all to see and discuss. Quite freeing in a way."

"It seems to me that being free is the best part of being attached to a scandal," Gemma pointed out.

"There are good parts," Lady Clare agreed. "And there are bad. Quite bad."

More than an hour flew by as Clare regaled them with stories of how she'd been ostracized, diminished, ignored, un-invited, and essentially treated with a complete lack of manners for the last decade. None of it was news to Gemma, but hearing some of her tales did make Gemma gulp.

"But…but won't your true friends, your good, *real* friends, remain by your side even after a scandal? Like Meredith did for you?" Gemma prompted. She had to hear another bit of good news after hearing all the bad. The bad had been quite discouraging.

"I'll stay by your side, Gemma," Cecily promised, grasping Gemma's hand and squeezing it. "No matter what Mama says."

"I know you will, Cecily," Gemma replied, returning her friend's pat.

They both waited for Lady Clare's answer.

"It's true," the older woman said. "Your real friends *will* remain steadfast."

Gemma breathed a sigh of relief.

"But you must ask yourself," Lady Clare continued, arching a brow. "Are you prepared to find out how few of them there truly are?"

CHAPTER THIRTY-ONE

L ater That Afternoon, The Duke of Grovemont's Study
When Lucian stepped into his study to see Gemma bending over his desk, rifling through a stack of papers, he stopped short.

"Good afternoon," he said in his most cheery voice. The one he'd been using whenever he saw her now. Honestly, it hadn't been easy pretending to be the soul of happiness these last several days, but he was committed to changing his demeanor for his wife's sake.

Gemma dropped the papers and shot upright. She slung an arm around her waist and used her other hand to innocently scratch behind her ear. "Um. I was just…uh…"

He bestowed her with an easy smile. "No need to explain. I trust you."

He enjoyed watching her mouth fall open and then her struggle to close it. It might not be easy to pretend to be cheerful, but he had to admit it was fun defying Gemma's expectations.

"You trust me?" she echoed, frowning.

"Of course, I do." He walked around to the front of the

desk and glanced at the papers. Some accounting information from his solicitor. Nothing particularly interesting. Though he doubted that was what Gemma had been looking for. It was plain as day on her face. She was nosing through his office to find out if he was up to something. She'd been treating him like this all week. As if he was hiding something. And he knew why she was suspicious. She didn't trust why he was acting so differently toward her. It was comical to watch, actually.

"May I help you find anything?" he offered.

She rocked back and forth on her heels. "No. I just…"

"Have you decided whether you'll go riding with me? Just say the word, and I'll have the curricle put to."

Her mouth snapped shut, and she was clearly contemplating the matter for several moments before she finally asked, "Why do you *want* to go riding in the park with me?" Her tone was accusatory.

Lucian allowed the hint of a smile to play around his lips. "I'm told it's a pleasant experience."

Her suspicious eyes narrowed further. "It is. But why would you want to go with *me*?" She pointed at herself.

"I believe married couples do these sorts of things," he supplied.

She perched a hip on the edge of the desk and crossed both arms over her chest. "That's just it. We needn't pretend we're a regular married couple. Have you made your decision? About the divorce, I mean?"

Had he made his decision? Of course, he'd made his decision. There wouldn't be a divorce if he had any say in it, but he'd spent the last several days coming up with an intricate plan. One he hoped she couldn't refuse. He had only to present it to her.

"I have," he said with a solid nod. "And I'm happy to explain it to you while we ride in the park."

GEMMA NARROWED her eyes to slits. What in the world was he up to? Before he'd arrived, she'd been in his study for the better part of twenty minutes, and she hadn't found anything about a divorce. If he had hired a solicitor to thwart her plans, there was no sign of it. But what if he'd anticipated that she would go snooping through his study? Perhaps she'd have to look in his bedchamber or even his wardrobe for such documents.

It hadn't been a full sennight, but she'd asked him if he'd come to a decision to get the focus off herself and her nosing about his study. He'd surprised her by saying that he *had* come to a decision. Then he'd surprised her even more by asking her to go riding in the park to discuss it. She supposed she could demand an answer here and now, but she did like the park. Very well. If it meant he'd continue to act pleasant, she would go with him. She had to admit that over the last several days, his attentiveness had been far preferable to his previous surly orders. But her deep suspicion made her question everything he did and said. She would go riding in the park, but she would *not* trust him.

"Very well," she said. "Let's go."

CHAPTER THIRTY-TWO

One Hour Later, Hyde Park

Gemma tilted back her head, closed her eyes, and clutched the crown of her bright-yellow bonnet as Grovemont's well-sprung curricle jostled its way through Hyde Park. She breathed in deeply, taking in the lovely scent of the late summer flowers and grass in the park. It was always so much better here than on the streets in town. And the park was the best of both worlds. The countryside itself was far too remote and dull, but she did love to be outdoors. Even having Grovemont by her side would not dim her happiness this afternoon.

She had to admit he looked good today. But then again, he always looked good. He was wearing simple dark-brown buckskin breeches, black boots, a white shirt, and a sapphire waistcoat and overcoat. His white cravat stood in stark relief to the tan he'd acquired in India, and his hooded blue eyes and sharp jawline were as captivating as ever. Why did the man have to look like the devil had carved him out of stone to tempt ladies everywhere? It was truly unfair. And just another reason why he couldn't possibly believe she hadn't tried to trap him into marriage. A man as handsome as Grovemont had probably been born with women fighting over him. But she was only too willing to toss him back into the pond. Another woman was welcome to catch him.

She may have agreed to this outing, but she had no intention of speaking to him. At least not the silly little pleasantries they'd exchanged over the last week. It had all been so obviously false. She refused to pretend as if they were happy. He might want to act as if they were something they were not, but she had no interest in it. Instead, she settled into her seat and watched as chipmunks chased each other through the meadow. He would have to speak first.

They'd trotted about for the better part of an hour before Grovemont pulled the curricle onto a dirt road near the Serpentine. Hmm. This seemed *too* private. She watched him from the corner of her eye. He appeared to be entirely nonplussed, shaking out the reins and issuing commands to the finely matched pair of horses pulling the conveyance. She'd had to grudgingly admit the man was an excellent driver. A rubbish husband, but good with horses. Too bad for him she wasn't a horse.

When they reached the water's edge, he stopped the curricle and leaped to the grass. Oh, dear. Was this it? Did he want to talk now? Fine. But she refused to speak of anything other than when they'd get their divorce.

He bounded around the side of the curricle and offered her his hand.

"I'm fine. I don't need your help," she said as she gathered her sunny skirts and jumped to the grass.

Grovemont stepped back and shook his head. "I can see that."

"Not the way you think a duchess should behave?" she sniped. Ugh. She'd let him goad her into saying something ill-mannered. She needed to remain completely unaffected by him. Indifference!

"Behave however you like," was his even reply.

Gemma merely side-eyed him again. Of course, he didn't mean that.

They walked slowly together toward a large chestnut tree and once under its shady branches, Gemma turned sharply to her husband. "Why did you bring me here?" She couldn't help herself. She could no longer stand the suspense.

He chuckled. "Not enjoying the park?"

"Oh, I'm enjoying the park. It's the company I find lacking." Oh, drat. She could *not* stop.

"Ouch." He put a hand over his heart.

Gemma turned away from him so he couldn't see the frustration on her face. Why couldn't she seem to control herself around this man? She took a deep breath and shook her head, ready to try again to be civil. She turned back to him, hoping her face was a composed mask of indifference. "You could save us both a lot of time by just coming out with what you're up to."

One of his dark-blond brows shot up. "What I'm up to?"

She lifted her chin. She would not allow him to make her doubt her sanity. "I think we both know you haven't suddenly begun enjoying rides in the park with me."

"You're suspicious of my motives." It wasn't a question. It was a statement. And a correct one at that.

She blinked at him. "Why shouldn't I be?"

Grovemont tilted his head to the side and contemplated her. "I like that about you, Gemma. You're forthright."

Oh, that was it. Using her Christian name? Giving her a compliment? Too much. She rolled her eyes. "Flattering me is a waste of your breath."

He shoved his hands into his coat pockets. "Fine. Then allow me to get directly to the point."

She straightened both of her shoulders, preparing herself for the inevitable impact of his words. "Please do."

"I am willing to grant you your divorce," he said simply.

Her head snapped to the side to stare at him in wonder. What was that? Had she heard him incorrectly? She must have.

"I said I'm willing to grant the divorce," he repeated as if reading her thoughts.

She narrowed her eyes to slits and plunked her hands onto her hips. "And?" She drew out the word slowly.

He scratched his jaw. "And what?"

"And what is the condition upon which you will grant it?" She blinked at him, glaring as if she still didn't believe what he'd said. Because she didn't.

He chuckled and bit his lip. "That obvious, am I?"

"Out with it," she demanded.

Grovemont removed his hat and scrubbed his hand through his unfairly thick hair before replacing the hat. "Fine. I will grant you your divorce in two months' time if… you spend that time with me pretending to be happily married."

Of all the things she thought the man had been about to say, *that* had certainly not been one of them. Now she *knew* she was hearing things. That or perhaps her ears weren't working correctly. "Pardon?" was all she could muster.

"I'm asking you to spend the next eight weeks pretending to be happily married to me."

Was it her imagination or did he look worried, vulnerable even? As if he was concerned she would refuse. She pressed her palm to her forehead. A hundred questions flew through her mind. Where to begin? "Pretending? Why would you want that?"

He folded his arms behind his back and nodded once. "I have my own reasons."

"Your own reasons?" she echoed. What in heaven's name did that mean?

"Yes. And I'd like to keep them private…for now."

Her brows shot up. "I bet you would," she mumbled.

"Pardon?"

"Nothing." She gave him a beatific smile. "But I don't think—"

He didn't let her finish. "If you agree to pretend that we're happily married, I will not only grant the divorce at the end of the two months. I will also provide you with a hefty settlement of, say, fifty-thousand pounds?"

First, Gemma gasped. Then she struggled to breathe. Fifty-thousand pounds was twice as much as her extremely generous dowry. It was a fortune. And Grovemont knew that. Why would he offer her such a sum? And with nothing more than having to *pretend* to like him for two months? It was unorthodox, strange perhaps. It might even make her stomach revolt, but it was certainly worth *fifty-thousand pounds and an uncontested divorce*. Still. She didn't trust him. Not one whit.

She straightened her shoulders and glared at him. "What is the catch?"

"Catch?" He blinked at her innocently.

"Yes, what precisely will be involved with my 'pretending' to be happy?"

He leaned back against the tree trunk and drew up one knee to rest the flat of his boot against the bark. "I've been thinking about that."

"And?" she prodded.

"You must agree to go places with me, dance, laugh, drink, have fun. In short, we will carry on as if we are a happily married couple."

More narrowed eyes. "What would *you* get out of such an arrangement?"

"I will get your company and the good graces of my wife, if for a short period of time."

She swiveled on her heel and began marching back to the curricle. "No. You're lying. The answer is no."

Moments later, he came flying around her, laughing. "Why are you so suspicious?"

"Why would you ever think I wouldn't be?" she shot back.

"Fine. I admit that I'm not telling you my entire reason, but I swear that I am not lying about wanting your company and to be in your good graces."

"When will you tell me the rest of your reasoning?" she demanded.

"I can only say I hope it shall become obvious after we begin."

Gemma crossed her arms over her chest once more. She drummed her fingertips near her elbows as she contemplated his words. It sounded too good to be true. Of course, it was too good to be true. On the other hand, what choice did she have? A divorce without his cooperation might not happen at all and fifty-thousand pounds was nothing to dismiss.

But there was one question burning a path through her brain. One that had to be settled immediately. "What about conjugal rights?"

More innocent blinking from Grovemont. "What about them?"

"Ugh." She huffed. Did she have to say it so clearly? "Will you expect me to pretend to be happy…" She tugged uneasily at the neck of her pelisse and forced the two words from lips. "In bed?"

He cleared his throat and gave her a sly smile. "I *hope* you won't be pretending."

First, something about the look on his face made heat

gather between her legs. Unwelcome heat. Unwanted heat. But *undeniable* heat.

Second, that was *not* the answer she'd expected. "What?" She wanted to stamp her foot on the grass. "You must be jesting. You honestly think we should share a bed? What if I become heavy with child?"

~

LUCIAN HAD BEEN WAITING for this argument. And he was fully prepared with his counter. "If we divorce after the two months have passed, I will have no hope of securing an heir. These eight weeks may be my last chance."

She lifted her chin. Her eyes were dark slits. "That's not true. You can remarry."

"I won't remarry," he assured her.

She clenched her jaw and turned away from him. Clearly, this last bit was difficult for her to agree to. But it was non-negotiable. He could only await her answer.

"And if I don't agree to this plan?" she finally asked.

"I will make it as difficult as humanly possible for you to divorce me," he said in a matter-of-fact voice. Damn. That was his last card. He'd just dropped it on the proverbial table. He hoped this worked.

She strode away from him quickly and then nearly as quickly strode back. "While we are in bed, do you expect me to...participate?"

His grin was devilish. "Wholeheartedly."

She sucked in her breath. "But what if I—?"

"Look. Despite your claim that the marriage was not consummated, we both know it was. And we know that it was—ahem—enjoyable. Do you deny it?" He lifted his brows, challenging her.

She looked as if she wanted to slap him. But thankfully

she said, "No. I don't deny it." He admired her for her honesty.

"Good, then we can agree that despite our failure to begin on the right foot as a married couple, we are compatible in bed. Which means we might as well enjoy ourselves while we're there. I don't want an unwilling wife. There is absolutely nothing attractive to me about forcing a woman."

She tapped her fingertip on her jaw, alarm obvious in her eyes. "Wait a moment. You said, 'if we divorce after the two months.' Does that mean you are hoping—?"

"That you'll change your mind by the end of it? Yes. I am. I admit it."

Gemma closed her eyes and sucked in a long, deep breath. When she finally opened her eyes again, she met his steady, inquiring gaze. "Why do you want this?" Her voice was strained, quiet.

Despite the nerves that jangled through him, Lucian forced his own voice to remain perfectly calm. She would be suspicious of anything but the unvarnished truth spoken plainly. He owed her that. "Because I realize I made a grave mistake in judging you, and I want another chance."

The tiniest gasp flew from her lips. She stared at him as if he'd just descended from a cloud. An unknown being she'd never seen before. Clearly, she didn't believe him. "Another chance at what?"

"Influencing your opinion of me." He pulled off his hat and turned it around and around in his hands. Damn. He was nervous again.

She lifted her nose in the air. "It could not be worse."

"Which is why I have nothing but hope." More hat turning. He bit the inside of his cheek. She had to agree to this. She *had* to.

She dropped her gaze to the grass. "*If* I agree to this, I will still want to leave at the end of the eight weeks. Do not fool yourself."

He nodded slowly. "If you still want to leave, I will abide by your wishes."

Her hands moved back to her hips and she lifted her gaze to meet his, her eyes bright with determination. "I want all of this in writing."

His crack of laughter bounced off the nearby trees. "I'm sure you do." He cleared his throat, forcing himself to calm down. She was going to say yes. *Thank God*. Relief poured through him. "I will have my solicitor draw it up. He's quite discreet. Which reminds me of another stipulation. No one else can know about this besides us."

Her brows shot up. "No one?"

"No one."

Her chin lifted once more. "And if I am with child by the end of the time period and still want to leave?"

"You may raise the lad until the age of, say, eight, and then he'll come live with me."

She rolled her eyes. "Of course, you think it'll be a boy."

"If it's a girl, you may raise her if you prefer, but I will want to visit from time to time. To know her."

She shook her head incredulously. "You're saying all of this as if it will be easy to give up a child."

He met her gaze and held it. "Gemma, I hope we'll raise our children *together*." He did his best to infuse sincerity into his words, to keep his gaze locked with hers.

She turned her head away, breaking their eye contact. "You're mad. You know that?"

Success was within his grasp. He could feel it. He was thankful for it. "Do we have an agreement?"

She swallowed hard, the thin column of her throat working. *Say yes, Gemma. Say yes.*

～

GEMMA EXPELLED A SHAKING BREATH. This was madness. Nothing but. Only she didn't have much of a choice. Sticking it out eight weeks and then insisting upon the divorce was the best way to get what she wanted. The alternative was unthinkable. She took another very deep breath. This is what it felt like to make a deal with the devil. She knew it in her bones. "Yes, we have an agreement."

A wide smile spread across his too-handsome face. "Good, then I'll have the papers drawn up immediately."

CHAPTER THIRTY-THREE

One Night Later

Gemma pushed the last bite of lemon pudding around her bowl. She'd eaten so much she thought she might pop, but if lingering over dinner delayed the inevitable, so be it.

The moment supper ended, she would have to go upstairs and change into a night rail...and wait for Grovemont to come to her bedchamber. The mere thought sent gooseflesh scattering along her arms and down her chest.

She didn't know if she could do it. Spend the night in bed with him, that is. She'd signed the paperwork this morning, and everything had been in order. She'd asked a hundred questions and added a dozen stipulations. But in the end, she had promised to pretend to be Grovemont's loving and faithful wife for two entire months. She could tell no one, and she had to act at all times as if they were nothing but happy together. In company and alone. Which reminded her. She'd agreed to call him Lucian from now on.

She was so full of nerves she was vibrating. Grovemont—

ahem, Lucian—was mad. That's all there was to it. He'd promised to trade fifty-thousand pounds and a divorce for the chance that he *might* be able to charm her into agreeing to stay. The man didn't have a charming hair on his head. Every time he attempted to be charming, the strain in him was obvious. It was ridiculous. But it was also the easiest way to get her divorce. She'd thought about it more all night. He could make things untenable for her if he decided to fight the divorce. But the contract was clear. The moment the two months were up, she would get her money, her divorce, and her freedom.

As for whether she wanted to have a baby, she was torn. Part of her hoped she wouldn't conceive. At least not with a boy child whom she would have to give away to his father one day. But Gemma couldn't help but wish for a girl. A girl she would be able to keep forever. The thought made her tear up. But each time she thought it, she shook her head. There were ways to prevent pregnancy. Even ways to end a pregnancy. She'd heard the maids talk about such things upon occasion. Of course, the notion worried her, and if Grovemont found out, there was no telling what he'd do. But it was an option, if worse came to worst.

"More pudding?" Grovemont offered from his side of the table with a bright smile. He'd had nothing but bright smiles for her all day. Apparently, she would have to endure two months of his cheerfulness.

She was tempted to say yes to the additional pudding. But ugh. She was already so full. If she ate one more bite, she might cast up her accounts. "No, thank you." She stood and spent an inordinate amount of time folding her napkin. She couldn't meet his gaze. "I suppose I should…"

He stood too. "Retire for the evening?" he offered.

Her only response was a curt nod. "I'll see you…later." By way of an invitation to bed, it wasn't particularly encouraging, but what else was she to say? She turned and strode from the dining room.

~

AN HOUR LATER, Gemma was pacing next to her bed. With Anna's help, she'd put on the night rail from her wedding night. And tonight, she was just as filled with nerves as she'd been that night.

Gemma swiped the back of her hand across her brow. She was sweating. And breathing heavily. What if she'd... forgotten how to go about it? They'd only done it once, after all. She didn't have enough practice to be any good at it. She winced. What if she did it wrong?

And she hadn't merely agreed to lie there and accept Lucian's advances. The contract had been clear. She had to be a *willing*, if not eager, participant. Thankfully, the solicitor had gone over the details of the contract exhibiting a completely stoic demeanor. But Gemma had read every word multiple times. There would be no getting this over with quickly.

Which frankly meant that she might as well enjoy herself. Though *that* thought made the nerves even worse.

The soft knock at the door between their rooms made Gemma jump. She promptly forced herself to smooth her hands down the front of her lacy night rail and take a deep breath. She counted to five. "Come in," she called, hoping the worry didn't sound in her voice. Only the words came out so faint, she wasn't certain he'd heard them.

When the door opened, her doubts were put to rest. Lucian was there, standing in the candlelight, wearing the linen breeches he apparently always wore to bed. His chest was even more defined now than it had been the last time she'd seen it. All sinewy and covered with muscles. Only now he was also tanned. She swallowed hard.

He slowly made his way over to her. "You're shaking?" Concern lit his eyes, and he reached out to gently cup her shoulders. "How do you feel?"

"I'm frightened," she admitted, hating herself for the tremor in her voice, hating herself for showing him her vulnerability. Though she had to admit it felt better to say it aloud.

Lucian pulled her into his arms and hugged her, resting his chin atop her head. "Shh. Don't be frightened. I promise you I won't hurt you."

His warm skin heated hers. "I know that, I just…" She just *what*? She didn't even know how to end that sentence.

He pulled away from her slightly and met her eyes. "Come, sit down," he offered, taking her hand and leading her to the bed.

They sat side-by-side on the mattress facing each other. His warm hands rubbed up and down her bare arms. "Are you cold?"

"A little." Gemma watched him with wide eyes and swallowed again. He was being so solicitous. And gentle. Careful with her. It made it difficult to stay angry with him. He didn't feel any differently about her, she reminded herself. He just wanted her to remain married to him to save face. He couldn't stand the *ton* knowing his wife had left him. As soon as the two months were up, he'd go back to being the cold, uncaring man she'd known before. This man, this man who hugged her and rubbed her arms and asked after her feelings, didn't exist. She *had* to remember that. She had to remember the truth. His attempts at being charming were improving, and *that* was dangerous.

"Come, get under the blankets," Lucian offered.

They both stood. He pulled back the covers and lifted them, and Gemma slid between them. Lying on the bed, she turned on her side to face him and wiggled backward, leaving room for him to join her. He moved to lay beside her, also on his side facing her. The warmth from his body surrounded her. She sucked in her breath and lowered her eyes to his muscled chest.

"Don't worry," he breathed, rubbing her left arm that lay atop her side. "I have no intention of pouncing on you. And if you want me to stop, you only have to say so."

She nodded, but gooseflesh was already spreading all over her body from his touch. The heat radiating from him made her relax. He smelled good, like soap and pine. She closed her eyes. She remembered it, remembered this, the feel of his hands on her, the way her skin reacted to his touch, the way her breathing hitched when his fingers found a sensitive spot. "I'm more worried that I won't want you to stop," she whispered.

His firmly molded lips tugged up in a smile. "I hope so," he said, catching his bottom lip with his teeth.

Gemma closed her eyes. She felt him move closer, knew his face was only inches from hers. His lips finally touched hers, a soft brush at first. Then another. No pressure. No demand. He was asking her if she wanted it. And damn herself to hell, she did. She scooted closer to keep the contact and pressed her lips to his more fully. Sparks of desire shot through her body, centering between her legs. When her hand curled around his neck and her fingers sifted through his hair, his groan echoed through her head.

Oh, yes, she wanted him. Maybe she shouldn't, but she did.

One strong arm wrapped around her waist, and he pulled her into contact with his body. She felt him hard and hot against her belly, pressing against her intimately, making her ache. The kiss exploded then. His tongue pushed into her mouth and tangled with hers as his hand moved down to her backside to press her even more tightly against him. She moaned.

"Gemma," he breathed against her mouth. "I want you." His voice was deep and rough and intoxicating.

Her answer was to deepen the kiss, to cling to him more tightly.

"Do you want me?" he asked, the slightest hint of vulnerability in his tone.

Tears stung her eyes. His voice sounded slightly…tentative. As if her answer mattered more than he would ever admit. She couldn't lie.

"Yes," she admitted, and God help her, she did. She wanted him so badly. She'd wanted this man from the moment she'd first seen him in the study that night at Griffin's wedding, looking so caught up in his faraway thoughts, a little sad, and a little broken. He was extraordinarily handsome, but that wasn't the only reason she wanted him. She wanted him because moments like this felt so real. As if they were truly sharing themselves with each other. And she wished it were true. For the moment, for tonight, she would pretend it was real. It was the only way to keep her sanity.

He pushed her gown to her thigh and lifted her bare knee. He pulled it atop his hip, ensuring that the part of her that ached with need came into even tighter contact with his hard length. They both groaned when he moved his hips against her, pressing into her again and again.

The friction in the place she wanted it the most made her whimper into his mouth. "Please," she begged, wanting even more.

In seconds, he had her gown up over her head and tossed to the floor. Then her hands were tangled in the waistband of his trousers, tugging them down. They, too, were on the floor in moments, and Lucian rolled atop her, pushing her onto her back as his hot, hard body covered her. Her legs spread, and she welcomed his heat between them. Their kiss continued, wet and all-consuming. She clung to his hard shoulders, digging her fingernails into them. She couldn't get enough of him. "Please, Lucian. Take me."

LUCIAN HAD HAD every intention of going slowly with Gemma tonight. He wanted to give her pleasure and plenty of it. Unrelenting pleasure she would remember and want more of. But the explosion between them from the moment they'd touched was undeniable, and when she said his name while begging him to take her, he was lost.

He moved his hand down between their bodies to ensure she was ready for him, and the wet heat he felt there left no doubt. Nearly mindless, he pushed into her to the hilt in one swift thrust and then gasped, pressing his forehead to hers hard. He stayed like that, unmoving for several seconds, waiting for her body to have time to adjust. But the ungodly heat and tightness of her made his eyes roll back in his head.

It had been a long time. So long. He hadn't told her, hadn't wanted to give her the satisfaction before, but Lucian hadn't touched another woman the entire time he'd been in India. Partly because he'd been so focused on his work, and partly because he hadn't been able to bring himself to touch another woman. He may have believed she was a scheming liar, but unlike his father, Lucian was no cheater. Now that he knew the truth about Gemma, he was thankful for his discretion. But it certainly wasn't helping his performance at the moment that he hadn't had a woman in over a year. He'd taken himself in hand, of course, but since he'd been home, each time he pleasured himself, it was his wife's gorgeous face he'd seen hovering in his fantasies. Now, the real woman laid before him, her head thrown back in passion, her body stretched with his cock, would be his undoing.

It was Gemma who began to move. Beneath him she thrust up her hips and Lucian bit his lip in agony. "Gemma, I can't—"

"Can't what?" She had a downright mischievous grin on her full, kiss-swollen lips.

"If you move again, I can't be held responsible for my actions," he panted, doing his damnedest to control his breathing, to control himself. It wasn't easy.

"Ooh." She licked her bottom lip and thrust up her hips again. "Promise?"

The damn broke then, and Lucian took over. He grabbed both of her hands that were clutched to his hips and pinned them above her head against the mattress as he took control and began thrusting into her. Once. A groan. Twice. Another. Soon his groans were intermingled with her sharp cries of pleasure bouncing off the headboard as he thrust again and again into her his lush body. He was sweating with the exertion it took to keep from coming when all he wanted to do was explode into her hot, wet warmth.

Lucian took a deep shivery breath and moved his hand down between their bodies again. This time he used his finger to touch the spot he knew she needed him to. He drew little unending circles around and around the center of her pleasure while Gemma's brow furrowed and her head tossed fitfully against the pillow. "Please," she begged.

Oh, he could watch this all day, Gemma taking her pleasure. She bit her lip and whimpered deep in the back of her throat. He purposely slowed his thrusts so she could concentrate on chasing her orgasm, and moments later, when it overtook her, her entire body shook. Her eyes rolled back in her head. Her breath caught in her throat and the delicious tremor that made her shiver spread through Lucian too. He threaded his fingers through hers and pushed the backs of her hands against the mattress on either side of her head as he took up his deep thrusts again. Over and over, he drove into her, letting go and allowing the overwhelming perfection of being buried deep in her tight body consume him until his body shuddered one last time and he spilled his seed deep inside of her with one last rumbling groan.

When his brain finally worked again enough for him to open his eyes, he kissed her ear, the side of her face, and her neck before rolling off of her. But he kept one of her hands in his, holding it tightly, never wanting to let it go.

SWEATY and satisfied and still breathing heavily, Gemma stared unseeing at the ceiling above her bed. Oh, God. She was in trouble. Because *that* had been good. *So good.* Life-alteringly good. The man knew precisely what he was doing. She'd just experienced pleasure she didn't even know she was capable of. If she allowed herself to, she could get used to this. Which was why she could *not* allow herself to get used to it. Because she still wanted a divorce. No matter how good they were together in bed.

CHAPTER THIRTY-FOUR

L ucian woke up to an empty bed. He pushed himself up to his elbows and frowned. Where was Gemma? She had sneaked out in the middle of the night? Like a doxy? That wouldn't do. And *why* had she gone? He was *certain* she'd enjoyed herself last night.

And so had he.

Lucian fell back on the pillow as the memories of last night returned to him in vivid detail. He hadn't imagined it. Gemma had been just as uninhibited and passionate as the first time. More so, since she knew what to expect. She hadn't been a bit shy about what she wanted. She'd taunted him, actually. He liked that. A lot. He was hard again just thinking about it.

Far from being a timid innocent, Gemma had given and taken pleasure as if it was something to revel in. She was unexpected that way, his bride. He'd misjudged her about so many things. He wouldn't make that mistake again.

And it wasn't just her lovemaking that surprised and delighted him. In addition to the physical compatibility, Lucian had learned that Gemma was savvy. She'd been immediately suspicious of him when he'd changed his behavior toward her, and she'd asked every question she'd been able to think of when negotiating their contract. She'd even thrown in some things he hadn't thought of.

In addition to her beauty, she was clever. Clever, savvy, witty, and gorgeous. Not to mention strong. He shook his head. No wonder she'd become the darling of the *ton*. No wonder men like Pembroke threw themselves at her. *Not* that Lucian intended to allow Pembroke to throw himself at her ever again. No. She was *his*, and he intended to treat her like a precious gift from now on. To earn her respect and admiration. That would take time, he knew. But he was committed to his task.

And he would begin with a luncheon picnic in the garden.

GEMMA POKED a lock of hair under the edge of her bright-pink bonnet. She'd spent far too much time this afternoon poking at her hair. There was nothing left to poke, but she still couldn't help herself. She and Lucian sat on an ice-blue quilt beneath the shade of an elm tree in the gardens behind the town house. A lovely picnic consisting of bread, meat, cheese, and grapes had been spread out before them. The servants had left them alone, per their master's request.

Gemma sat primly with her back resting on a pillow that she'd propped against the tree trunk. She didn't say anything. She couldn't say anything. And she couldn't look at him. All she could do was think about last night in bed with Lucian. Oh, God. She'd even begun *thinking* about him as *Lucian*.

It was one of the reasons she'd rushed out of bed this morning. The moment she'd awakened to see her gorgeous husband splayed out next to her, her skin had heated. The things he'd done to her last night. After they'd had sex the first time, fast and frantic, the next time he'd taken his time with her. Touched her slowly and made her burn for him before making her beg him to take her again. It was as if he wouldn't give them what they both wanted until she was a pleading mess of heat and wetness, clutching at his hips and mindlessly murmuring his name. Only then had he slid into her, giving her relief from the deep ache between her legs. He'd given it to her *twice more* before they'd both fallen into a deep sleep.

And that was the problem. Despite being satisfied *four times* last night, when she'd awakened and saw him lying there, she'd wanted him *again*. Madness. And it frightened her so much, she'd quickly slid from beneath the blankets, wrapped a dressing gown around her nakedness, and hied off to a guest room where she'd called Anna to get the footmen to draw her a bath. It had been cowardly of her, but Gemma didn't care. It had given her the reprieve she desperately needed. And when she returned to her bedchamber over an hour later, Lucian was gone.

But he'd soon sent a note asking her to meet him in the gardens for a luncheon at noon. Which promptly reminded her that in addition to spending the nights in bed with him, she would have to spend the days with him too. Doing things like picnic lunches and rides in the park, apparently. All while he did his best to charm her.

These would be the longest two months of her life.

"Would you like some food?" Lucian asked pleasantly as he sorted through the items sitting atop the quilt.

How could he do that? How could the man act as if they *hadn't* spent the entire night tangled in a sweaty heap in each other's arms, giving each other pleasure unlike any Gemma had known? She could still hear his groans and the way he called her name when he —

Not helpful.

She cleared her throat and made a show of poking some more non-existent errant hairs into her bonnet. "Yes, please," she finally managed.

Why was this so awkward? Would it always be this way? If so, the next two months would be excruciating. And as for the two months, they weren't even going about their arrangement properly by having lunch in their own backyard. "If you wanted us to be seen, we should have gone to the park," she informed him as he piled bread and cheese on her plate.

He frowned. "What do you mean?"

Gemma nodded toward the grapes. "I mean our own gardens are hardly a place to make a show of things."

His frown intensified as he pulled a cluster of grapes off the pile and placed it on her plate. "A show of things?"

She took the plate from him and lowered her voice to a whisper. "I assume the reason you want me to pretend to be happy is to keep up appearances for the *ton*."

Lucian sat back on his heels and blinked. "Is that what you think?"

She arched a brow. "Isn't it the truth?"

He reached down and plucked a grape from the cluster and popped it into his mouth. "Are you always so suspicious?"

She lifted her chin. "No, actually. I'm normally not suspicious at all."

He smiled at her and it did things to her insides, things she didn't want to examine too closely. "Only with me then?"

"Normally, I see the good in everything and everyone. Until they show me any differently. Like Lady Mary did for instance."

"And like I did," Lucian said solemnly.

Gemma nodded and pushed a grape around her plate. "I'm not myself around you. I can't be."

"Duly noted," he said, rising back to his knees to pour the wine. "And thank you for your honesty." He handed her the first glass of wine and met her gaze with a truly remorseful expression. "Look, Gemma. I'm sorry. I'm sorry I didn't trust you before. I'm sorry I thought the worst of you. I realize now that I was wrong."

Gemma couldn't help her eyes widening in surprise.

He must have seen the skepticism on her face because he continued, "But I'm mostly sorry that I'll have to re-earn your trust because of my stubborn pride."

Wine glass in hand, she eyed him carefully. Lucian Banks was saying he was sorry. And not just sorry, but sorry *and wrong*. She wouldn't believe it. Only it had to be more of his act to charm her in order to make her abandon the divorce. It was going to take much longer than the first few days of their agreement for her to believe he was anything other than an actor who would stop at nothing to save his family's reputation. Anyone could pretend for a day or two. But two months was quite a long time.

Still, she watched him from beneath her lashes, intrigued by both what he'd just said and his appearance. She'd never seen him like this. So casually attired. His waistcoat was gone and so was his jacket. He didn't even have a hat. He wore dark-brown breeches, black top boots, and a white shirt. He'd even forgone a cravat. He looked relaxed. He could be any man pouring a glass of wine while lounging atop a quilt in the grass. He certainly didn't look like a duke, the leader of one of the most powerful families in the country. And he didn't look like the overbearing, controlling ass she knew him to be either. Which reminded her how dangerous he was when he acted this way.

He settled back onto the quilt with his glass of white wine and crossed his legs in front of him. Such an unexpected pose. It made her smile, but she quickly hid her smile behind her wine glass when she took a quick sip.

Lucian settled into the quilt and sighed. "So, Gemma Brooks Banks, in addition to rides in the park and playing the pianoforte, what else do you enjoy doing?"

Her brows shot up. "There's no one else here," she pointed out.

He glanced around. "I know."

"So...." She drew out the word slowly.

"So? What?" He cocked his head to the side and narrowed his eyes on her, clearly confused.

She sighed and fluttered a hand in the air. "So, you don't need to pretend to care about things such as what I enjoy doing."

He pressed his lips together as if trying to squelch a smile. "What if I'm not pretending?"

She narrowed her eyes on him. "What do you mean?"

He chuckled. "I mean I would truly like to know what you enjoy doing."

Gemma popped her mouth closed and contemplated his statement for a few moments. He'd disoriented her, confused her. But she supposed she could answer his question. What harm would it do? "Well, I *do* quite like to play the pianoforte," she admitted, allowing the hint of a smile to touch her lips.

"And you're quite skilled at it." He nodded.

"Thank you." She couldn't help the blush that slightly heated her cheeks. She took another sip of wine. "And I do like rides in the park, but *not* in the countryside."

His eyes narrowed, and he cocked his head as if he found that bit of information interesting. "Why's that?"

She settled back against the trunk once more, warming to her story. "Oh, I've never much cared for the countryside. It's far too dull if you ask me. That's why I was so opposed to it when you wanted to send me to Cumberland."

"I'm sorry I did that," he said quietly, his face taking on a serious mien.

She waved her hand in the air again. "It's fine."

He reached out and gently grabbed her fingers and squeezed. Warmth spread up her arm. "No, it's not fine, Gemma. I'm truly sorry. I didn't know who you were back then. I greatly want to learn, however."

She shook it off and pulled her hand away. She had to. She couldn't stand the look of genuine remorse on his face. Not meeting his eyes, she traced a fingertip along the intricate pattern of the quilt. What could she possibly say to that? Of course, her mind told her he was lying. He was trying to get her to give up the idea of a divorce. He'd told her that was his plan. And here she was spilling secrets to the man who was essentially her opponent. She shouldn't have told him she hated the countryside. Now he could use it against her.

"Now for what you dislike," he said, taking a long sip from his glass. His eyes remained trained on her. Watchful. Curious. "What else? Besides the country?"

She scrunched up her nose, contemplating the matter. She opened her mouth to reply when he surprised her by snapping his fingers and saying, "I've noticed you never wear earbobs."

Gemma's pure surprise felt like a blow to her chest. "You noticed that?"

"Yes. Even the night in your brother's study. I noticed that about you. And you haven't worn them since, at least that I've ever seen."

A stiff breeze could have lifted her and blown her away. Her shock was so great. She hadn't thought he'd noticed anything about her. Especially not the night they'd been forced into marriage. "I — I—" She was at a loss for words. And that *never* happened.

"I'm curious why you don't like them." He leaned forward and watched her intently as if truly invested in her answer. If this was an act, he was a scarily good actor.

Unthinking, she plucked at her bare earlobe. "They've always hurt my ears...unmercifully," she explained. "Mama and I argued over my refusal to wear them on many occasions." Why was she sharing this with him? Something about the way he was looking at her, the way he was asking her questions no one had ever asked before. Mama knew why Gemma disliked earbobs, but only because Gemma had told her, not because Mama had asked. It felt strangely comforting to have someone ask. It felt better than she ever would have expected it to.

"Makes sense then," Lucian continued. "It's the same reason I'm not wearing a cravat right now."

"Cravats do look awfully uncomfortable," she added with a tentative smile.

"They are, believe me. But I expect they are no more uncomfortable than earbobs and stays."

At the mention of stays, her ears heated, which made no sense because they were far beyond the "stays" part of their relationship. He'd done things to her last night that left stays far in the dust. But it felt as if they were newly discovering each other today. Almost as if he was...courting her.

"What else, Gemma?" he asked, pouring a bit more wine into her glass. "What else should I know about you?"

She spent a few more moments poking at her hair. *Think. Think. Think of something neutral to say. Something that doesn't involve stays* or feelings.

"I've always wanted a dog," she finally blurted. *There. That was a neutral topic.*

His eyes crinkled at the corners and he poked out his cheek with his tongue. "A dog? Really."

"Yes." She nodded and took a sip. "And not a big lumbering hunting dog either. I want a smaller one, a terribly loyal one, who'll sit in my lap and be my constant companion."

Lucian tugged at his bottom lip with his teeth, and Gemma had to glance away.

"What would you name this dog?" he asked.

She stared down into her wine glass, but a smile soon lit her face. "Oliver, of course."

"Oh, of course," Lucian replied, laughing. "How silly of me not to know it."

Gemma laughed. She never would have imagined a man as proper as Lucian using the word *silly* or laughing at himself the way he was doing now.

"I've had the name picked out since I was nine years old," she continued. "I always quite liked the idea of the Lord Protector. I think it's an excellent name for a dog."

"Ah, so named after Cromwell?" Lucian said. "I see you know your history. And knew it at nine years old? Impressive."

"I see you know your history too," she countered, unwilling to examine the pride that had swelled in her chest when he praised her knowledge. "Did you ever have a dog?" she quickly asked.

Lucian took a sip of wine and nodded slowly. "I did," he said. "My father quite enjoyed hunting fowl. He had a pack of spaniels to fetch the birds."

"And did you like the dogs?" She was fully prepared to hear him say they'd been a loud, dirty mess that he left to the servants.

Which was why her brows shot up when he replied,

"Indeed, I liked them so well I went chasing after them the first time I saw them go after a bird," he said, laughing again.

Gemma couldn't help her own laugh. The idea of a young Lucian chasing after a pack of dogs was humorous indeed. "How old were you?"

"Let's see." He drew up his knees and hung his arms over them. Another completely unexpected pose. "I couldn't have been more than six or seven."

Now she was truly curious. She couldn't help it. "What happened when you caught up to them?"

Lucian sighed. "My father had failed to inform me that the dogs knew precisely what they were about, so when I saw them in the stream, I jumped in after them, thinking they needed help. I was worried about them, you see."

Gemma's hand shot up to cover her mouth. She wasn't sure which was more surprising: that Lucian had been worried about dogs or that he'd jumped in a stream. Surely, he'd never been young or impetuous enough to do such a thing. "You didn't!"

"Oh, yes, I did," he assured her, nodding.

"What happened next?" Gemma searched his face, suddenly quite interested in hearing the rest of the tale.

"My father finally came looking for me and found me treading water in the freezing stream, wondering where all the dogs had gone. Meanwhile, they fetched the bird and returned to father's side. I was the only one foolish enough to remain in the stream."

Self-effacing? Was this truly Lucian Banks? He didn't have a twin brother, did he? "How did you get out?" she prodded.

Another long sigh. "Father whistled and sent one of the dogs in to fetch me. It's quite sobering to be rescued by a dog, I can assure you."

Gemma laughed again and shook her head. "My father

had hunting dogs too," she told him, taking another sip of wine. "But he would never allow me a special pet."

"That seems wrong," Lucian said, frowning again. "But I understand perfectly. My father never allowed me anything that would reflect poorly on him. His hunting dogs were prized, of course."

Gemma nodded. Their fathers sounded quite alike, actually. And it explained quite a bit that Lucian's father had been obsessed with his reputation. No wonder his son was too. "My father never did anything for anyone other than himself...or Richard." The moment she'd said the words, Gemma regretted them. Why was she sharing this much with Lucian? They may have had arrogant, entitled fathers in common, but Lucian would only use that knowledge against her and her family.

Lucian's smile vanished. "Richard was your eldest brother who died?"

Gemma nodded. "Yes, several years ago. Honestly, I barely knew him. He was much older than me." There. That was vague enough. And true. What she did remember about Richard was that he had been treated like a prince in their household, while Griffin was ignored. She shook her head at the unwanted memory. If only Father had known that Richard would be killed and Griffin would be the duke. He would have treated Griff much better. Father had never done anything that didn't benefit himself. It sounded as if Lucian's father had been the same.

"I'm sorry your brother died," came Lucian's deep, solemn voice. "I met him a time or two at school."

"Then you know he was—" She really shouldn't speak ill of the dead.

"Difficult?" Lucian offered.

"Yes." She nodded. Difficult was the perfect word. She shook her head. She *hadn't* been particularly close to Richard, but the memory of his death made her throat tight just the same. Now, she wanted to change the subject as quickly as possible. "May I ask you a question?"

"Of course."

"What was India like?"

TWO HOURS LATER, Gemma realized that she'd been completely mesmerized by Lucian's ability to tell stories. He'd related tale after tale about his time in India. The sights, the sounds, the colors, the scents. It was nearly as if she'd been there herself, tasting the food, feeling the sticky heat, and hearing the buzz of insects at night. And Lucian had spared no detail. He answered question after question about his journey to India while Gemma paid rapt attention the entire time. They'd finished the entire bottle of wine.

When there was finally a lull in the conversation, their eyes met, and sparks leaped between them. Gemma caught her breath and glanced away.

"I suppose we should go in," she said nearly wistfully, glancing toward the back of the house. "We've been out here quite a long time." Only it hadn't felt like it. She was just realizing how long it had probably been. No longer directly above them, the sun had dipped toward the west.

"You must be tired," Lucian said as he gathered up the remnants of their picnic and placed everything back in the basket. He stood and helped her to stand. The touch of his hand sent a thrill through her body. Scenes from their night together flashed unbidden through her mind.

Shaking her head, she moved off the quilt and into the grass so he could pick up the blanket.

Gemma was back upstairs in her bedchamber before she realized that the feeling lingering in her chest after any entire afternoon spent in her husband's company was…excitement. She bit her lip. He was witty today. He'd seemed caring. He'd even made fun of himself a bit. *That* had been surprising. Even more surprising? She'd actually enjoyed herself at the picnic and hearing all his stories about India.

Was it possible that she had misjudged him?

CHAPTER THIRTY-FIVE

Tonight, Gemma didn't even question it. The nerves were gone. The doubt was gone. She only knew she wanted him. The moment Lucian came through the adjoining door wearing those revealing breeches slung low around his hips, she rushed into his arms and kissed him.

Without saying a word, he turned her toward the door and pushed her against it, his mouth ravaging hers. He leaned down and grabbed the backs of her thighs, easily lifting her. Then he shifted himself, pushed down his breeches, and let her slide onto his hot shaft.

"Oh, God," she breathed. She braced both hands atop his wide shoulders as he lifted her hips again and guided her down over and over. His eyes were closed, and a pained expression made his features hard. Gemma looked her fill at his sculpted chest, his rigid muscles. She ran her fingers over him, memorizing his muscles. She pressed her face into his neck and breathed in his now-familiar scent.

He pumped into her again and again. But then he

stopped, and she cried against his throat. "Don't stop," she begged.

"I want to make it good for you."

Oh, God. Didn't he know it was already good for her?

He carried her over to the bed and laid her upon it before pulling off her shift and his breeches and tossing them both to the floor. He began a slow descent down her nude body, kissing her cheek, her chin, her jaw, her neck. He lingered, dipping his tongue into the hollow of her collarbone. Then he moved down to cup both of her breasts in his large hands. "You're so beautiful, Gemma."

She tried to reach for him, to pull him atop her—she wanted him, *now*—but he leaned down, his hot mouth finding one nipple and sucking it until she moaned and writhed beneath him, arching her back to move her breast into closer contact with his mouth. How did he know how to do that with his lips? His teeth?

He plucked at her nipple with his tongue, circling, biting, and drawing up the tight bud until he nipped the tip of it, which sent a jolt of pleasure directly between her legs. He moved his mouth to the other nipple and gave it the same tender care. By the time he was through, Gemma was mindless. Mindless and wet and wanting. She grabbed at his hips, but he moved them away.

Instead, he lowered his torso between her legs. He caught her thighs and slowly pulled them apart, leaving her open to him. Gemma gasped and then held her breath. Oh, God. He was going to kiss her *there*. What—?

When his tongue dipped between her folds to find the nub of pleasure centered there, Gemma arched her back and cried, "Lucian." Her hands moved down to tangle in his soft hair. "Please," she begged. Though she didn't exactly know what she was begging for.

But Lucian did. He licked her in circles until her hips were thrusting of their own accord. Then he traced a hand up her inner thigh and slid one finger inside her, pressing against that spot along the front of her inner wall that sent her hurtling over the edge of oblivion in seconds.

After her body stopped shaking and her limbs no longer felt liquid, Gemma lowered her gaze to see Lucian still propped between her legs, a smug smile on his face. He was obviously proud of himself. She longed to replace that smile with pleasure-pain, the same intense look of desire she'd seen in his tight jaw last night just before he'd taken his pleasure.

She planned to torture him.

Pushing herself up to her knees, she pointed at the mattress. "Lie down," she demanded.

Lucian's brows shot up, but he did as he was told. He easily flipped onto his back and laid there while Gemma moved around his body and straddled him. He would have liked nothing more than to pick her up and drop her on his throbbing cock, but apparently she had other plans.

Slowly, so damn slowly, she did to him what he'd done to her. She started at his neck, dropping kisses upon his shoulders, his jaw, his collarbone. Then she licked his nipples and nipped at them. When she went even lower and drew her tongue down his belly, Lucian thought he would go up in flames. The closer her tantalizing mouth got to his cock, the more his hips jolted. She moved lower, lower, until...

"Tell me what to do," she said in a throaty voice. "To make you feel good."

Fuck. He couldn't tell his *wife* such a dirty thing. Could he? Honestly, he'd never contemplated doing such things with a *wife*. He'd been raised to believe wives were to be swived in the dark with a few thrusts until heirs were begotten. But Gemma hadn't allowed any of that. From the first moment he'd touched her, it was as if her body came alive under his fingers. She'd already been far more exciting in bed than he'd ever expected or hoped for. And all he wanted was more.

"Tell me," she demanded. She'd already figured out enough to wrap her hand around his cock and squeeze. A jolt of desire shot through him. He was going to die. It was that simple.

"Should I kiss you?" she said, lowering her mouth to his tip and kissing it.

He groaned, his hands grasping the bedsheets on either side of his hips.

"What if I lick you?" she asked next, her voice breathy and hot against him.

Her tongue slowly lapped at the crest of his cock. Lucian clenched his jaw so hard he saw stars. "No," he begged.

Her brows shot up. "No, you don't want me to?"

"Oh, I want you to." His own voice was husky.

She licked him again and he groaned.

"Then no, what?" she repeated.

"No, you shouldn't..." His breath was coming out in desperate pants.

"Who says I shouldn't? What rule book is there for such things?"

"*Fuck*. Gemma, please."

"Please, Gemma, what? Do it again?" She lowered her mouth and licked his tip.

His hips bucked.

"If you tell me what to do, it will feel even better," she whispered, sliding her tongue up and down his length.

That was it. She'd convinced him.

"Suck me," he demanded.

A wide, victorious smile spread over her face. She quickly moved her mouth over him and lowered her lips until he was halfway to the back of her throat. She sucked his length, moving her head up and down until she nearly swallowed him.

Fuuuuck. How had the woman learned so quickly? She was doing far too good a job of it. His hands clenched the sheets so hard his knuckles cracked. He was going to come in her lovely, hot mouth if she didn't stop.

And then she did the most unexpectedly sexy thing in the world. She took one of his hands and placed it on the back of her head. "Show me," she whispered, her lips hovering over his cock. "Guide me."

Lucian didn't need further encouragement. He fisted his hand in her luxurious dark hair and guided her sweet mouth down the length of his throbbing cock. Then he gently tugged her back up again. He wanted to ask her if it she was all right, but the enraptured look on her face told him she was enjoying it, and he was too far gone to stop. He guided her again and again up and down the length of him, driving himself mad with want until he could take no more. He finally pulled her away, flipped her easily onto her back, and slid all the way inside of her in one sure thrust. She was so wet and hot. It was an easy slide.

"Lucian," she cried into his ear, making him even harder. He hadn't thought it was possible. But he was quickly learning that with Gemma, anything was possible.

He threaded his fingers through hers just as he'd done last night. He couldn't get close enough to her in this moment. He wanted his body to meld into hers. He pushed himself up on his elbows and stared deep into her fathomless eyes while he thrust into her again and again, watching the pleasure play across her face.

Finally, he pumped into her one last time, fiercely growling her name. And when he was finished, he fell to a heap beside her, certain that he'd just had the most fulfilling sexual experience of his entire life.

With his wife.

CHAPTER THIRTY-SIX

Four Days Later

"I am going to visit my brother and sister-in-law today," Gemma announced at the breakfast table.

This morning, she hadn't slunk away from bed. In fact, just as she had the last three mornings, she'd stayed. Lucian had woken up and begun kissing her neck and, well, that's why they'd been late to breakfast.

It had become his favorite part of the day, their morning lovemaking. At night, they drove each other wild and couldn't get enough of each other fast enough. But in the mornings, he slowly slid atop her and then into her. He rocked his hips while staring deeply into her eyes. No matter when they did it, they both ended up satisfied, but there was something about the intimacy of their morning lovemaking that made it special to him.

This was the first morning she'd mentioned visiting her family.

"May I come with you?" Lucian asked. He'd long ago discarded the paper after only glancing at the headlines.

Trentham's words echoed in his head. "Pay attention to your wife," the marquess had said. That's exactly what Lucian intended to do. *In and out of bed.*

At first, Gemma had seemed surprised that he'd begun asking her questions at breakfast. But now that they'd been carrying on long conversations for three days in a row, it seemed like second nature. As if they'd never not shared breakfast together. And Lucian found that he truly enjoyed her company.

Gemma's brows shot up. "You want to…come with me… to see my family?" Surprise sounded in her voice.

"Yes. I'd very much like to." They'd spent a great deal of time together over the last few days, talking and laughing. They'd gone on another ride in the park. They'd gone shopping on Bond Street where Gemma had ordered a new hat from the milliner. They'd enjoyed each other's company, or at least Lucian thought so. But he could tell that even after moments where they shared stories from their childhoods and laughed with each other while enjoying their favorite sweets at Gunter's, Gemma continued to eye him with caution. He didn't blame her, of course. She'd told him she couldn't be herself around him. He suspected she was the most herself around her family, and he'd been looking for an excuse to see her with them. This was the perfect opportunity. Of course, he *asked* her if he could come with her. He hadn't *told* her he would come.

Gemma pushed bits of potato around her plate with her fork for a few moments. "All right," she finally allowed.

"Thank you," Lucian replied, inwardly breathing a sigh of relief. "Oh, and before we go, I have a surprise for you."

NOT HALF AN HOUR LATER, while Lucian was helping Gemma up into the coach, a movement under the seat caught her eye. She looked again to see a ball of brown fluffy curls just before the furball hurtled itself at her. She fell into the velvet-covered seat with a wiggling puppy grasped in her arms.

"What's this?" she cried, absolutely delighted.

A smile spread across Lucian's face. "What? I thought you'd know Oliver when you met him," he said with a wink, settling into the seat across from her.

"Oh, Oliver!" Gemma grasped the squirming pup under his top legs and held him up in front of her. He didn't look like any dog she'd ever seen before. He was a mess of both curls and long hair that fell into his eyes. He was tiny, no bigger than her foot. "Of course, I recognize you, you darling boy." She clutched him to her chest possessively, which made Lucian throw back his head and laugh.

"What sort of dog is he? Not a spaniel?" she asked, supporting the puppy with a hand under his bum, the other clutching the barrel of his little puffed out chest.

"No. I found him in Covent Garden. They were selling him as a rat dog. I think he may have a bit of terrier in him. I told the seller my only requirements were a dog that was small and cute and happy."

First? "*You* went to Covent Garden to buy this dog for me?"

"Of course," he replied as Oliver jumped out of Gemma's arms and bounced over to Lucian's lap. He caught the pup and laughed. "How else was I to know which dog was Oliver?"

An unexpected tightness expanded in Gemma's chest. She couldn't quite picture Lucian, in his expensive clothing. strolling about Covent Garden with the vendors and sellers hawking their wares. It was loud and crowded and dirty, a place servants were sent to purchase things. Not a place a duke would normally be found. Especially not a duke as concerned with his reputation as Lucian was. But apparently he'd gone there...for her. For Oliver.

"I believe he's a mixed breed," Lucian continued, further surprising her.

Second? "A mixed breed?" she echoed. "*You* purchased a mixed breed."

Lucian cuddled the puppy to his chest and patted him on the head. "I don't want Oliver here to have any expectations placed upon him. He is a companion. His job is to be joyful. And to make you joyful, my lady."

Their eyes met and the sincerity in Lucian's gaze made Gemma glance away. He was being more and more unexpected with each passing day. She never would have thought he would put down the newspaper to talk to her each morning, or ask her what she wanted for dinner, or want to accompany her to visit her family. Now, he'd done the least expected thing of all. He'd given her a puppy without a care to its breeding. Most noblemen were quite particular about their dogs. They bought and sold from certain bloodlines the same way they did with horseflesh. But Lucian had purchased a mixed breed dog from Covent Garden with no greater order than to ensure it was small and cute and happy. That seemed to be completely unlike the uptight man she thought him to be. In fact, it was more difficult each day to recall that man.

"Do you think your mother and brother will approve?" Lucian asked as Oliver bounded back over to Gemma's lap.

"I don't know," she replied, grinning and cuddling the squiggly puppy once again. "But we're about to find out."

~

Two hours later, Lucian sat in Southbury's drawing room next to his wife. Southbury, his mother, and Meredith were all there too, and much of the afternoon's conversation had centered on the newest addition to the family. Oliver Cromwell Helios Banks, Gemma had named him.

"He's clearly got a bit of the Greek God in him and he's full of sunshine, so Helios seems the most fitting," she'd said when she'd picked the name.

Southbury had rolled his eyes. Meredith had declared it quite a fitting name indeed. But Lucian had just watched Gemma with pride bursting inside him. Her mind worked in such an interesting way. She looked on the bright side of everything, he realized after having spent as much time in her company as he had the last few days. The mistrustful way she'd treated him was truly not her normal style. It made him feel guilty for ever causing her to feel that way. For ever causing her to doubt his sincerity.

He'd been right about one thing. She was clearly never happier than in the company of her family. In fact, ever since he'd arrived here today, Lucian had been staring at them all in wonder. They laughed and jested and talked to each other as if they all were the best of friends.

But they were family. A very different family than the one Lucian had, to be sure. He'd quickly learned that Gemma's family had scores of secret sayings and jests that only they understood. But instead of making Lucian feel like an outsider, to the contrary, Gemma's mother and sister-in-law had explained every reference to him, and now he found himself longing to be part of such a close and fun-loving group.

His own family had been nothing like this. They'd barely spoken, let alone spent hours in each other's company laughing. Lucian finally understood how alone Gemma must had felt when she'd first come to his house. It had been a tomb compared to Southbury's rowdy, cheerful drawing room. But with Gemma there now, it was no longer a tomb. It was a place filled with smiles and laughter and pleasure and joy. The thought made his throat tight.

Lucian stared at his wife in awe. His arm curved around her back as they sat side-by-side on a settee with each other. He was so intent on watching her profile that he barely noticed when the talk turned to an event the family had attended.

"You should have seen Cecily at the Wiltshires' ball last night, Gemma," Meredith said. "She looked radiant."

"Oh, I'm sure she did," Gemma said, her own face radiant with a wide smile. She was petting Oliver, who was asleep next to her thigh, tiny snores emitting from his fluffy little head. "She's had her eye on Lord Albion this Season."

"Ooh, I think I saw her dancing with Lord Albion," Meredith replied, nodding.

"Is Lord Albion good enough for our Cecily?" the dowager asked, stirring another lump of sugar into her tea.

Lucian wistfully shook his head. This family cared about its friends the same way it would care about a member of their own. Lucian was further surprised when the dowager set down her teacup, leaned across her seat to Gemma, and smoothed a lock of dark hair behind her ear. Then the dowager cupped her daughter's cheek. The look of pure happiness on the dowager's face was a revelation to Lucian. His own mother had loved him. He knew she had. But she'd never smoothed his hair or cupped his cheek. His father hadn't allowed it. And by the time father had died, well, they'd been set in their ways. Stoic to the end, he'd merely squeezed his mother's hand when she lay on her death bed.

An ache gathered in his chest. One that was quickly and thankfully dispelled by Meredith changing the subject and the dowager drawing her hand away from Gemma's cheek.

"Lord Pembroke asked after you," Meredith said, directing her remark to Gemma.

Lucian shifted in his seat, his arm reflexively pulling his wife closer. He would have to have a talk with Pembroke if that fool didn't stop showing his wife undue attention.

"Is Pembroke a sore subject?" Southbury asked, his astute gaze not missing Lucian's protective embrace.

"Pembroke is only a friend," Gemma said, glancing up at Lucian and giving him an exasperated look as she shook her head at him.

Lucian cleared his throat but said nothing. Mainly because the only thing he had to say was that he *would* have given Pembroke a piece of his mind last night had they opted to go to the Wiltshires' ball. Instead, when Lucian had arrived at Gemma's bedchamber to fetch her for the ball, he'd taken one look at her revealing ruby-red gown, and they'd begun kissing and had never made it out of the bedchamber last night. Not, perhaps, subject matter to share with Gemma's family, however.

"Well." Meredith stood and quickly launched herself into her husband's lap. She wrapped her arms around Southbury's neck and kissed him thoroughly on the mouth. "I know Griffin wouldn't like it if Pembroke had looked at me the way I've seen him look at you, Gemma."

"He'd better not look at her that way again," Lucian growled, suddenly wishing Gemma would stand and plop herself into his lap with the same carefree ease he'd just seen her sister-in-law exhibit. And to be kissed on the lips by one's wife in the middle of the day in front of company? He could imagine both of his parents rolling in their graves at the prospect. But for the first time in his life, Lucian wanted something different. He *wanted* this ease. He *wanted* this comfort. Dare he admit…he wanted this *love*?

The unexpected thought nearly knocked the breath from

his chest. But when he glanced over at his beautiful wife, who was happily smiling down at her new puppy, he knew it was true. He wanted Gemma's love. And he would stop at nothing to earn it.

ANOTHER HOUR LATER, when the coach door shut behind them as they left Southbury's house, Gemma had another bright smile on her face and an alert puppy in her arms. Lucian sat beside her this time, their thighs touching.

"Meredith looks good," Gemma said. "You'd never know she's to have a baby in the winter."

"Is she?" Lucian's brows shot up.

"Oh, yes. In February. Didn't you see how solicitous Mama was being? She is beside herself with happiness."

Beside herself with happiness? Lucian considered his own mother. He couldn't imagine ever describing her as "beside herself with happiness." He'd been raised to believe that duke's families were special, different. They must carefully control their reactions, their feelings. No one could see anything other than the careful façade they erected. And yet…Southbury was a duke. He hadn't been raised to the position, to be certain. His older brother had been killed in a horse race while Southbury had been gone to the Continent with the Army. But they'd all been raised in the same home. It stood to reason that all three of the Southbury children were given same instruction. Gemma had already proved herself to be quite without compunction when it came to showing emotion. Which could only mean one thing… Lucian's father hadn't been telling the truth when he'd told Lucian that to show no emotion was the responsibility of a duke.

"What did you think of my family?" Gemma asked as she settled Oliver onto her lap for the ride home.

"I thought they were all quite wonderful. They're all so warm and loving." *Unlike my family.*

"Well, of course, they are." Her smile brightened the coach.

Lucian cleared his throat. "I'm… It's different from how I was raised."

Gemma's brow immediately furrowed. "Your family didn't laugh?"

My family didn't speak. Lucian nodded tersely. Why did he have a lump in his throat? Why did he suddenly feel sorry for the boy he'd been? "Not often."

"That's sad," Gemma replied. She reached up and gingerly laid a hand on his cheek.

Lucian swallowed hard. "I didn't know any different."

Gemma bit her lip. "I've always had the impression that you are very concerned about your family's reputation."

"I am."

"Because of your father?" she asked quietly.

Lucian nodded. "My father pounded it into my head that a family's name and a man's reputation are all that he has at the end of the day. He was quite clear that they both should be guarded at all costs."

She tugged at the ribbons hanging from her bonnet. "At the cost of your relationships?"

He narrowed his eyes on her. "Pardon?"

She shrugged. "You have always seemed as if you care more about what people think in public than how people behave—how they treat each other—behind closed doors."

Lucian rubbed his jaw as he contemplated her astute words. "A more perfect description of my father I'm certain I'll never hear."

"Your father?" she prodded. "But not you?"

Lucian blinked. He hadn't ever questioned why he'd always been so preoccupied with his family's reputation. It had simply been drilled into his head since birth. A man protects his family. A family is nothing without their name. A duke's name is his reputation. It was the duty of a ducal family to be preoccupied by how they were perceived by others.

Or so he'd thought.

Lucian found Gemma's hand beside his thigh. He twined his fingers through hers and lifted them to kiss the back of her hand. In addition to being gorgeous, his wife was also funny, clever, and wise. But the best part of Gemma was her warmth. It shined from her skin and made him want to bask in its glow. To be away from her was to be left in the cold. Ever since they'd married, he'd been trying to get her to fit into *his* mold. Now he realized that hers was so much better. "If I did want to be like my father, I don't anymore," he breathed.

She eyed him carefully, biting her lower lip. "May I be honest with you?"

"Please do." He held his breath.

"Every time you say things like that, I *want* to believe you, but I can't help but think you're only saying it because you want something from me."

This time, Lucian reached out and cupped her cheek. He rubbed his thumb softly against her jawline and pressed his forehead to hers, meeting her eyes. "I do want something from you, Gemma. I want *you*. I want you to come to me willingly and give our marriage a chance."

CHAPTER THIRTY-SEVEN

A Fortnight Later, The Duke of Grovemont's Town House

Gemma already knew she was in trouble. Each night in bed, Lucian didn't stop pleasuring her until she called out his name. Until tears ran from her eyes. Until she was begging him for release, and then he gave her the most intense orgasm, making her forget the one from the night before.

He was a selfless lover, a master in bed. He touched her in the right spot every time. He knew what to do to make her body sing with pleasure. What to say to make her ache with wanting. Within the first fortnight of their arrangement, she was a slave to him in bed, body and soul. She couldn't get enough of him. How would she ever be able to leave his bed when the time came? The thought preoccupied her more and more of late.

But it was outside of bed that had her even more concerned. It had been a fortnight. *Two entire weeks* and Lucian was still solicitous and caring. He talked to her each morning, made love to her each night. They'd gone for walks in the park, picnics by the lake. They'd spent lazy afternoons lying in the grass, watching Oliver hop through the gardens behind the house. And they'd danced countless waltzes while staring into each other's eyes, the entire ballroom fading away around them. It was no longer easy for Gemma to remind herself that Lucian was trying to keep her by his side. In fact, he'd all but convinced her that he *wanted* her there.

Which made the notion of being with child even more poignant.

Because after all of their lovemaking, she might well already be with child. And if she wasn't, it was highly likely she would be by the time the two months were over, given the amount of time they spent in bed.

Gemma made her way down the corridor to the nursery with Oliver trotting at her feet. Mrs. Howard had briefly pointed out this room when she'd given Gemma the tour of the house last year. At the time, Gemma hadn't paid much attention, but now she sought it out.

She placed her cold, shaking hand on the door handle and gently pushed it open. The door creaked wide, and Gemma and Oliver stepped into the large room. There was a wooden cradle, a rocking horse, and a cushioned rocking chair. She made her way to the wardrobe and opened it. All the tiny clothes were still there, lined up. She touched them gently, running her fingers over the aged cloth. Had Lucian worn these once? It was difficult to imagine he'd ever been so small.

Oliver made his way to the window, where he curled into a ball in a spot of sunlight and promptly fell asleep.

Gemma stepped back from the wardrobe and wrapped her arms around herself. Could she do it? Could she give birth to a child and leave him here to live with his father? What if Lucian raised her son the way his own father had raised *him*? To be preoccupied with reputation at the cost of relationships.

The man who made love to her at night was loving and warm. The man who'd treated her so solicitously the past fortnight was too. But the man who'd been raised in this room to an indifferent father was someone else entirely. A cold, heartless person who only cared about status, not people.

Footsteps sounded in the corridor, and Gemma turned to see Mrs. Howard step through the doorway.

The housekeeper stopped short when she saw Gemma. "Oh, Your Grace. I'm sorry. I didn't realize you were in here. I thought perhaps the door came ajar."

Gemma nodded. "It's all right, Mrs. Howard. I wanted to see this room again."

A tender smile came to Mrs. Howard's lips. "It's been empty since His Grace was a lad."

Gemma cocked her head to the side and forced herself to ask the question that was on the tip of her tongue. "What sort of a boy was His Grace?"

The tender smile turned into a bright one that lit the entirety of the older woman's face. "Oh, he was a handsome one," Mrs. Howard said, the skin around her eyes crinkling.

"I bet he was," Gemma replied, laughing.

"Always up to something." Mrs. Howard shook her head. "Always trying to make something or figure out how something worked."

"That sounds right too." Gemma's smile grew. She took a deep breath. This might just be her best opportunity to get answers to the questions about Lucian that continued to gnaw at her. She lowered her voice. "What was he like...with his parents?"

Mrs. Howard glanced back into the corridor before shutting the door behind her. Then she hurried over to where

Gemma stood. A solemn look shone in her eyes. "If I tell you, you must never tell His Grace that I did so."

Gemma nodded.

Mrs. Howard glanced back over her shoulder, then she expelled her breath and threaded her fingers together tightly in front of her. "His Grace grew up in a very strange household," she began.

Gemma nodded again. "I'd gathered that much."

"Yes, well. You see, his parents would go out into Society and smile and pretend they were happy together, if not madly in love."

This time Gemma shook her head. "I can't imagine anyone in this family being madly in love."

A wistful smile touched the housekeeper's lips. "His mother loved him dearly, but his father would not allow outward signs of affection. She had to sneak into this nursery to hold her son and hug him."

Gemma gasped, her hand instinctively cupping her mouth. "No."

Mrs. Howard nodded. "Yes. And if her husband found out, or even suspected, he wouldn't speak to the duchess for days."

Gemma's eyes widened. "Days?" It was worse than she'd thought.

"That's right. If she did anything he disapproved of, she was met with complete silence. He wouldn't speak to her or even look at her. Sometimes weeks passed that way."

Weeks? Oh, God. The indifference. That's where it had come from. Lucian's father. She'd suspected as much, and she'd been right.

"That's awful," Gemma said solemnly, trying to picture a young boy with no siblings growing up in a house devoid of love and happiness. "So they lived separate lives, the duke and duchess?"

Mrs. Howard shook her head. "No. That's what's so strange. They would have meals together. Sit in the drawing room together. They just wouldn't speak."

Gemma frowned. How would such a thing even work? She couldn't imagine not speaking to Griffin or Meredith or Mama while they were having meals.

But then she remembered…the paper. It was possible to sit in the same room with a family member and not speak. She just hadn't ever seen it until she'd come here.

Mrs. Howard cleared her throat. "As he grew older, His Grace was only allowed to see his parents upon occasion."

Gemma bit her lip. Pain shot through her chest as she thought of a little boy being locked away in a nursery without his family. She'd grown up with Mama and Griffin and scores of servants she counted as friends. How must it have been for young Lucian? "I suppose he wasn't allowed to speak to the servants?"

"Only me," Mrs. Howard confirmed. "And his tutors when they came. If the old duke saw his son speaking to servants in a friendly manner, he was severely reprimanded."

Gemma expelled her breath. *That* was why Lucian treated the servants so cooly. He'd been taught to keep his distance. Punished for doing otherwise. It made her shudder.

"Of course, I was relieved when he was sent to Eton," Mrs. Howard continued. "That's where he met his friends. Including your brother, I believe." Mrs. Howard winced. "I can't tell you how many nights I spent with him before he left for school while he cried himself to sleep, wanting to know why his parents wouldn't visit him. After a while, he just stopped trying to earn their love."

Gemma gasped. The ache in her chest grew wider, making it difficult to breathe. "That is positively dreadful. Love shouldn't have to be earned."

"I agree." Mrs. Howard's voice was low and sad. "And

I'm only telling you this now because I know you're the sort of lady who can convince His Grace to try to love again."

Gemma sucked in her breath. She'd never contemplated such a thing. In fact, just the opposite, she was trying to *leave* the man. Or she had been. Now she was confused about her feelings. Still, she had no intention of telling Mrs. Howard about their arrangement, even if she hadn't signed a contract keeping her from it. Lucian was proud. He didn't deserve that sort of humiliation. When she did leave—*if she did leave* —she would take the blame.

"Did he—?" Gemma took another deep breath, shook her head, and tried again. "Did he *ever* spend time with his parents?" she ventured, already afraid of the answer. She couldn't help but remember Lucian's story about the hunting dogs and how his father hadn't explained to him what they could do. But clearly, he'd been in his father's company sometimes.

"His father would take him hunting upon occasion. Shooting or some other pursuit the old duke deemed as manly, but they never did much else together."

Gemma swallowed the painful lump in her throat. She hated the idea of a little boy being told what was "manly." Everything Mrs. Howard had told her made Gemma's heart ache for the child Lucian had been. "Nothing else?" she prompted.

"I'm afraid not." Mrs. Howard shook her head again. "And His Grace's father wouldn't allow His Grace's mother to do anything with him either. Aside from the secret visits, she rarely saw him. And when His Grace did see his father, he was punished for showing any emotion."

Tears fell from Gemma's eyes. She couldn't help them. She didn't try to hide them. "That's dreadful."

"It was," echoed Mrs. Howard. "After the old duke died,

His Grace and his mother became closer. He always loved her very much. It was difficult for him when she died."

Gemma sucked in her breath and slowly exhaled. The things Mrs. Howard had just told her were awful. Now Gemma understood why Lucian had been the way he'd been.

But one thought throbbed viciously through her brain, pounding her skull with its importance.

I will not allow my *son to be treated that way.*

She might not even be *enceinte*, but it didn't matter. She had to have Lucian's promise, or she could not continue with their agreement. She would *not* allow her children to be raised without love.

CHAPTER THIRTY-EIGHT

The Next Morning

Lucian awoke in his wife's arms. A feeling of
contentment unlike any he'd ever known swept
through him. He nuzzled his face into her hair and
breathed in her intoxicating scent. What was this wonderful
feeling? Happiness? Contentment? He'd never known it
before. He pulled her close and kissed her atop the head.

These last two weeks with Gemma had been the best of
his life. Better than anything he'd imagined. And she was
beginning to trust him. He could feel it. It wasn't only in the
way she responded to him in bed. It was in the way she asked
him questions and listened to his answers. It was in the way
she laughed when he made a jest, and the way her eyes crinkled when she smiled at him over breakfast in the morning.
She was still wary—and probably rightfully so—but he'd
made progress in gaining her trust. He'd asked her to give
their marriage a chance. And she was. He felt it. Each day,
she was opening herself up to him a little more. Trentham

had been right. Being charming wasn't difficult, after all. And there was no trick to it. Just respect and interest.

"Good morning," came Gemma's sleepy voice muffled by the covers.

"You're awake?" He smiled and pulled the covers away from her lovely face.

She drew her fingertip across his chest and glanced up at him from beneath her lashes.

He swooped down to kiss her, but she ducked and laughed. "Wait, Lucian. I need to ask you something."

He looked down at her and smiled. "I like it when you say my name."

She bit her lip and glanced away.

There was something wrong. He could feel it. Last night, they hadn't spoken and had merely fallen into bed together, ravenous for each other as usual. But now there was tension in her drawn-up shoulders. There was hesitancy in her gaze. "What is it?"

"Will you tell me something?" She still did not look at him directly.

"What?" His heart hammered, panic rising in his chest. His gut told him he wouldn't like what she was about to say.

She pushed herself up against the pillows and crossed her arms over her middle. She stared down at the covers silently.

Lucian pushed himself back against the pillows next to her, but he searched her profile. "What is it, Gemma? Say it?" Fear made his voice sound angry.

She swallowed. He watched as her throat worked. "I've heard a few things," she began tentatively. She uncrossed her arms and plucked at the quilt with her thumb and forefinger but still didn't look at him. "Things that concern me. Servants' gossip, mostly. But I want to ask you directly." She sucked in a breath. "What sort of parents were your mother and father?"

Lucian's face hardened into a mask of stone. "Servants shouldn't gossip." His parents were not a subject he was willing to talk about. And to hear that his servants had shared anything about his family with her incensed him. Gemma didn't need to know details of how he'd been raised or how his parents had treated him. All of that was a long time ago. It had nothing to do with their future.

"It's not just the servants," she clarified, her voice rising with what sounded like alarm. "When you and I went to Griffin's...you said my family was warm and loving. You said yours was different."

"It was different." The words shot out of his mouth as if they came from a pistol. His jaw was clenched. What the hell did any of this have to do with *them*?

"They didn't show you affection, did they?" she prodded.

The overwhelming emotion that had invaded Lucian's chest was spreading now. And it was unmistakable. Anger. Anger that this was coming up. Anger that his servants had gossiped. Anger clawed at his insides. He never discussed his parents with anyone. Ever. No one ever asked. "What does it matter what my parents were like? They are both *dead*," he nearly spat.

Gemma winced, drawing away from him slightly. "It matters quite a lot." Her voice was raw with sadness.

"I don't see how." Along with the anger, discomfort was also spreading quickly through his veins. He was used to being in control of everything. But he couldn't control this. He couldn't control her questions or her reactions to his answers. He couldn't control what she thought of him. He scrubbed a hand through his hair.

Gemma turned toward him and placed a cold hand on his shoulder. Her voice held a note of steely resolve. "You want a child with me. But I will not allow a child of mine to be treated as if they are nothing more than a possession."

Lucian's jaw clenched so hard it popped. What was she trying to say? Was she pushing him away? She still wanted the divorce, didn't she? She was using this as an excuse. It was clear as day. *"We have a contract,"* he growled.

She quickly drew back her hand as if it had been burned. "I know we have a contract. I'm asking for an amendment to it." Fire flashed in her dark eyes and her voice was angry.

His eyes narrowed. "What sort of amendment?" What was she getting at? What did she want?

"If we have a child...I don't want him to be subjected to the sort of treatment that..."

Lucian slashed his arms through the air. "You make it sound as if I was beaten."

Gemma tossed back the covers and stood, glaring at him from the side of the bed, her hands on her hips. "You might as well have been. If your parents withheld affection. If they—"

Lucian ripped the covers back and stood too. His hands were clenched into tight fists at his sides as he glared at her from the opposite side of the bed. "My parents have nothing to do with us."

"Yes, they do! I don't want our child to be kept away from me when he is young. I want to hold him and hug him and kiss him and tell him I love him every day."

Lucian paced away from the bed. Dark spots of anger covered his eyes. Who the hell had told her about his parents? And why had he trusted that she was allowing him to get closer to her? He'd been fooled into thinking she was letting him in. He was almost happy, a foreign feeling. One he'd thought he was enjoying. But now he realized that *he* wasn't the one who'd been acting. *She was.* Her actions these last two weeks had all been an act. Performed by an actress who had no intention of staying in their marriage. She still intended to leave him, which was why she'd gone messing about in the servants' hall, digging up gossip to use to renegotiate their contract.

Damn it. He pressed the palms of his hands against his eyes. He'd been a fool. This was no more than he deserved. For believing even for a moment that Gemma's feelings for him were real. And the worst part was that...all along, his despicable father had actually been *right*. Lucian should have kept Gemma at arm's length. *One doesn't fall in love with one's wife.* Love wasn't an emotion for the Grovemont heir. His father had warned him. But Lucian had been too blinded to listen.

"There will be no renegotiation!" His words came out as nearly a yell. The panic and pain clawing at his chest made him fearful, loud.

Gemma's next words came from somewhere behind him, and they were filled with anger too. "What are you saying? You *want* our children to be raised like you were? Without love?"

"I'm saying there will be no renegotiation," he shot through his clenched jaw, turning to glare at her again.

Gemma grabbed her dressing gown and pulled it on. She waved a hand in the air toward the bed. "This has all been an act. You've only been pretending to be nice to me to make me stay, haven't you? You didn't want the divorce because of your precious reputation. You don't care about me or the child we might have."

Lucian grabbed his breeches and quickly pulled them on. Oh, how clever of her. Accusing him of doing the exact thing *she* was doing. "If anyone is an actress, it's you. I'm leaving."

"You are heartless!" she cried.

"You're right," he ground out. "I *am* without a heart. Don't forget it." And wasn't it better that way? Less painful? He turned on his heel and stalked from the room.

CHAPTER THIRTY-NINE

Later That Morning, Bond Street

"Just one more stop, Mr. Bigley," Gemma called through the window to the coachman. "Madame Renard's, if you please."

She was on her way home. She'd taken Anna and gone out shopping today. Anything to keep her mind off her argument with Lucian this morning.

The man was beyond frustrating. Just when she'd begun to open up to him. Just when she'd begun to *hope* that perhaps he was able to be a good husband, the kind of husband she'd dreamed about, he'd gone and said all of those awful things this morning. He wasn't even trying to hide the truth any longer. He'd admitted he had no heart. He'd said as much!

She couldn't regret bringing up his parents though. She'd known she was betraying Mrs. Howard's trust by mentioning it, even if she hadn't shared the housekeeper's name. But Gemma had seen no other way to directly address her concerns. And her concerns had grown until they overpowered her, until she could think of nothing else.

Now she realized that in bringing up her fears, she'd escaped an awful fate—the fate of believing that Lucian was a kind, loving man, when, in reality, he was as cold-hearted and indifferent as she'd always feared. If she hadn't brought it up, she might never have seen his true character. He might have gone on pretending to be loving and kind for the rest of their contract. Only to stop the act after it was too late for her to leave with everything she'd been promised.

He *was* a cold, indifferent man, and she would do well to remember that. It was truly chilling that he'd been able to pretend otherwise for as long as he had.

The coach pulled to a stop in front of the milliner's shop. When the footman folded down the steps, Anna made to accompany Gemma into the store.

"Oh, don't get up, Anna. I'll just be a moment," she said. "I'm only picking up an order."

The footmen could do it for her, of course, but Gemma was restless. She wanted to get out of the coach and walk a bit. In fact, she wished she could run all the way to Hyde Park and keep running. To get away from the life she was trapped in for at least six more weeks.

Oh, why had she ever agreed to that contract in the first place? She'd *known* he was pretending. He'd never intended to give her a divorce or any money. He knew she'd conceive and that she'd never be able to leave her own child. It had been his plan all along. It made sense now. And like a fool, she'd begun to believe he actually cared. In fact, the part that hurt the most was realizing that she'd actually begun to believe that he was falling in love with her.

The way she'd begun falling in love with him.

Tears stung her eyes at the thought. But none of that mattered now. It wasn't real. When she got back home, she intended to tell Lucian that she would be seeking the divorce immediately, with or without his agreement. She'd have her brother's backing. That would have to be enough. She refused to live a lie with Lucian.

After the footman helped her down, Gemma lifted her skirts and made her way the short distance from the road to the front of the hatmaker's shop.

"We'll come back around for you, Your Grace," Mr. Bigley called from atop his perch.

"Thank you," Gemma replied, dismissing the coach with a wave of her hand.

The coach took off in the afternoon traffic. As usual, they would circle around the nearby stores and return for her.

A bell fastened to the top of the door rang when Gemma stepped into the milliner's shop. The space was filled with rows and rows of lovely hats. Ladies' hats on one side, gentlemen's on the other. Rows of bows, and feathers, and reams of ribbons graced the wall behind the ladies' side. Gemma spent a few moments looking over all the pretty baubles. She did so love a beautiful hat. She'd commissioned the one she was here for not a fortnight ago. With Lucian smiling by her side. She shook her head. No. She would not remember such things. It did no good to act as if any of that had been real. The man didn't have a real hair atop his head.

"There you are, Your Grace," came Madame Renard's voice from the back of the shop. "I've been expecting you. Zee hat came out perfectly, if I do say so myself. Let me get it." The woman disappeared into the back of the shop and Gemma continued to browse through the ribbons and feathers while she waited.

She didn't have to wait long. Madame Renard promptly returned with the green concoction in her hands. "Here it is," she said, handing it over to Gemma.

"It's lovely," Gemma breathed. "Just as I imagined it would look."

The hat was green velvet, shaped in a circle, and adorned with a bright-white bow and matching feather. It would go perfectly with a certain emerald-green gown she owned.

"Shall I send zee bill to your husband?" the milliner asked with a knowing smile.

"Please do," Gemma replied with a decided nod. She didn't like being reminded she *had* a husband, but the least he could do was pay for her pretty new hat.

Gemma waited a few more moments while Madame Renard packed the hat into a box with tissue paper, wrapped a string around the box, and gave it to her.

"Thank you, Madame," Gemma said as she headed toward the door.

"My pleasure, Your Grace." The milliner waved at her.

When Gemma stepped back out onto the street, her coach was not there. She pushed herself up on tiptoes and craned her neck, doing her best to search the heavy midday traffic in the congested area. She still didn't see it.

No matter. Mr. Bigley would be around as soon as he was able. She turned to look into the window of the patisserie next door.

She'd been salivating over an éclair for a few moments when a familiar voice rang out from behind her.

"Gemma? Is that you?"

She turned to see Lord Pembroke, of all people, pushing through the crowd toward her. Odd that he'd used her Christian name. But they *were* friends.

"Your Grace, you're looking well," Pembroke said when he finally made it to her side.

"Good afternoon, Lord Pembroke," she said, smiling at her old friend. "I haven't seen you since…" She let her voice trail off, realizing as she spoke that she hadn't seen him since her husband had rudely told him to go away at the Chadworths' ball.

"It's been quite a while," Pembroke replied with a smile that didn't reach his eyes.

"I'm sorry," Gemma began, feeling true regret at the way Lucian had treated her friend. She should have known what a scoundrel her husband was based on his treatment of this man, who'd never done anything more than be kind to her.

"No apology necessary," Pembroke said, shaking his head. "May I drive you home? My coach is just here." He motioned to the conveyance that sat in the street behind them.

Gemma shook her head. "No, thank you. My coach should be back momentarily," she assured him. She didn't mention that if Lucian saw Pembroke's coach drop her off, he'd be anything but happy. *Not* that she should give a toss what Lucian thought.

"It's no bother," Pembroke added. He splayed a hand toward his coach again.

Gemma eyed him warily. "No, thank you," she repeated. Had he not heard her the first time? Or was he just being overly polite?

Just then, Pembroke crowded toward her and grabbed her arm. Gemma made to step back when she saw the flash of metal at her side. Panic shot through her. Pembroke was brandishing a *pistol*. He wrapped his arm through hers and pressed the weapon to her ribs. "Don't move. Don't say anything. Come with me."

Gemma's breath caught in her throat. Her heart pounded unmercifully. A hundred different thoughts raced through her mind. This wasn't happening. Pembroke was her friend. What in the world was he doing with a pistol?

"You must be jesting," she said. "But honestly, it's not very funny."

He jammed the pistol into her ribs, making her grunt. The pain demonstrated how very real it was.

"Do as I say," Pembroke demanded. His eyes, which had darkened considerably, were scanning the crowd.

The street was busy. Scores of people were walking about, but none of them knew there was a weapon pressed to her side. How could they? Gemma's pelisse and Pembroke's coat obscured it. Not to mention, Pembroke had a wide smile on his face, as if they were doing nothing more than having a pleasant chat. Gemma tried to catch the eye of the passersby, but none of them appeared to notice her.

Pembroke pulled her roughly alongside him a few paces to his coach. "Get in," he demanded. The door was already open, and the steps were down, so Pembroke was able to help her up and push her in without the aid of a footman. He kept a hold of her arm, the pistol still clutched in his other hand. He pushed into the coach directly behind her, so she didn't have time to try to jump out the opposite door.

The moment the door closed behind them, Pembroke banged on the ceiling, yelling to the coachman to go. Moments later, the coach rolled into the crowded street. And with every turn of its wheels, Gemma felt more trapped.

She forced herself to breathe and count ten. She could handle this. This was Pembroke, after all. They'd shared wine and laughs and dances for the better part of the last year. He couldn't possibly mean to harm her.

"What are you doing?" Gemma asked in as calm a voice as she could muster.

"I'm getting what I deserve," Pembroke replied. He sat on the seat opposite her, but the pistol was firmly trained on her.

Gemma swallowed. What in God's name did that mean? "What you des—?"

"Shut up," Pembroke demanded. "No talking until we get home."

She drew her brows together. "Home? Are we going to your home?" What in the world was happening?

"No talking," Pembroke ground out.

She'd never heard his voice angry. She didn't like it. Apparently, Pembroke was an actor too.

Gemma took another deep breath to calm her nerves, then she turned to look out the window at the crowded street. Everyone was going about their day completely normally. And why wouldn't they? None of them knew she was being held at the end of a pistol in Pembroke's coach. No one knew she was in the middle of a nightmare.

She had to think. What could Pembroke possibly want? What did he think he deserved from her?

The only thing she knew for certain was that whatever he was up to, it couldn't end well. He couldn't let her go without harming her. Unless... She would just have to try to reason with him.

She folded her hands carefully in her lap and spoke in a calm, quiet voice. "You don't have to do this, you know? I would visit you if you asked."

"Shut up. You cannot visit me now that your *husband* is back." He sneered at the word *husband*.

"That's not true," she insisted. "I don't tell my husband everything I do." She wasn't lying. She hadn't even told Lucian she'd gone out shopping today.

"Your husband won't like what I want from you." Pembroke's stare was positively leering.

Cold sweat beaded down Gemma's back. Oh, God. Did that mean—? Did Pembroke intend to *rape* her? If so, he'd have to kill her first. She would fight him without end.

"My husband will come looking for—"

"SHUT UP!" Pembroke's voice was so loud the carriage shook.

Gemma sucked in her breath. Her eyes widened with fear. She'd never seen him like this. It was as if something had come over him, a rage unlike anything she'd seen before. His eyes had gone dark. He'd turned into a completely different person. One she was truly frightened of.

Swallowing hard, Gemma turned back to stare out the window. Given the extent of his anger and the fact that his finger was on the trigger of a pistol, it was probably best not to rile him further. She would wait to see where they were going. Perhaps there would be a chance to escape on the way out of the carriage.

Within the hour, they pulled to a stop in front of Pembroke's town house. Gemma had never been inside his home before, but she had waited outside for him upon occasion. It wasn't that far from the milliner's shop, but the traffic had been so thick, it had taken a long time to make it here.

Just like when he'd hustled her into the coach, Pembroke took no chances. Pulling her from her seat, he wrapped his arm through hers and stuck the pistol to her ribs. "Let's go," he said the moment the footman opened the door and let down the steps. "And don't try to run or I'll shoot you."

Gemma gulped. The metal pressing into her side proved how serious the man was.

The moment they made it up the stone stairs and into the town house, Gemma wrenched from his arm. "What do you intend to do with me?" She glanced around frantically, but there was no butler or any other servants to be found.

"I must hide you."

"Hide me." Fear gripped her spine. "What do you mean?"

He shrugged. "Only temporarily. Until the news breaks."

She furrowed her brow again and shook her head. The man wasn't making any sense. "What news?"

"The news of your impending divorce, of course." His smile was dark.

"My what?"

"Your divorce," he repeated. "There's been a rumor for quite some time now that you want a divorce from your dear husband, the duke."

What? How in the world had *that* rumor spread? Gemma, Cecily, and Lady Clare were the only three who knew about it, and Gemma would stake her life that Cecily and Clare hadn't said anything.

"That's not true," she insisted. "I—"

Oh, God. Wait. Now that she thought on it, she'd mentioned to Pembroke upon occasion that while divorce would be frowned upon, it was an option. Which meant Pembroke knew she'd been considering it. It was her own fault. The rumor had been spread by Pembroke himself.

"When has the *ton* ever cared about the truth?" Pembroke scoffed. "I only need the rumor, not the truth. Now walk." He pointed the pistol toward the staircase.

Oh, God. They were going upstairs.

By the time they made it to the landing on the third floor, Gemma was shaking so badly she could hardly walk. But Pembroke pushed her ahead of him, and they went all the way down to the far end of the corridor, to the last door in the hallway. Pembroke opened it and pushed her inside. "I'll be back for you later."

The door closed behind her, and Gemma barely had time to register relief at the fact that she wasn't about to be imminently raped before she rushed over to the nearest window. It was locked. Nailed shut from the outside, apparently.

She took a deep breath before trying each of the three other windows. They were all the same. Apparently, Pembroke had planned this little abduction well. But how had he known she'd be shopping today?

Oh, God. He must have been following her. He could have been waiting for her for days. Hadn't Meredith said that he'd asked after her recently?

Doing her best to calm her nerves, Gemma made her way over to the bed and took a seat atop the mattress. She needed to think. Surely, there was a servant here who could help. Or had Pembroke dismissed the servants? She hadn't seen a butler. Or anyone else, for that matter. What was Pembroke's plan? And how exactly would the rumor of her divorce help it?

Would Lucian figure out where she'd gone? How could he? No one had seen her with Pembroke. Not even Anna.

Gemma was still miserably contemplating her options when the door cracked open again and Pembroke's head appeared. It was almost as if she'd conjured him with her thoughts. "I paid a maid to leave a note for your husband telling him you want a divorce. He *won't* be looking for you."

CHAPTER FORTY

Later That Afternoon, The Duke of Grovemont's Bedchamber

Lucian crumpled the blasted note in his fist. It had been left on the foot of his bed. He'd found it just now after returning from his club. Alongside the afternoon edition of *The Times*.

Both the note and the paper had been clear. Gemma wanted a divorce. She was leaving him.

His eyes narrowed to slits. She couldn't do this. She'd signed a blasted contract. Didn't she realize she was forfeiting their agreement?

He paced away from the bed and scrubbed a hand through his hair. Damn it. He shouldn't have been so crass this morning. He should have stopped and thought about what he'd said to her. He knew he'd be setting back his own objective, but he'd been so angry and uncomfortable when she'd begun asking questions about his childhood. Any mention of his parents put him on edge. And, of course, his reaction had been to lash out at her, incorrect though it had been.

Now he wouldn't have the opportunity to make things right. And, honestly, did he even deserve another chance?

She wasn't entirely without fault either, of course. He'd thought they'd been getting closer these last several days. But the first sign of any trouble, and she'd left him. Disregarded their contract and taken off.

And here he'd been falling in love with her. Oh, what a fool he'd been to believe love was in his grasp. Gemma had left the moment she had a chance. And she hadn't just left. Oh, no. She'd ruined his reputation first. The story in the paper had seen to that. In addition to making him a laughingstock, the scandal of a divorce would ruin his family's name.

He'd first seen the story in the *Times* when he'd got home this afternoon, and his first inclination was to rip the bloody thing to shreds. Then he'd considered going to the paper's offices and burning them down, or at least threatening the editors until he was given the name of the chap who'd printed the blasted story.

But it didn't matter, Lucian had finally determined. Gemma would just find another way to humiliate him. She must have believed that giving the story to the papers would help her cause and convince him to allow her the divorce. Only she was sorely mistaken. She'd just started a war. A war that he fully intended to win. Now he would never grant her the divorce. Never.

When he first realized she'd gone, he'd considered tearing apart the town to look for her. But that wouldn't do. That would just cause more of a scandal. Besides, no doubt she was at her brother's house. Where else would she be? If Lucian had anything to say to her, he could find here there. And he would. He would find her and inform her that he intended to make her attempts at securing a divorce nearly impossible.

But first, he'd make her wait.

He stalked to the window and glared out onto the street below. He'd never been more aware of his struggle to quell his emotions. He wanted to shatter the bloody window with his fist. He wanted to howl at the top of his lungs. He wanted to —

A knock on the door startled him.

He blew out a deep breath. "Come in," he called.

Mrs. Howard stepped into the room. "Your Grace, Anna came home quite upset."

"Who is Anna?" Lucian barked.

"Her Grace's maid. She was with her on her shopping expedition today. Anna said Her Grace made a stop at the milliner's and went in alone. The coach was delayed in traffic, and when they came back around, Her Grace wasn't there. They couldn't find her. Anna's quite worried."

Lucian looked down at the crumpled note in his hand, stalked over to the fireplace, and tossed it inside. Bloody hell. It missed the flames and fell to the side untouched.

But what did he care? To hell with his wife and her deceptions. "Tell Anna not to worry," he replied in a deceptively calm voice, carefully readjusting his mask of indifference. "Her Grace has gone to visit her brother."

When Lucian heard the door close behind him, he assumed Mrs. Howard had left. But a slight noise caused him to turn, only to see the housekeeper still quietly standing there.

"I have something to tell you, Your Grace," Mrs. Howard began.

Lucian scrubbed a hand through his hair again and bowed his head. "I don't think I want to hear it."

"You must," the housekeeper insisted.

At Lucian's nod, she took a deep breath. "I found Her Grace in the nursery yesterday."

Lucian closed his eyes. Now he *knew* he didn't want to hear this. He gave only a curt nod.

"Her Grace was worried about your future children."

Lucian made a noise halfway between a growl and a pained groan.

"I know I shouldn't have done it," Mrs. Howard continued, "but she asked me questions about your childhood. And I answered them."

Lucian kept his eyes closed. Damn. Damn. Damn. If it had been any other servant. *Any* of them but Mrs. Howard, they would be out on their ear right now. He opened his eyes. "What did you tell her?" he asked, his jaw clenched.

"I told her the truth, Your Grace." There were tears in the older woman's eyes. "I told her that your father wouldn't allow you to be touched, and your Mother had to sneak in to hold you. I told her that you were alone until you went to school, and you were punished for showing emotion. I told her that His Grace was the type of man who only cared about appearances and who punished your mother by refusing to speak to her for days, sometimes weeks, at a time."

Lucian's teeth were clenched so tight his jaw ached. "You had no right."

Mrs. Howard hung her head. "I know that, Your Grace. And if you wish to send me away without a reference, I will understand. But I must tell you that there was something I didn't tell Her Grace. Something I've known since you were a baby. Something that makes all the difference."

Damn it, if those weren't tears stinging the backs of his eyes. But he'd *die* before he allowed them to fall. "What is it, Mrs. Howard?"

"That you are *nothing* like your father, Your Grace. He was a cold man who never showed love a day in his life. You are a man who is filled with love but was forced to hide it. And at the risk of saying even more than I should, I believe your wife is the woman who can finally allow you to share that love."

Lucian's throat worked. This was excruciating. What could he possibly say? "Mrs. Howard—"

"Wait," Mrs. Howard continued, holding up a hand. "I'm not finished. I told you a bit before, but I've had an entire year to get to know Her Grace and what I've learned, what *all* the servants here have learned, is that a more gracious, kind-hearted woman does not exist. She knows every servant by name. She asks after their children. She asks after their health. She knows when they are having a bad day and sends Cook with treats to make them feel better. The entire staff adores her, Your Grace. And it was clear to me soon after you left that you could love her too. You may not have meant to, but you chose the perfect bride. And at the continued risk of being sacked, with all due respect, I must say, I do not want to see you ruin your chance at true happiness. She will give you the love you've always longed for if you let her."

Lucian slowly lifted his head. He blew out a long, painful breath and shook his head. "It's not often that I'm at a loss for words."

"That's true," Mrs. Howard acknowledged, the edge of her mouth tilting up in a smile.

Lucian lifted the corner of his mouth in a half-smile too. "You're not sacked, Mrs. Howard."

She nodded. "You must know I never would have shared such details with Gemma if I didn't know for certain she would only use them to help you."

"Gemma?" He crinkled his brow.

"She asked me to call her that a long time ago." Mrs. Howard winked at him.

"That sounds like her." He expelled his breath again and scrubbed both hands through his hair this time. "I suppose

I'll have a servants' riot on my hands if I don't convince her to stay with me."

"I believe so, Your Grace." Mrs. Howard walked over to him, reached up, and put a hand on Lucian's shoulder. "I am certain she is in love with you. Even if she doesn't know it yet."

Her gave his long-time servant, his long-time *friend*, a wry smile. "And I'm fairly certain I've ruined things with her." He shook his head sadly.

Mrs. Howard patted his shoulder. "Where there is love, there is always hope, Your Grace."

Lucian nodded. Slowly. "Thank you for telling Gemma the truth, Mrs. Howard. I never would have been brave enough to do it myself."

"Yes, you would." She turned to leave.

"And please," Lucian added, "if you're going to call my wife Gemma, call me Lucian. At least when we're alone." He returned the housekeeper's wink.

"Oh, I can't do that, Your Grace." Mrs. Howard shook her head forcefully. "Old habits, you know?"

"Seems we'll both have to try something that makes us uncomfortable then," Lucian replied.

Mrs. Howard smiled and nodded.

Lucian tipped back his head and pinched the bridge of his nose. He paced away from Mrs. Howard. It was all so obvious now. Now that Gemma was gone. He'd pushed her away. He'd been frightened when she'd asked about his child-hood. He'd been looking for a fight, a reason to mistrust her. Because he hadn't been able to believe, to *accept*, that she was as wonderful as she was. And that she could love him as deeply as he had begun to hope she could. But the most frightening part of all had been when he'd realized how deeply he'd begun to love her.

After all, if you push someone away with a stupid fight,

they can't prove you were right about them all along. You pushed away the chance at being hurt. And Gemma hadn't been acting. Just as Mrs. Howard said, Gemma had merely been frightened for their unborn child. A child that even now might be growing inside of her. And how he hoped it was so. Of course, Gemma had been concerned. Any loving mother —and Gemma would be the *most* loving mother—would want an assurance that her child would be treated with love and kindness.

"I'm madly in love with her, you know," Lucian admitted. As soon as the words were past his lips, it felt as if a hundred-stone weight had lifted from his shoulders.

"Oh, I know." Mrs. Howard opened the door and glanced back at him. "And I also know that you need to find that woman and treat her as if she is more important than anything in this world for the rest of her days."

Lucian hung his head. "She is. She truly is."

CHAPTER FORTY-ONE

That Night, The Earl of Pembroke's Town House

For just a moment—a fleeting second—right after she woke, Gemma thought she was in her bed at Lucian's town house. Snuggled and warm. If she would just reach out, she could touch him, and —

She blinked open her eyes to be confronted with the awful realization that she was not at home. She was in Pembroke's town house. Locked in a bedchamber. And no one knew she was here.

She pushed herself up sharply and scanned the room. She was alone, thank heavens. Darkness had descended outside. She'd fallen asleep on the bed, and according to the clock on the nearby mantel, it was past nine.

Pembroke had not yet returned. Gemma was thankful for the reprieve from his odious company, but she'd been left to guess at why he'd done this outrageous thing. What could he possibly think he would do? Keep her hidden in his home? It made no sense.

He'd said he would only keep her here temporarily. But

what did that mean? Did he plan to hurt her? Kill her? Take her somewhere else? She had no earthly idea, and with each passing moment, her anxiety grew.

A knock sounded on the door, startling her. Should she pretend to still be asleep? If it was Pembroke, that might be the safest measure.

"Me lady," came a female voice a few moments later. "I brought you some food and drink."

Gemma hopped off the bed and hurried to the door. "Thank you," she said through the portal. She tried to open the door, but it was still locked.

"Please go sit on the bed, me lady. Tell me when you're there, and I'll open the door."

Gemma frowned, but after a few moments' thought, she decided to do as she was told. After all, she had no way of knowing if the housemaid was alone or if Pembroke or another servant was with her. And Gemma would have to convince this maid to trust her if she had any hope of convincing her to help her escape this madhouse.

"Very well," she called when she was sitting on the bed again. "I'm on the bed."

The housemaid had clearly heard her voice coming from farther away and must have been satisfied with that because the lock turned and the door opened. The maid entered with a tray of food held in front of her. Gemma thought she saw a glimpse of a footman in the corridor before the door closed. But thankfully, Pembroke wasn't there.

"Here you are, me lady," the maid said as she placed the tray on a sideboard to the right of the door. She turned, wiped her hands on her apron, and blinked at Gemma, who remained on the bed.

"Oof. They said ye was a real beauty, but I had no idea," the maid admitted with a crooked smile. She was petite with blond, curly hair and a shy smile.

"Thank you," Gemma replied. "What is your name?"

"Louisa, me lady."

"Who did they tell you I am, Louisa?" Gemma asked, truly curious if Pembroke's household was aware they had a duchess trapped inside.

Louisa waved her hands in front of her, palms out. "I don't ask any questions like that, me lady. The only thing I heard was that ye was a lady, and by the looks of ye, that's certainly true."

Was this Pembroke's attempt at being discreet? If so, it was bizarre.

Now that they were alone together, Gemma hopped off the bed and hurried over to Louisa. "I *am* a lady," she confirmed. "A very wealthy one. And if you'll help me leave here, I can promise you a fat purse."

The maid began backing toward the door, waving her hands in front of her again. "Oh, no, no, no. No, me lady. I couldn't. Me family has worked for the Pembrokes for generations. I wouldna do nothin' ta put me job in danger."

"But Lord Pembroke is keeping me here against my will, Louisa," Gemma continued, trying to appeal to the woman's sense of justice. "Please."

"Oh, I don't believe Lord Pembroke would do anythin' so unbecoming of 'im," the maid said. Her back was pushed up against the door now, and she rapped her knuckles against it twice without turning her back to Gemma.

"Then why am I locked in here?" Gemma cried as the door opened and the maid nearly flew out of it. Gemma leaped toward it, hoping to grab the knob before it closed, but she missed. And the door was quickly locked.

Grr. Next time, she would just have to be less hopeful Louisa would help her willingly. God only knew what Pembroke had told the obviously frightened servants.

Turning in a frustrated huff, Gemma glared about the

room once more. There had to be *something* she could do to escape. She just had to think. She barely spared a glance at the food on the tray. She wasn't hungry…but…could she use the fork or knife to pry open the door?

She rushed over to the tray, only to find that the food consisted of pastry and tea without any cutlery whatsoever. Not even a spoon. Pembroke must have anticipated her thoughts. Damn him.

She walked over to one of the windows and was pulling hard at it with all of her weight when another sharp, quick rap at the door startled her again.

This time, there was barely time to turn around before the door opened and Pembroke stalked in. Gemma clutched at the window frame behind her back while Pembroke strode determinedly into the room and tossed a copy of the paper on top of the writing desk. "Here you are," he said, smiling. "All is going precisely to plan."

Dread slowly filled Gemma's middle. What did that paper say? She pried her fingers off the windowsill and calmly pressed her hands together, willing them to stop sweating. Sweating never helped anything.

Swallowing, she slowly walked to the desk and looked down at the headline.

Duchess of Grovemont Seeks Divorce!

She gasped and her accusing gaze flew to Pembroke. "Who told the papers?"

"I did." Looking smug, Pembroke grasped his lapels and rocked back and forth on his heels.

She plunked her fists on her hips. "You had no right."

"The sooner everyone thinks you've left town, the better. Now." He opened the desk drawer, pulled out a piece of vellum, and set it on top. Then he splayed his hand toward the chair in front of the desk. "Write your brother a note telling him you're spending time with friends."

Gemma had no intention of writing Griffin a note. "I demand to know why you've done this."

Pembroke crossed his arms over his chest. "Isn't it obvious? I've done this because I've been patiently waiting for you all these months, and I'm tired of waiting."

She stared at him, brow furrowed. "Waiting for what?"

But the moment Gemma asked the question, she regretted it. He stepped closer and slid a hand down the side of her face, letting his gaze dip to her décolletage. "I thought it was obvious, but apparently not. I've wanted you for months now. I always knew what a beauty you would become. Your mother is a beauty, after all. My father told me your mother bloomed late. Surprised everyone. Your husband was a fool, leaving you alone. But when you told me you were going to leave Grovemont..." Pembroke nearly spit her husband's name. "You lied to me. I am just trying to make things right."

"I *am* going to leave him," Gemma insisted. Of course, she hadn't been planning on leaving Lucian for *Pembroke*, and she had no idea why the earl believed she would. But now was hardly the time to point that out to him.

"As if I'd believe you now," Pembroke sneered. He dropped his hand to her cleavage and rubbed a finger along the tops of her breasts.

She fought the urge to pull away from his repugnant touch. "What do you intend to do with me?"

His smile was diabolical. "You shall be my mistress for as long as I desire. And when I tire of you..." His lips curled higher. "I'll think of something to do with you. Perhaps I'll sell you to the highest bidder."

Gemma winced. It was worse than she'd ever imagined. She clutched her hands together. Perhaps pleading with him would be more effective. "You must believe me, Pembroke.

Take me home. I'll return to you after the divorce has been granted. I promise."

Of course, she had no intention of returning to this madman, but if pretending to be on his side would cause him to trust her again, she would do it.

"It's too late," he snapped, pulling his hand away from her breasts. "Besides, I *know* you're lying."

Gemma shook her head. "How can you possibly know that?"

"Because Lady Mary told me."

Gemma's blood went cold. What did *Lady Mary* have to do with this? "I assure you whatever Lady Mary said was a lie," Gemma retorted.

Pembroke arched a brow. "She told me you'd say that."

Gemma tossed an infuriated hand in the air. "I don't even speak to Lady Mary. How would she know what I'm planning to do?"

"Lady Mary said she overheard you telling your family how in love you are with Grovemont." Pembroke's voice rose. "He *left you* for over a year. You told me he never wrote. How can you love him?" The earl's face clouded with anger. His voice was accusatory.

"I *am* planning to leave," she reiterated. That much was true. Perhaps if she kept repeating it, Pembroke would believe her.

Pembroke shrugged. "Now that the story is in the papers, you'll have no choice. *Now*, write your brother a note." He pointed at the vellum again.

"No." The word escaped her lips before she had a chance to think.

Pembroke's eyes grew dark. He grabbed her arm roughly and swiped the newspaper to the floor. Then he forced her into the seat. He pulled the quill from the inkpot and handed it to her. "Do it," he demanded.

Gemma lifted her chin. "If I refuse?"

He grabbed her by the hair and yanked her head back so sharply she was looking straight up into his inhuman eyes. *"You won't like the consequences."*

Tears stung her eyes from the pain. "Fine," she ground out.

He released her and turned toward the door. "I'll be back in an hour. The letter had better be finished."

CHAPTER FORTY-TWO

Later That Night, The Duke of Grovemont's Study

Lucian paced in front of the windows with Oliver nipping at his heels. A movement outside the window caught his eye, and he moved over to look outside. Was that Southbury's coach?

There was one sharp rap on the door before it opened and Southbury entered the room.

Lucian frowned. What was his brother-in-law doing here? The truth was that Lucian had been about to pay a call on his friend. Or more correctly, on his wife at his friend's house.

He'd been preparing his speech all night. He knew he couldn't just show up and ask Gemma to forgive him or give him another chance without some truly spectacular groveling on his part. He'd been practicing all afternoon. He'd nearly asked Mrs. Howard to give him some ideas.

But now Southbury was here, and his friend looked harried. Had he come to tell Lucian that his sister wanted a divorce? He already knew that. Hell, the whole town knew it because of the papers.

Had Southbury come to discuss the *details* of the divorce? If so, Lucian would have to explain to him that he intended to win back his wife. He would do whatever he had to. If only Gemma would give him one more chance. Southbury would see reason in that.

Hopefully.

Lucian shook his head. "If you've come to tell me—"

Southbury didn't let him finish. Instead, he tossed a folded piece of vellum onto the desk. Lucian glanced at it. It was a handwritten note.

"I don't understand," Lucian said.

"The note is from my sister saying she's gone to the countryside," Southbury explained.

Lucian arched a brow. "So? She's not with you?" Surprising, but if Gemma wasn't with him, why was Southbury here?

Southbury hunched over the desk, bracing the knuckles of one hand atop it and pointing at the note with the other. "No, she's not with me, and there's a problem with this note."

Apprehension licked at Lucian's gut. Damn it. His gut was never wrong. Something bad had happened. "What is it?"

"In this note, Gemma goes on and on about how she cannot *wait* to get to the countryside because she likes it so much. Fresh air. Trees. It's practically a *poem* to the countryside."

Fuck. Lucian briefly closed his eyes. "Gemma *hates* the countryside."

Southbury nodded. "Precisely. Which means—"

"Something *is* wrong," Lucian finished for him, expelling his breath.

"When is the last time you saw her?" Southbury asked.

"She went shopping earlier today. She left a note telling me she was leaving me. I assume you've seen the paper."

"Yes, and this note came not an hour ago. Both seemed odd. Gemma never mentioned a divorce to me. The last time I saw the two of you, you appeared to be happy. And there's no way she would leave Oliver."

Lucian glanced at the little brown puppy, who had jumped up on the leather couch near the window and was moving his head back and forth, watching the two men speak as if they were playing a game of battledore and shuttlecock.

Lucian cursed under his breath. Of course, she wouldn't leave Oliver. He should have realized the moment he'd heard she was gone that Oliver would have been with her had she truly decided to leave. At the time, Lucian had been too blinded by his own stubborn pride to think of it.

He didn't relish admitting to his brother-in-law that his wife *had* wanted a divorce, but now there *was* something about the note she'd left him that didn't make sense.

Southbury narrowed his eyes. "Do you still have the note she left you?"

"Wait here." Lucian left the room. By the time he made it to the staircase in the foyer, he was so worried that he took the stairs two at a time. He'd assumed Gemma was with her brother and been so sure of it that he hadn't even bothered to confirm it. But now that Southbury was here...the sick feeling that had begun in Lucian's middle earlier was spreading throughout his body, making him numb with fear. Dear God. What if he'd made a mistake? What if Gemma hadn't left on her own accord? There could only be one reason Southbury wanted to see the note Gemma had left for Lucian.

He pushed open the door to his bedchamber and made his way to the fireplace with ground-devouring strides. The note was still there. Thank God. He'd never been more relieved to have missed a toss in his life. He grabbed the small ball of vellum lying off to the side and hurried back down to the study, smoothing it out along the way.

Once he re-entered the room, he strode over and pushed the piece of paper onto the desk in front of his brother-in-law.

Southbury studied the scrap for a few moments. "This isn't her handwriting."

Lucian cursed under his breath. He wouldn't know his wife's handwriting because he'd never written her. God damn it. "You're certain?"

"Positive. She must be in trouble." Southbury shook his head and narrowed his eyes. "But who would do something to her?"

Lucian's hands curled into tight fists. "*I know who.*"

CHAPTER FORTY-THREE

The Earl of Pembroke's Town House

"The footmen are preparing the coach," Pembroke said as he walked into the bedchamber.

Gemma groggily sat up and rubbed her eyes. She hadn't been sleeping, but she was exhausted, and it was still the middle of the night. Apparently, Pembroke had decided to slip her from town under the cover of darkness.

She hoped if she acted compliant, he might treat her as if she were still his friend. She'd written the blasted note he'd demanded of her last night. And she'd done the only thing she could think to do, which was to spend an inordinate amount of time extolling the virtues of the countryside to Griffin. Griffin, of course, knew she detested the country. She could only hope her brother was wise enough to wonder what was wrong.

But she wasn't counting on it. No. She'd made up her mind in the hours since Pembroke had taken that note. In the long hours sitting alone in this room, she realized that she might be able to hope that Griffin would come looking for her, but there was no guarantee her disappearance would be traced to Pembroke. For the first time in her life, no one was here to help her. Gemma would have to save herself. And the realization felt oddly...good.

And that wasn't the only thing she'd realized as she'd stared out the darkened window. She'd made a great many discoveries tonight, actually. She was through with everyone else telling her how her life would be. She was a grown woman, and it was up to her to determine her destiny. As the youngest in the family, she'd been treated like a child by all of them. Mama and Griffin and even Meredith had looked after her during her debut. Griffin had chosen her husband and negotiated the contract. Meredith had informed her of the secrets of a wedding night. Her husband had left her for a year, never written her, and returned to try to tell her how their marriage would be. Everyone was eager to tell Gemma what to do and how to do it. But she was done with all of that. She was in control of her future from now on, and she'd be damned if she would allow another person, least of all Pembroke, to tell her how her life would be. She'd deal with her husband afterward.

And she *did* want to deal with Lucian, she realized. All those hours alone in the dark had given her plenty of time to replay their argument in her mind. She'd had no right to ask Mrs. Howard for the secrets of his childhood. If Lucian wanted her to know, he would tell her himself. And that was what she wanted too. She wanted him to open up to her. She wanted him to tell her how he felt. She wanted him to be honest and giving and loving and kind to her.

Because she knew he was capable of it.

He wasn't a cold-hearted monster. He'd merely been startled when she had brought up his childhood and demanded a different life for their baby. No doubt he'd felt as if he were under attack. She'd threatened to call off their agreement.

If she was going to start acting like a grown woman, she needed to do it in every way. Which included not getting angry at Lucian for expressing his feelings. Lucian had the right to tell her he'd been angry when he learned she'd talked about his childhood with a servant. She may not have liked what he said, but she had signed a contract. She'd agreed to stay with him for two months. A grown woman honored her commitments and that meant her commitment to the marriage too.

And now she realized how much she wanted to stay in her marriage. At first, she had been scared witless. She'd been so worried she would discover that Lucian was as awful as his father that she'd accused him of it without even speaking to him. It was the exact thing he'd done to her after they'd married, when he'd refused to listen to her explanation of why she'd been looking for him in study. She'd been angry about that the entire time he'd been gone to India, yet she'd just done the same thing to him. She'd refused to give him a chance to explain himself.

She may not have liked how her husband reacted to knowing she'd been told about his childhood, but she owed it to him to discuss it with him. Not run away, demanding a divorce. Because the truth was that these last two weeks with Lucian had been the best of her life. She'd fallen in love with him. Truly. She'd seen beneath the façade he'd carefully crafted for the world and glimpsed the man who had missed his parents' love but still had so much love to give. He'd been taught to be cool and indifferent. He'd been told it was the right way to act. But she knew him. She knew his heart, and she knew he was capable of the deep and lasting love they both deserved.

Lucian was a good man. A very good man. And she would tell him as much, just as soon as she got away from Pembroke.

"Where are we going?" she asked her captor as she pushed herself up on one elbow on the bed.

"I cannot tell you that. But it's far from here," Pembroke replied. "A place where I can have you all to myself."

"Your country estate?" she ventured.

"That would be too obvious, don't you think?" He laughed. "Now, be a good girl and prepare yourself. Use the convenience if you must. It's a long journey, and we won't be stopping often along the way. I'll be back to fetch you shortly."

The moment the door closed behind him, Gemma surged to her feet. Her nerves made her exhaustion disappear. She couldn't go with him. Wherever he was taking her, it was far away and obviously somewhere no one would look for her. She *had* to escape before he got her out of London. It was her only hope.

She rushed over to one of the windows. Could she break the glass and jump? No. She'd already thought of that and discarded the notion. It was a three-story drop directly into an alley. She might well break her neck. And that was if she *didn't* fatally cut herself on the glass first.

She raced over to the door and tugged the handle as hard as she could. Still locked, of course. She lifted her slipper and kicked the handle as hard as she could. So forcefully an ungodly pain shot through her foot. It was no use. It was clearly bolted from the outside.

She turned around in a desperate circle. What else could she do? Pound on the door? Scream? Bring the household running?

Suddenly, loud voices sounded from far away. She guessed they were coming all the way from the foyer three stories below. Booming voices. And one that was…familiar. She'd know it anywhere.

Lucian? Could it be? It seemed unlikely and yet…

A glimmer of hope kindled inside of her.

~

"Where is she, Pembroke?" Lucian demanded. He was about to smash this idiot into bits, but first he had to find out where he was keeping Gemma.

Pembroke clutched at his lapels and lifted his bony little chin in the air. "I don't know what you're talking about. Please leave." He pointed toward the door.

"I'm not leaving without *my wife*," Lucian snarled.

Pembroke pulled at his earlobe. He wouldn't meet Lucian's eyes. He was obviously lying. "Why would you think your wife was here?"

"I *know* she's here," Lucian replied. "I'm giving you the chance to tell me where before I begin smashing things, including *your face*."

~

Gemma pulled the bellpull as hard as she could. She wasn't about to wait around for Lucian to rescue her. But she *would* use his arrival as the distraction she needed to escape. She could only imagine that Pembroke was even now downstairs in the foyer, pretending as if he had no idea she was here. She had to get out of this room. Had to let Lucian know she *was* here.

A few minutes later, the voices were still booming downstairs, but there was a tentative one on the other side of the door. "Yes, me lady?" Louisa asked.

Gemma bit her lip. This *had* to work. "Please come in, Louisa. I need help."

"His lordship told me to stay out, me lady," Louisa replied, her voice shaking with what was clearly fright.

Gemma was frantic. She *had* to convince Louisa to open the door. Time was of the essence. What could she say to get the girl to open the door?

"Please, Louisa. I tried to break the window. I cut myself on the glass. My arm is bleeding…badly."

"Oh, dear," came Louisa's response. "Let me go fetch some rags to—"

"No!" Gemma nearly shouted. "Please. I need help immediately. I've already ripped apart the sheets."

The moment the door inched open, Gemma breathed a sigh of relief. It worked. Her ploy had worked. She waited for the maid to step inside the room before she smashed the bedpan over her head. Poor Louisa crumpled to the ground in a heap.

"I'm quite sorry, and I hope you don't have a large knot," Gemma whispered to the girl as she stepped over her prone body. She couldn't help but add, "Next time, you should listen when another woman tells you she's in trouble."

This time, there was no footman behind her, thank heavens. Limping, Gemma made her way into the hallway and down the corridor, toward the staircase in the front of the house, toward the raised voices. When she got there, she grabbed the balustrade with her free hand, leaned over it, and looked straight down. In the foyer below, three footmen were trying to bodily push Lucian out the front door. Meanwhile, Pembroke hovered against the wall nearby, cringing in fear. Despite the efforts of three grown men, Lucian was standing his ground.

"I will not leave without her," Lucian thundered, his legs firmly braced apart while the footmen grabbed his arms.

Gemma's heart clenched. He'd figured it out. He'd figured it out and was here for her. "Lucian!" she called. "I'm here!"

His head snapped up at the same moment that Pembroke gathered enough courage to punch him in the face. Not at all brave of him, given the fact that Lucian was being held by three men. Gemma went racing down the stairs toward the scene as Lucian shook off the punch *and* the three footmen to grab Pembroke by the collar. "I shall happily murder you now," he bellowed.

By the time Gemma reached the foyer, Pembroke was a bloody mess who'd fallen to the marble floor. Lucian was still kicking him. In addition to the three footmen, a group of servants, including another maid and what looked like a butler, stood nearby, clearly with no intentions of intervening.

"Lucian, stop!" Gemma screamed as she flung herself into his arms. "He's already stopped fighting."

The hatred in Lucian's eyes abated as he wrapped his arms around her. Another look entirely lit up his face. *Relief.* Relief and—dare she hope—love?

"Gemma." His voice was rough. He tucked her head beneath his chin and squeezed her tight. "Gemma. Are you all right? Did that bastard hurt you?"

"I'm all right," she sobbed against his shoulder. "I'm all right, Lucian."

Still clutching her to his chest, Lucian glared at the servants. "Which of you knew about this? I'll be returning with the constable."

The servants all backed away and quickly scattered, disappearing into the bowels of the house.

"Take me home, Lucian," Gemma whispered. "Please just take me home."

CHAPTER FORTY-FOUR

Later That Day, The Duke of Grovemont's Town House

Gemma was propped up in her bed, a smile on her face. She'd taken a long, hot bath, and Anna had braided her hair. She'd also taken a much-needed nap and was wearing a fresh night rail. Lucian sat at the foot of her bed, bandaging her sore foot. He'd insisted on doing it himself.

"I should have killed that bastard," Lucian grumbled as he applied the balm the maids had given him to her bruised skin.

"No, he's not worth it," Gemma replied. "He's going to gaol."

"Gaol is too good for him."

Gemma winced as Lucian rubbed the balm into her foot. "How did you know he had me?"

Lucian spent the next several minutes tending to her foot while explaining what had happened. He began with how Griffin had arrived on his doorstep last night.

"I'm only sorry I didn't figure it out myself," he finished, shaking his head.

"You couldn't have known. I sent the letter to Griffin."

Lucian stood and moved closer to her. Then he sat next to her, leaned forward, and pressed his forehead to hers. He cupped her shoulders in his hands. "I'm sorry, Gemma. I'm sorry for everything. That morning, when we argued, I didn't mean to—"

"No, Lucian. *I'm* sorry. I was angry with you. But I wasn't going to leave you without telling you. After shopping, I had every intention of coming back home. But now I realize that I signed the contract, and—" Tears dripped down her cheeks.

He pushed a hand up into her hair and cradled her head against his chest. "I don't care about the bloody contract."

"Neither do I," she sniffed, shaking her head and pulling back to look at him again. "Not anymore. While I was locked in Pembroke's house, I realized that I missed you. And when I thought I might never see you again, I realized that you have my heart. I think you've had it since the night I saw you in Griffin's study looking so alone."

Lucian's eyes filled with tears, then he grabbed her and kissed her. "I realized the same thing, Gemma. I love you."

Gemma's tears fell even harder now, and she was sobbing. "You do?"

"Yes, I do. I love you. I cannot live without you. I don't want to, at least."

"I thought you'd hate me forever for bringing shame on your family with the divorce news in the paper."

"Oh, darling. I don't hate you. And I *don't care* what's printed in the paper. I finally understand that what happens behind closed doors is so much more important than what people think. You made me understand that. I have you to thank for it."

She wrapped her arms around his neck, still crying. "Do you mean that?"

He smoothed a hand over her hair and nodded. "The papers can write whatever they want. All I care about is *your* opinion of me. And I'm hoping you love me as much as I love you."

She sniffed and nodded. "I do, Lucian. I truly do." Then she lifted her chin. There was something she needed to say to him. "But I am a grown woman, and I refuse to be treated like a child or a piece of property *ever again*. I came back to you because I love you. I want a true partnership with you. We are equals. If you cannot give me that, I will not stay."

He nodded and kissed her. "I understand, and that's what I want too. Besides, I've been told by a very wise woman that I am to treat you as if you're the most important person in the world from now on. And I intend to do exactly that."

"Mrs. Howard?" Gemma asked, smiling through her tears.

"Mrs. Howard." He nodded.

"You aren't angry with her...for telling me about—?"

"No." He shook his head. "But I should have told you myself. I didn't want to appear weak, and—"

"Oh, Lucian. How could I ever think you are weak? A little boy who could withstand what you had to withstand? You're the strongest person I know." She rubbed his rough cheek with her palm. "I'm in awe of you."

He grabbed her and hugged her tight. Tears ran from his eyes. "I love you, Gemma. Now and forever."

EPILOGUE

Two Months Later, October, The Duke of Southbury's Drawing Room

"Four more months until the baby comes," Meredith said, rubbing her hand over her belly.

"I cannot wait to meet him," Griffin said, placing his hand atop his wife's stomach too. They were sitting on the settee together in the midst of a large gathering.

In addition to Griffin and Meredith and Gemma and Lucian, Mama was there and so was Cecily. And Oliver, of course. Lady Clare Handleton had even sneaked away from her mother for a visit.

Gemma and Lucian had employed Lady Clare, actually, to help them mitigate the scandal from the papers. She told them the exact rumors to spread to the exact people. Having gone through a scandal herself, Lady Clare knew precisely how to manipulate not only the papers but the right gossips in town to turn any story in a person's favor. Which, of course, begged the question as to why Lady Clare hadn't employed her skills to restore her *own* reputation. Gemma had asked her once, and Lady Clare's slow wink and sly smile were her only answer.

"Him?" Lady Clare's eyebrow arched. "I, for one, am *certain* the baby is a girl."

"Not possible," Griffin replied with a wide grin. "Isn't that right, Mama?"

"A boy would be nice," Mama allowed.

"I shall be equally happy with a girl or a boy," Meredith informed them all, rolling her eyes.

Rubbing her fingers over Oliver's soft fur, Gemma exchanged a private look with Lucian. Just this morning, she'd informed him that she was certain she was also with child. They were waiting for the right moment to share their news. But every time Gemma looked at her husband, his eyes glowed with all the warmth and love he had for her.

And that was what the last two months with Lucian had shown her. Gemma had no doubt she was loved as much as she loved. Lucian had proved to be the same loving, kind-hearted man he'd been when he'd been trying to woo her. And in return she'd shared with him all the love in her heart, and he'd opened his to share right back. Their unborn child —whether a male or female—would know how loved she was. Gemma reached down and squeezed her husband's hand.

"If the baby is a girl," Meredith continued, "someone will have to break it to my brother. He told me he has quite a few bets on the matter at the club."

"I can confirm that's true," Lucian added with a laugh, settling back into the settee and crossing his booted foot over his knee.

Gemma watched Lucian interact with the rest of her family with happiness bursting in her heart. Ever since the night she'd escaped from Pembroke, Lucian had been more relaxed and affable. He laughed more easily and smiled more readily. He took himself less seriously. They had all noticed it. Griff had remarked on it more than once.

"I may have a bit of money on the matter myself," Lucian said with a wink to his new family. "Though I refuse to admit which gender I chose."

"What? Exactly how many bets has Ash placed on his niece or nephew?" Meredith asked Lucian, feigning outrage.

"I cannot say," Lucian said with another laugh. "I owe Trentham a favor. He taught me to be charming, after all."

Gemma, who had long ago heard the story of how Lord Trentham had given Lucian lessons in charm, threw back her head and laughed. "And a good teacher he was."

Lucian winked at his wife, and she gave him a subtle nod. He cleared his throat. "I think now may be the perfect time to tell everyone that Griffin and Meredith's child will have a cousin next year."

"What?!" The room erupted into congratulatory remarks and hugs all around. Mama's eyes got teary, and it was several long minutes before they all settled back into their seats.

Gemma placed a hand on her own belly. "And to think this all started with a dare."

"A dare I'm awfully glad you accepted," Lucian replied, leaning down and kissing his wife on the nose.

Gemma let out a long, happy sigh. "I do love to think of Lady Mary unhappily contemplating how it all went wrong for her that night." She shook her head. "I do hope she's learned her lesson about trying to tell other people what to do."

"After you berated her at the Whitmans' ball, I should think she has," Meredith said with a laugh.

Gemma bit her lip. It was true. Not long after Lord Pembroke's arrest, Gemma had spied Lady Mary at a ball and had wasted no time marching up to the woman. She'd informed Mary in no uncertain terms that if Gemma ever caught her name or the names of her family members on Mary's lips again, she would live to regret it.

Mary had turned pale, grabbed her long-suffering husband, and promptly left.

"Now that Gemma is happily matched, I suppose you don't have anyone else to matchmake, Meredith. What *shall* you do with your time before the baby arrives?" Griffin asked, grinning.

"On the contrary, my darling. I believe you're forgetting that *Ash* made you a promise." Meredith had a decidedly sly smile on her face.

Griffin frowned. "A promise? What was that?"

Meredith smoothed a hand over her belly again. "Did my brother not say he would take a wife *this* year if you admitted to the woman you love that you love her before the Cartwrights' Midsummer Night's Ball *last* year?"

A huge smile spread across Griffin's face. "By God, he did! And you, my lovely wife, have the memory of an elephant."

"And did you not tell me you loved me before said ball?" Meredith continued, clearly beyond pleased with herself.

"I did." Griffin nodded.

"Then the search is on for Ash's marchioness," Meredith replied gleefully. "And before I get too large to walk, I intend to host a country house party in two weeks' time in order to see to it that he finds the right match."

"I should have known you would have a plan," Griffin said to his wife, kissing her soundly on the cheek.

"I shall invite the cream of the crop of debutantes and eligible young ladies," Meredith announced. "Starting now. Cecily, please say you'll come. I'll be sure to invite Lord Albion for you." She waggled her eyebrows.

"Oh, yes, please do invite him," Cecily said, clapping her hands together in glee.

"And before you say no, Clare, you *must* come. To help me. I'm going to need you, and I refuse to take no for an answer."

"Are you jesting? To see the notorious bachelor Ashford Drake succumb to the marriage mart?" Clare said, arching a brow. "*I'll be there.*"

THANK YOU FOR READING. I hope you enjoyed Gemma and Lucian's story. The next book in the Love's a Game series is *The Marquess Match*. Find out what happens between Ash and Clare at the country house party. CLICK HERE FOR "The Marquess Match".

ALSO BY VALERIE BOWMAN

Love's a Game
The Duchess Hunt (Book 1)
The Duke Dare (Book 2)
The Marquess Match (Book 3)

The Whitmorelands
The Duke Deal (Book 1)
The Marquess Move (Book 2)
The Debutante Dilemma (Book 3)
The Wallflower Win (Book 4)

The Footmen's Club
The Footman and I (Book 1)
Duke Looks Like a Groomsman (Book 2)
The Valet Who Loved Me (Book 3)
Save a Horse, Ride a Viscount (Book 4)
Earl Lessons (Book 5)
The Duke is Back (Book 6)

Playful Brides
The Unexpected Duchess (Book 1)
The Accidental Countess (Book 2)
The Unlikely Lady (Book 3)
The Irresistible Rogue (Book 4)
The Unforgettable Hero (Book 4.5)
The Untamed Earl (Book 5)

The Legendary Lord (Book 6)

Never Trust a Pirate (Book 7)

The Right Kind of Rogue (Book 8)

A Duke Like No Other (Book 9)

Kiss Me At Christmas (Book 10)

Mr. Hunt, I Presume (Book 10.5)

No Other Duke But You (Book 11)

Secret Brides

Secrets of a Wedding Night (Book 1)

A Secret Proposal (Book 1.5)

Secrets of a Runaway Bride (Book 2)

A Secret Affair (Book 2.5)

Secrets of a Scandalous Marriage (Book 3)

It Happened Under the Mistletoe (Book 3.5)

Thank you for reading *The Duke Dare.* I hope you enjoyed Gemma and Lucian's story.

I'd love to keep in touch.

- Visit my website for exclusive information about upcoming books, excerpts, and to sign up for my email newsletter: www.ValerieBowmanBooks.com or at www.ValerieBowmanBooks.com/subscribe.
- Join me on Facebook: http://Facebook.com/ ValerieBowmanAuthor.
- Reviews help other readers find books. I appreciate all reviews. Thank you so much for considering it!

Want to read the other Love's a Game books?

- The Duchess Hunt
- The Marquess Match

ABOUT THE AUTHOR

Valerie Bowman grew up in Illinois with six sisters (she's number seven) and a huge supply of historical romance novels.

After a cold and snowy stint earning a degree in English with a minor in history at Smith College, she moved to Florida the first chance she got.

Valerie now lives in Jacksonville with her family including her two rascally dogs. When she's not writing, she keeps busy reading, traveling, or vacillating between watching crazy reality TV and PBS.

Valerie loves to hear from readers. Find her on the web at www.ValerieBowmanBooks.com.

facebook.com/ValerieBowmanAuthor
instagram.com/valeriegbowman
goodreads.com/Valerie_Bowman
pinterest.com/ValerieGBowman
bookbub.com/authors/valerie-bowman
amazon.com/author/valeriebowman

Printed in Great Britain
by Amazon